"He asked if you understand."

Connor looked up. "I heard him."

"Then answer the man," growled the sumo wrestler.

Connor stood. "Let's go, Blister."

The fullback, stepping in close, put a thick finger against Connor's chest. "But you ain't said you understand."

Blister McGraw simply sat, mesmerized.

"Blister?" Connor said.

The boy jumped to his feet, knocking over his chair in the process, the sound incredibly loud in the silenced room.

"Say you understand," growled Sumo, "or you don't leave. Standing up."

Blister wet his lips with the tip of his tongue. A fight! Big Connor Gibbs, alone against three guys! Wow! Wait'll he got back to school, he'd get free Jell-O for a week off this story.

The players moved in, spreading out a little, flexing their hands, posturing for the crowd. This was gonna be easy, they thought.

They didn't know Connor Gibbs . . .

DEADBEAT

Leo Atkins

BERKLEY PRIME CRIME, NEW YORK

DEADBEAT

A Berkley Prime Crime Book / published by arrangement with
the author

PRINTING HISTORY
Berkley Prime Crime edition / March 1999

All rights reserved.
Copyright © 1999 by Clay Harvey.
This book may not be reproduced in whole or in part,
by mimeograph or any other means, without permission.
For information address: The Berkley Publishing Group,
a member of Penguin Putnam Inc.,
375 Hudson Street, New York, New York 10014.

The Penguin Putnam Inc. World Wide Web site address is
http://www.penguinputnam.com

ISBN: 0-425-16781-X

Berkley Prime Crime Books are published
by The Berkley Publishing Group,
a member of Penguin Putnam Inc.,
375 Hudson Street, New York, New York 10014.
The name BERKLEY PRIME CRIME and the BERKLEY PRIME CRIME
design are trademarks belonging to Berkley Publishing Corporation.

PRINTED IN THE UNITED STATES OF AMERICA

10 9 8 7 6 5 4 3 2 1

This book is dedicated to the lovely Wanda Faye Hiatt, a serendipitous gift, a blessing undisguised . . .

and to Sandi, Tyler, Rikki Anne, and Michael Ashley—my elder sister's kids, who, despite her influence, turned out pretty good; none is in jail and none is a lawyer. God bless them.

ACKNOWLEDGMENTS

I'd like to acknowledge the following gentlefolk:

My nine-year-old son Chris, who wrote a song, precocious and mazy and somber, sang it for me bold and proud and bittersweet, then let me steal it. Thanks, babe.

My niece Rikki, who chauffeured and doctored and bolstered during my debilitating nadir; in a word, saving me.

My sister Anne, my cheerleader in New Jersey, who taught me all I know, except for the good stuff.

My pal Mike, like Gibraltar always there, even for hours in a hospital waiting room. Everything a friend should be, except rich.

Neighbor Nancy Fleming, a bubbly savant whose internal clock reads seventy, still a kid. And can she make soup . . .

Faithful Debbie Ortiz, whose support never wavers, critiques are spot on, and whose punches are never pulled. Sometimes she hits hard, too.

Jean Turoff, the consummate professional, whose careful copyediting has freed me more than once from an embarrassing sandtrap.

Sandy Wingate, who praises and encourages, exhorts and

encourages, proclaims and encourages. Balm for a writer.

Emma Layne. When her ageless eyes sparkle, memories of lengthy bouts with the muse slip silently away. It's all her doing, anyway.

Jackie Ritter. No one could have a more exuberant reader, or a more perceptive one, or one with better taste in dogs.

Ed Humburg, who directs me through police procedural matters, prods me to keep pecking at the keys, and allows me to tell people I know him.

Dr. David Best, who attempted to keep me on the medical strait and narrow.

And Tom Colgan, who gets paid to put up with me, but not nearly enough.

She was at the kitchen sink when her water broke. (Thank goodness; the fluid will mop up easy later.) She phoned her husband at the bowling alley. Busy signal. Got her suitcase (already prepared) then tried again. Still busy. It was only 2.3 miles to the hospital; her husband had checked it on the odometer. Not so far. Better go. Up with the suitcase, not really heavy, then down the porch steps, slowly.

Cranked the car, careful not to flood. (Lord knew the last thing she needed was a flooded engine, what with dilation beginning and the baby shifting position!) Light touch on the gas to avoid kicking off the choke, then reverse—clunk—and out the driveway, the steering wheel barely clearing her distended abdomen, all filled with life wanting out. Ouch, second contraction! Grin and bear it, it wouldn't be the last. Gathering speed. "Hospital, here we come," Christy said, then her breath caught—another contraction—and she began to breathe like they'd taught in Lamaze, which helped some, and she switched on the flashers and went to greet her baby.

Able Johnson ran the light at Third and Forrest, barely missing a Trans Am who had green on his side. The irate driver honked angrily, five seconds of stridence in the night.

"Fuck you!" shouted Able, and flipped the TA jockey the bird. "It's two fucking o'clock! Y'oughta be home in bed!" he slurred, slobber coating his stubble. "Sheiutt," he said philosophically, then took a pull from his bottle, amber dribble diluting the spit on his chin.

He headed for Warren G. Harding Boulevard, weaving erratically, at eighty-three miles an hour.

ONE

The door said CONNOR GIBBS—CONFIDENTIAL INVESTIGA-
TIONS, and the prospective client said, "I hear you find
people."

"Occasionally," replied Gibbs, who was slightly smaller
than a yeti but not as hairy. "Who do you want found?"

"Noah Sizemore. Here's his picture," the prospective
client replied, leaning across the desk to relinquish a bent,
worn, faded, wallet-sized photograph of a young man with
a blade of a nose, sallow complexion, and a cleft chin. The
man depicted wore a red shirt with Elton John on the front.

"How long has Mr. Sizemore been missing?"

The prospective client casually surveyed the room—its
numerous framed photos, bust of Jackie Robinson, an ancient gramophone. "Didn't say he was missing. I just ain't
exactly sure where he is."

"He a relative of yours?" asked Connor Gibbs, crossing
one long leg over the other.

Pointing to the bust, the prospective client said, "That
Tiger Woods?"

"No. It's not James Earl Jones, either."

Feigning indifference, as befit a person of means: "Do
you charge a whole lot?"

"Depends on the client," replied Gibbs.

Various emotions played across the unshaven face; decision time. "Yeah, he's kin. So will you help me?"

"Tell me why you want to find this Sizemore gentleman."

With more than a hint of bitterness the prospective client eructed, "Because he's my dad, and he prob'ly ain't no gentleman," then tried to cross his legs like Connor had, but his feet wouldn't reach the floor.

Which was not really surprising.

He was only nine.

"Tell me about your dad."

"Don't know much. Ain't seen him since I was two."

"Do you go to school?" Connor asked.

"Just got out for the summer a couple weeks ago."

"What grade did you complete?"

Proudly: "Third."

"They teach you to say 'ain't' in school?"

Fidgeting a little: "Naw."

"Then don't say it. They teach you to say 'naw' as a negative response to an adult?"

Defiant, the determined chin tilting up: "You ain't my daddy."

"That's true, not that I might not like to be. Your daddy the only grown-up you intend to treat respectfully?"

Ambivalence now; after all, the boy needed this man. "I suppose not."

"Good. I don't like cocky. You epitomize cocky."

"What's ' 'pitomize' mean?"

"To be a perfect example of. And it's *e*pitomize."

Eyebrows nearly meeting in the center. "You saying I'm cocky."

"You bet."

The prospective client thought it over. Still truculent, he said, "Well, you're bigger than me."

Connor shook his head. "That has nothing to do with whether you're cocky, only whether I can get away with saying it to your face. If I take this case, you don't act cocky with me, and I won't patronize you. Mutual respect, okay?''

"What's 'patronize'?''

"Acting as if you're better than someone else. It's impolite.''

The boy grinned impishly. "Even when you are?''

Appreciating the repartee, unusual from one so young, Connor responded with a grin of his own. "Even if.''

"So I gotta say 'yes, sir' and 'no, sir' to you?''

"No, that's too formal. The key is respect, not pomposity. You can simply say 'yes' or 'no' to me, not 'naw' or 'yeah' or some other response suitable for peers. We're not peers. I'm an adult, and I'm in charge when you're with me. Always. Deal?''

"I know what 'peer' means.'' Pride again, after the moderate dressing-down. The boy had bottom.

"Good. Your education to date has not been a total failure.''

"I learned 'peer' on TV, not at school.''

"Television can be educational. Now, since you don't seem to have much to offer about your dad, tell me about you. Your name would be a good start.''

"My full name's Cody Wainwright McGraw, but you can call me Blister.''

"You're not partial to Cody? It's a fine name.''

"I ain't no cowboy.''

"Neither was he. An army scout and a showman, but he warn't no cowboy.''

The boy smiled at the locution, as Connor had intended. A thaw; slight, but the ice was melting.

"What about Wainwright? That's an honorable name.''

"I ain't no general, neither.''

"True. But did you know a wainwright is a wagon maker?''

"Nope, I didn't . . . I mean no . . . sir.'' Mildly flustered; the boy was obviously not accustomed to close attention from a man.

"So why 'Blister'?''

Hesitation. Should he tell the truth? Decided against it. "Because I like it. You like Connor?"

"Better than Warren."

The boy grinned. "That your middle one?"

Connor grinned back. "Great, isn't it."

"You get picked on about your name when you were a kid?"

Aha. "Not much. I was always pretty big, and athletic. And I started aikido when I was seven."

Up came the chin. "Well, I ain't big and all I can play good is kickball and I don't even know what aikido is but I suppose it's some kind of fighting crap and even if I did know what it was I prob'ly couldn't do it," all a-rush, but from the heart, revealing.

"Size isn't very important, and athletics are good for enjoyment and keeping in shape and adopting an attitude, but not much else, and fighting seldom solves anything."

Head down now: "Sure, you can say that, because you're big, and athletic, and can fight. Try looking at it from this side sometime."

Connor saw the hurt, applied balm. "Good point. Maybe the aquisition of fighting skills can be useful after all. Occasionally."

"Maybe you could teach me." Hope there, a glimmer of water to a desert traveler.

"Maybe, but let's concentrate on finding your father. Who do you live with, your mom?"

Instant cloud. "My mom's dead."

"I'm sorry to hear it."

"She died when I was born."

Connor just listened. What could he say?

Cody, recovering: "I can pay, you know. I got money in the bank. I cut and sell holly every Christmas, and put all I make in a savings account. I got this passbook at home that says how much."

Connor smiled in admiration of the boy's industriousness.

"Guess how much I got," Cody said.

Connor shook his head. "No idea."

"Sixty-seven dollars and twelve cents. All from cutting holly."

Connor's face exhibited the proper appreciation. "No kidding, that much?"

"You bet. And I'll give it all to you, every penny. Took three Christmases to get that much saved up." Not bragging but bargaining, enticing, offering all the money he had. For his father.

Now Connor had to fight down a lump.

"You got it," the big man said after a moment, climbing to his feet. "So who do you live with?"

"My aunt adopted me, Aunt Vera."

Connor looked at his watch: half-past noon. "She at work?"

"Yes, till five-thirty."

"She know you're here?"

Reluctant but honest headshake. "No."

"She know that you *planned* to come here?"

The nod was barely perceptible.

"She going to be unhappy about it?"

"Prob'ly."

Connor nodded. Coming around his desk, he placed a heavy arm around the boy's slender shoulders and said, "I've dealt with unhappy people before. Let's do lunch. We'll pretend we're CEO wannabes from Silicon Valley."

The boy shook his head in wonder. "Half the time I don't have any idea what you're talking about."

"Me neither, my child. Me neither."

TWO

On a scale of one to ten, Vera McGraw didn't rate the uppermost numeral. But she was no eyesore. A petite five-three and size four, with hair not quite blond, not quite brown, she had the greenest eyes Connor Gibbs had ever seen. She was fresh from work in a red dress (sashed, not belted) and matching flats (no Adidas), with cultured pearls and modest gilt adornments. Very attractive, and not far into her forties, he judged as she suggested the sofa and offered tea.

Tea, and Emperor's Choice, too. Should he propose now or wait a week?

"What do you want?" she jabbed, settling opposite him into a platform rocker, shapely legs curled beneath her, eyes hard as jade. Perhaps a proposal might be premature.

Blister had scampered upstairs after the briefest of introductions. Now Connor knew why.

"It's not what I want, it's what *he* wants," Gibbs answered, indicating the stairway up which the boy had retreated.

Vera McGraw said, "Don't mince words with me."

"He wants his dad."

"So?"

"So he asked me to find him."

She made an unpleasant sound deep in her bejeweled throat. "And what do you think he'll pay you with?"

"We struck a deal."

"I'll bet you did."

"Why the cold shoulder, Ms. McGraw? We don't know each other well enough for the disrelish to shine through."

"Really? You're a man, aren't you?"

"That's the rumor."

"Then I dislike you on principle."

"Is it my shirt? I was told it made me look smaller."

She tilted her head in appraisal. "You are a tall one. How tall, exactly?"

"Six-seven."

She whistled through a small gap between her incisors. "Wow. Muscular, too. What do you weigh, exactly."

"Two hundred forty-two pounds, three and a quarter ounces."

Her look dripped censure.

"You said *exactly*."

"So here you are," she accused, "just some huge attractive guy intent on helping my nine-year-old nephew on a quest for his deadbeat dad."

"Is Mr. Sizemore a deadbeat dad?"

The pretty face transmogrified into an incredibly contemptuous sneer. "He's much worse than that. If you only knew."

Connor leaned forward on the couch, elbows to knees. "If I only knew what?"

"Nothing."

The teapot's singing interrupted her venomous glare. She went to prepare the brew, returning momentarily with a pair of hefty mugs, not the dainty cup Connor expected. Steam rose as she handed him one; he sampled gingerly then placed the mug on a glass-topped end table, saying, "Tell me about Noah Sizemore."

"No."

"Why?"

She shook her head.

"You don't want the boy to find his father?"

Another shake, with more vehemence.

"Obviously Blister feels differently."

That got a rise. "Don't call him Blister!" she said through her teeth.

"That's what he told me to call him."

"And I'm telling you *not* to. His name is Cody, and that's what you're to call him in my presence."

"Okay. Why would you deliberately keep Cody from finding his father?"

"He won't find him," she insisted, sotto voce.

"Why not?"

"You're the hotshot PI, you find out."

"I have your approval to delve?"

"Delve? What kind of thick-necked palooka says 'delve'?"

"One educated at Duke, maybe?"

Again the whistle, spontaneous this time. "Big and gorgeous and a Dukey to boot. Aren't you a catch."

"So Cody and I have your okay?"

"What's the financial arrangement between you and him?"

"Nothing unusual. He gives me his life savings and I find his dad."

She snorted. "He has about seventy bucks in the bank."

"That's plenty."

"You work for seventy bucks a case? Maybe you aren't such a catch after all."

"I'm altruistic."

Again the derisive snort.

"How about giving me a clue, here?" he said. "Point me in Noah Sizemore's direction. For Cody."

After a moment's reflection Vera said, "Noah has a sister. Last I heard she ran a scabby tanning salon north of the city. Her name's Ellie. I think."

"She married?"

"Husband's last name is Murphy, as I recall."

"Thanks," said Connor Gibbs, draining his cup.

"It's not for you."

"I know. The tea was excellent, by the way."
She nodded in response, sinking deeper into herself.
"One more question?"
She looked up as he stood.
"What's wrong with men?"
"They suck."
On that vacuous note, he left.

THREE

The sign had once proudly proclaimed: TACO'S TANNING TIME. With four letters faded away, it now stated: T CO'S TA NIN IME. No matter; the sign was easy enough to spot. Above the name (what was left of it) was an artist's rendering of a tanning bed—which resembled a hotdog bun resting on a plate so small that the bun overlapped. Canary yellow with foot-high scarlet letters, the sad sign sat high atop a telephone pole, and was visible for quite a distance. Connor eased his van into a vacant parking spot, one of many. A lone blue Ford pickup shared the lot, whether belonging to patron or employee yet to be determined.

The building before him was designed to mimic a barn, but the illusion was fanciful; no one above the age of two would be fooled. Connor climbed three rickety steps and went in, ducking to avoid bumping his head. On the right: an ancient mahogany desk surrounded by potted palms; three straight-backed chairs; a magazine rack filled to overflowing; a low table becircled by beverage stains. On the desk was a mare's nest of papers, and behind it sat a woman with much curly red hair in evidence. She was coloring her nails. One foot was up on the desk's edge, so she could paint it without having to bend down. Acknowledging his

presence with a plucky grin, she kept on stroking, stopping
every few seconds to admire her progress.

Opposite the desk was a cabinet bustling with sunblock-
ers: Tropicana Tanning Lotion, one proclaimed; another
said Blame It on Rio; a third, less wordy, declared itself
Capacity. On the floor near a slick spot was a nonspecific
bottle of a nondescript unguent probably intended for
burns; on the wall nearby, adjacent to a large blue water
dispenser, was a poster of a bodybuilder showing off both
his muscles and his tan. He looked quite taken with himself.

Two mismatching doors separated the office from the
tanning rooms beyond. One of the doors stood ajar. Par-
tially revealed was an upright clothes rack, a potted palm,
and most of a white metal tanning bed. Nearly protruding
from one end of the bed was what appeared to be a giant
wiener, but was more likely a bald or carefully shaven head.
The place reeked of disinfectant.

Approaching the desk and its occupant, Conner tossed
his chin at the open door. "Customer?"

The redhead glanced through the door, dipped her coiffure, and said, "That's Frank."

Connor looked again at the protruding pate, pink from
the effect of too many ultraviolet rays. "You have to be
joking."

She put her foot on the floor, leaned forward for a better
view through the open door, then said, "Nope, that's Frank
all right."

"Is his last name Furter?"

"Beg pardon?"

Irony did not dwell in this place. "Can a guest have a
little privacy?"

"Sure. We got as little privacy as anybody." Cackling
at her wit, she hiked up another foot and began to dab.
"Frank's claustrophobic. Likes to leave the door open,
them rooms're so small. You wanna tan, you gotta fill out
a questionnaire." She shoved one over with an elbow, her
hands being engaged in artwork.

"Questionnaire?"

"State requires it. Asks stuff like do you burn easy, got

any skin allergies, do you get sun poisoning, do you tan both indoors and out, that kinda stuff." Dab of purple pigment.

"Actually, what I'd really like is information."

Dab. "About what?" She looked at him over her foot.

"Noah Sizemore."

The look turned sour. "What about him?"

"Aren't you his sister?"

Her lengthy hesitation augered ill for the future of this conversation. Finally: "Yeah, I'm his sister. Name's Ellie."

Connor nodded. "I'm pleased to meet you. Do you know where I can find Noah?"

She shook her head and painted away, stroking attentively, the tongue of concentration peeking from the corner of her mouth.

"No idea?"

"Nope."

"Might your parents know?"

"Doubt it."

"Where do they live? I could ask them."

"They move around a lot," she replied. Finished, she returned the foot to the hardwood floor and stared at him. If the effluvium of nail polish, cleaning solvent, and sweaty feet was unpleasant, her expression was even more so.

"How old is your brother?"

"Don't remember."

"You don't remember how old your brother is? Is he older or younger than you?"

"There was seven of us altogether. I can't recall."

"Can't? Or don't?"

"Whichever, this conversation's over." She stood, pushing the chair back with her buttocks.

"Do you know Noah has a son?"

"Can't say I do, can't say I don't. Can't say I give a toot either way."

"His son is the one trying to find him. The boy's nine."

"You hard-of-hearing?"

"I don't think so."

"Then you heard me say this conversation was over?"

Connor didn't reply.

"You leaving?"

Connor didn't move.

"*Frank!*"

The tanning bed opened and out stepped Mr. Clean. In six strides he joined Connor and Ellie at the desk.

"Whatsa matter, scrumptious?"

"I just gave this jazbo his walking papers. He won't take the hint."

Frank looked Connor up and down, and didn't like what he saw. Nonetheless he said, "You leaving on your own, or I got to toss you?"

"I'll leave." Gibbs turned to go, pausing at the door. "But I might be back."

"You do and it won't go so easy next time," Frank said.

"You could be right," Connor agreed, and left.

Connor had barely cleared the stoop when Ellie said, "Drive down to Eckerds, to the pay phone, and call Noah."

"Probably ain't nothing, sweetcheeks."

Ellie Sizemore Murphy looked her husband in the eye. "Do it."

He did.

FOUR

Connor Gibbs stopped at a shopping center for a hoagie. Two, actually. And chips, a shake. He was, after all, a large man. While slurping chocolate dregs through a straw, he noticed a familiar Ford pickup enter the parking lot. Going to the window of the sandwich shop, he watched the driver of the truck—old Frank Furter himself—quit the vehicle to use a pay phone. "Better to be lucky than good," Gibbs said under his breath, while the only other person in the store, the cashier—a slim specimen with blue hair, tight jeans, and a nose ring—observed surreptitiously and wondered, *Is he talking to himself again?*

As Frank conversed on the phone, Connor watched, still mildly hungry, with Blue Hair examining his backside. Abruptly Frank hung up, stalked heavily to the Ford, climbed aboard, and U-turned toward an exit.

Pointing, Connor said, "You recognize that Ford pickup?"

The cashier followed the pointing finger. "Nuh-uh. But I just love the color."

"That's because it matches your hair."

"How sweet of you to notice."

"See you, Marvin."
"Bye, Connor."

Connor Gibbs made a phone call of his own, then routed
himself to Country Park for a run. Five laps, one-and-a-
half miles per lap. The day was warm; at least a dozen
other runners sweated their way along, some passing, some
trailing. Having removed his shirt, Connor looked like a
bronze Schwarzenegger. Only bigger. More than one ad-
miring glance slid his way. And more than one of envy;
both males and females trod the tarmac. He sprinted the
last half mile, breathing heavily—in through the nose, out
through the mouth—feeling loose, light, and fleet of foot.
And curious: Just who had old Frank called, and why from
a pay booth? Was the tanning salon's phone on the fritz?
The residence phone, too? Was he afraid Ellie would eaves-
drop, or did Frank simply want a secure landline? Interestinger and interestinger.

He slowed to a fast walk, made the big circle once again,
then cooled down with some stretching exercises—to the
delight of a cluster of coeds picnicking nearby. All six fell
instantly in love. Or in lust, depending on proclivity. He
then sat with his back against the trunk of a giant oak and
drank nearly a quart of bottled water.

On the way back to the van, something caught his eye,
under a bush near the bottom of a grassy slope surrounded
by shrubbery of various shapes and sizes. He squinted
against the sun.

"And what are you doing down there?" asked Connor.
The you said nothing.
"Are you hurt? Cold? Hungry? Disenfranchised?"
Not a whimper.
"Do you speak English?" said Connor, visually scruti-
nizing for external damage.
Still no answer.
A gentle surface examination now; probe here, squeeze

there. No broken bones, festering fistulas; no missing teeth or Rush Limbaugh baseball cap.

So Connor gently picked up the collarless pup and took it home.

FIVE

Detective Estelle Lawson was having a bad day. She'd fought with Larry last night until the wee hours, and her throat was sore as a result. Plus her head hurt, not to mention her heart. Larry didn't drink, he didn't smoke, he didn't do dope, he didn't even cuss much. He didn't overeat, didn't stay out late, and cleaned up after himself at home. He dressed well, was moderately handsome, and he was great under the covers. Hell, he even had a terrific sense of humor.

Larry's problem was gambling. Over the years, it had gotten out of control, was consuming him, destroying their marriage, indebting him to the wrong crowd. She'd done her best by him, paying off thousands of dollars in markers, even going so far as to shake down some of the creeps he was indentured to, getting them to give up the vig, sometimes forgive the entire amount.

That was before. Now Larry owed some Chicago mob types, big time, and she couldn't help. Not with dough, not with clout, not with anything. He was up to his ass in alligators and he was on his own.

Where's the Advil? she thought, rummaging through her desk. *Eureka.* She washed a trio down with some warm buttermilk (*Yecch! At least it's wet.*), then checked her notes: "Noah Barry Sizemore, DOB 6-2-61," one read. Another: "Call Connor back."

Connor Gibbs. Bet he doesn't owe the mob fifty grand, she thought. *Hell, if he did, he'd just write them a check.* She picked up the phone and punched in seven digits. Amazingly the big galoot was at his office.

"Quixote, Incorporated," said the galoot.

"Do you really do business under that ridiculous name?"

"I prefer to think of it as a colorful cognomen."

"I'll bet you do. If I knew what the hell a cognomen was, I'd probably agree."

"How are you, Estelle?"

"Lousy."

"Domestic strife?"

" 'Domestic strife'? Why the hell don't you talk like normal people? Whydn't you just say, 'Is Larry porkin' his new secretary?' Or, 'You and Larry still beating the shit out of each other?' You know, stuff like that."

"Knew it. Domestic strife."

"Why couldn't it be PMS?"

"What did you find out, Estelle?"

"From NCIC, *nada.* City has Sizemore in their computer, though. As a kid, he was a bad boy. Grand theft auto at sixteen, expunged at eighteen because he kept his nose clean, relatively speaking; several assault charges at age eighteen, all dismissed. Nothing after that.

"I talked to Billings over in vice," she continued. "He went to high school with Sizemore. Told me the kid—he was by then twenty-three, look who I'm calling kid—met some straight arrow skirt, fell head over whatever, and toed the line from then on. They got married and all, just like grown-ups."

"How cynical you've become in your dotage. And nothing since then?" asked Connor.

"What'd I just say?"

"Simply letting you know I'm paying attention."

"Now, what do I get for doing your grunt work?"

"Undying gratitude?"

"Can't eat that."

"Two dogs and a Coke?"

"Better. No cigar."

"What then?"

"Pizza at Pie Towne. The works, including rattlesnake."

"It's not pure snake, Estelle. They blend in sausage for a more palatable texture."

"Whatever."

"Okay. Larry, too?"

"If I don't shoot him first."

"He drop some change again?"

"Fifty big ones."

Connor whistled into the mouthpiece. "Anything I can do?"

"Wipe out organized crime in Chicago, before it wipes out Larry."

"How soon?"

"Thanks for offering to help, jelly bean, but Larry's a big boy. He'll have to deal with the situation."

"Unfortunately, so do you."

"Probably not for long." She sighed.

"Now, Estelle. You two have been married how long?"

"Since Columbus. A shipboard romance."

Silence for a moment. Then Connor said, "Remember, I'm here if you need me."

Another sigh. "I know. And I appreciate it. By the way, Billings told me some creep by the name of Wacky Mavens used to work with Noah Sizemore at his—Sizemore's, not Wacky's—brother's restaurant. Sizemore was night manager. He hired Wacky to scrub dishes."

"What kind of a name is Wacky?"

"He used to peddle weed."

"Ah. 'Wacky tobaccy.' Isn't that special."

"Street names, Connor. They're required when you want to be cool."

"Think I should get one?"

" 'Gargantua' is taken."

"Good-bye, Estelle."

· · ·

After ringing off Sergeant Lawson, Connor Gibbs called a snitch he knew from his CIA days. The snitch told him that Wacky Mavens was around and about, but that he didn't know where; it seemed he moved a lot. Connor made a mental note to find him later.

First, the Yellow Pages. And there it was, big as life, Sizemore's Barbecue, Route One, barely a mile out of the city. He was heading for the door when the phone chirped insistently—once, twice, thrice. Halfway through number four he yanked it up, saying, "This is a recording. I was just leaving. Record a message after the tone." He then made a sound vaguely reminiscent of a foghorn.

"You really are there," said a nine-year-old voice.

"I didn't fool you?"

"Ha," expleted Cody Wainwright McGraw, sometimes known as Blister.

"Always fools my sister."

"Then she can't be too smart."

"I won't tell her you said that."

"Why? I ain't . . . I'm not afraid of her."

"That's because you don't know any better."

"Were you really leaving?"

"Yes."

"Where're you going?"

"Out."

"Out where?"

"Out, out."

"Will you take me?"

"No." Firmly.

"Pleeease?"

"Why?"

"You *do* work for me, remember."

"How could I forget?"

"Are you working on my case?"

"Even as we speak."

"Yeah? You tracking down a clue?" Excited now.

"Got a magnifying glass right here in my pocket."

"No kidding, can I come?"

Connor thought about it. "I have an errand to run."

"No problem. I can't leave till Aunt Veer gets here, anyway."

"You home by yourself?"

"Sure, but I'm not scared. I even been watching *Alien* with nobody here but us chickens."

Connor hadn't heard that expression in a long time. "What if there's an emergency?"

"Mr. Gibbs, I know how to dial 911."

"Sorry. No offense," Connor said, then agreed to take the boy along to the Sizemore eatery.

Which was a mistake.

At the vet's where Connor had left his canine foundling for professional perusal, he was informed of the pup's approximate age (eight or nine weeks), and its breed (Boykin spaniel). The dog had been dewormed and detoxed and defleaed, for which services Connor had to fork over cash commensurate with open-heart surgery, or at least human toenail removal. The veterinarian suggested running a lost-dog ad in the *Wendover Times Dispatch*, but doubted anything would come of it. "I suspect you've adopted a dog," he surmised. "She was probably abandoned."

"Why abandoned instead of lost?" Connor queried.

The vet picked up the pooch, cradling it against his chest, and lifted a hind foot. "See the white hairs between the toes?"

Connor looked. Closely. "I do, but just barely."

"Kiss of death to a Boykin breeder, at least financially."

"How so?"

"She can't be registered with the Boykin Spaniel Society. She undoubtedly is purebred, mind you, but only a modest blaze of white is allowed, and that on the chest. If she could be registered, she'd bring three hundred bucks, maybe more. With this little thatch of white between her toes, she'd be lucky to fetch half that."

"You mean someone figured that feeding her and anteing up for shots and deworming was a losing proposition fiscally," Connor speculated. "So they decided to remove her politically incorrect DNA from their kennel's gene pool by dumping her in the park?''

"Probably hoped somebody would find her, scoop her up, have her spayed, and love her forever. All would be well in Puppyland,'' agreed the vet.

The pup lay unmoving against the veterinarian's chest, intelligent yellow eyes on Connor's face. "Let's go, dog,'' he said.

On the way home to drop off the pup, Connor cell-phoned his closest male friend, an attorney named Holmes Crenshaw.

"Sur, Arthur, Cone, and Doyle,'' sang the receptionist.

"Hi, Laverne,'' Connor greeted.

"Whatcha doing, big fella?''

"Missing you.''

"Oh, goody.''

"It's love, Laverne, I can't help it. I faunch for your touch. Is the barrister in?''

She giggled like a schoolgirl. "One minute, please.''

After twenty seconds of George Winston, Crenshaw came on. "Hurry. I have clients waiting.''

"In lockup?''

"What, what?''

"I need the dope on a guy named Noah Barry Sizemore, born June twenty-sixth, 1961, right here in friendly old Wendover. He's got a record locally, from his late teen years, but Estelle turned nothing up with NCIC.''

"What do you want with him?''

"Just trying to find the guy, for his son. Kid's nine.''

"Sizemore skip on his child support?''

"Skipped altogether, looks like, seven years ago. The child's mother died.''

"Who raised the kid?''

"Mostly the maternal aunt, Vera McGraw.''

"Works at Cablevision?''

"I don't know where she works.''

There was a short pause, then Crenshaw said, "Something's nagging at me, but I can't retrieve it. But the caution flag definitely went up, *sufi*, I felt it. Walk softly until I can nose around and get back to you. Something's off-kilter.''

It was Connor's turn to pause; Crenshaw was renowned for having a sixth sense. ''I'm checking a minor lead this evening,'' Connor said. ''Then I'll go home and wait till you call.''

''Can I go now?''

They hung up and Connor went to pick up the boy.

Christy McGraw—perspiring profusely but performing her cleansing breaths while an impatient baby railed inside her swollen abdomen—was less than a mile from Warren G. Harding Memorial Hospital when a big black Buick ran the light at the Third Street intersection. She swerved hard to avoid a collision, but the Buick came straight at her, ramming her from the left front and sending her head into the windshield. The force of the crash jammed a jagged strip of plastic into her groin, puncturing her femoral artery as she slammed forward. With her car spinning wildly out of control, she braced herself with a hand on the steering wheel and an elbow on the support pillar directly to her left, doing her best to protect her stomach and its precious cargo. When her caroming vehicle jumped a curb so violently it began to tip over, she leaned sideways, using the seat back to help to cushion against further peril.

As the errant Buick hurtled past, intent now on its own self-destruction, Christy felt no animosity toward the idiot behind the wheel, only concern for her baby. When her car finally came to a skidding halt, she immediately climbed out through the front passenger door, blood spurting from her ruptured artery, and sought help. No one was near,

except maybe the dunce in the Buick, whom she could no
longer see in the car. She pressed a hand against her
wound, tightly, trying to stanch the blood flow, then nearly
doubled over from a contraction, suddenly terrified. What
if the paramedics failed to arrive before she bled to death?
Could the child survive in her womb if her own heart
stopped? If so, how long? Safer for the baby to come out
now; then an EMS crew could attend to it immediately, not
have to take her to the hospital for an emergency C-section,
one that might be too late . . .

So she squatted right there—beside her ruined car, out
in the open, no help from anyone but God, with her right
hand striving desperately to stem the insistent flow of life
from her body—and delivered to herself a baby boy. With
a hair ribbon, she tied off the umbilical, then used the same
misshapen shard of plastic that had imperiled her life to
sever the cord connecting her to her son, as his defiant,
red-faced cries swelled her heart.

But the rapid blood loss was taking its toll. Lying with
her back to the pavement, bloody clothing further soaked
by the gasoline pooling beneath her, she carefully placed
the infant on her depleted abdomen. But he wouldn't stay
still. Petrified that he might roll off her body, she rotated
onto her left side and curled into a fetal position, both arms
protectively cradling the newborn against her chest, and
waited for an ambulance to arrive. She did her best to keep
pressure on her gaping artery, but it was no use.

She never heard the siren.

Able Johnson piled out of his Buick and vomited all over
the sidewalk, on all fours like an animal. While he was thus
engaged, Christy McGraw was delivering her baby. After
a minute or two Johnson climbed laboriously to his feet,
staggered out into the street, and spotted the woman birth-
ing. "Ohmygod!" he exclaimed. "Ohmygod! Ohmygod!
Ohmygod!"

He marched erratically but purposefully across four
lanes and a median to a curb market. There he purchased
a six-pack of Bud, paying with a fifty-dollar bill and de-

nying the change. Then out the door, around the back, into a rest room, locking the door.

Wedged between an overflowing trash bin and the single sink, he consumed four of the six beers, smiling weasellike and belching comfortably. "Get me on a DWI now, mother-fuckers," he said, and toasted the toilet. On the fifth beer, he passed out.

SIX

Sizemore's Barbecue was surrounded by a gravel lot big enough to host all the cars attending a Chicago Bulls championship game. It was nearly seven o'clock on a sweltering Saturday eve, and a line of eager diners spilled out of the doorway. Connor found a parking spot not too distant from the thronged portal, then he and his youthful companion joined the queue. The building was nondescript: cedar siding, shake roof, dormers, and a sign that allowed no alcoholic beverages on the premises. Obviously a family place, according to Baptist mores, anyway. Probably didn't allow impure thoughts. No gays, either; Lord, no. VISA, MasterCard, and bigots accepted.

Finally in the door and seated at table. A perusal of the bill of fare—posted on two walls in big block letters, yellow on black—suggested that a collective cholesterol count could run to seven figures. Fried this and that, and gravy of course, plus pork cooked various ways; french fries and baked spuds and hush puppies; cobbler, coleslaw, collards. GREEN GARDEN SALAD, a sign touted, for that slimmer you.

The waiters were all teenagers, long on bustle but short on service. And hygiene. Connor watched a gangly yellow-topped example duck into the bathroom, to reappear only seconds later. *Wouldn't want him to touch my food,* Gibbs thought. After a ten-minute wait the same towheaded kid brought over a pitcher of water and an order pad. "Take your order?" he said, placing the pitcher on the table.

"Two hard-boiled eggs and a coconut," from Connor.

"Huh?"

"That way you won't touch the edible parts."

"I don't understand."

"Why am I not surprised? We'll have a dose of salad with baked potatoes à la carte."

"What's à la carte?" said Old Yeller.

"And hush puppies?" Cody W. McGraw requested.

"And hush puppies for my young companion, please."

"I still don't get the à la carte stuff."

"Perhaps the cook will. Is the owner in tonight?"

"Mr. Sizemore?"

"The same."

"I reckon he's in his office."

"You reckon you could request his presence?"

"What kinda presents?"

"With a 'C,' " Connor said helpfully.

The waiter's perplexity compounded.

"Never mind. Would you ask Mr. Sizemore to join us for a moment? I have something I'd like to ask him."

"I reckon I could."

"I'm so glad."

The flaxen-haired kid went away.

"What's à la carte?" Blister asked.

"That's when certain items are priced individually. I was pulling his chain a little, in payback."

"For what."

"Taking a leak without washing his hands."

"How you know he did that?"

"I saw him go into the l'il buckaroos' room. He was out too soon to have washed."

"Maybe he just did his hair."

"Good point, if he'd had a currycomb in evidence. Alas, there was evidence of recent urination. The telltale spot."

"The what?"

"I'll explain later."

Four men were approaching, one so thin and pale it seemed a miracle he could perambulate under his own power. The other three were neither thin nor pale. One wore a red tank top and was maybe six-four and two forty. The second was roughly six feet tall and built like a college fullback. A third was only five-eight, but hefted around three hundred pounds; despite his excessive bulk, he was very light on his feet, like a sumo wrestler. The quartet stopped five feet from Connor's table, where the thin pale man hooked a chair with his toe and spun it around, then sat slowly, apparently painfully, to place his narrow chin on the back of the chair. He sized up Connor Gibbs for ten seconds, then looked at the boy. His eyes went soft for a moment, then hardened again as he swung his gaze back to Gibbs. "Sean said you wanted to ask me something."

"Are you Sizemore?"

"Tate Sizemore, yes, but you can call me Mr. Sizemore."

"This is your nephew, Mr. Sizemore. He likes to be called Blister."

Once again the eyes betrayed, but only briefly. "And you are?"

"Connor Gibbs."

Thin, pale nod of recognition. "Heard you went to my sister's place, stirred things up."

"What things?"

"Never you mind." The eyes were suddenly hard again, like flint. "Here's the story. You quit looking for Noah. Starting five minutes ago."

"Why? His son just wants—"

Tate Sizemore slammed his open hand on the table so hard it grabbed the attention of everyone in the place. "Don't give a camel fart what his son wants! You keep asking around about him and you're gonna come to grief, boy. You understand?"

It had been a long time since anyone had called him boy, but Connor said nothing.

The red tank top said, "He asked you if you understand."

Connor looked up. "I heard him."

"Then answer the man," growled the sumo wrestler.

Connor stood. "Let's go, Blister."

The fullback, stepping in close, put a thick finger against
Connor's chest. "But you ain't said you understand."

Blister McGraw simply sat, mesmerized.

"Blister?" Connor said.

The boy jumped to his feet, knocking over his chair in
the process, the sound incredibly loud in the silenced room.

"Say you understand," growled Sumo, "or you don't
leave. Standing up."

Blister wet his lips with the tip of his tongue. A fight!
Big Connor Gibbs, alone against three guys! Wow! Wait'll
he got back to school; he'd get free Jell-O for a week off
this story.

The players moved in, spreading out a little, flexing their
hands, posturing for the crowd. This was gonna be easy,
they thought.

They didn't know Connor Gibbs.

Tate Sizemore got up to leave, turning his back on the
spectacle. Connor said, "Sizemore."

Sizemore turned to face him. "What?"

"I understand."

Sizemore did not smile triumphantly. In fact, he showed
no expression at all. He just said, "Understand what?"

"That you want me to stop asking about Noah."

Sizemore came over to stand toe-to-toe, if not eye-to-
eye. "What I said was if you keep pushing, you're gonna
come to grief."

Connor nodded.

"*Say it!*"

Connor glanced at the three men hovering nearby, not
only ready to pounce, but willing. He returned his attention
to the thin, pale man before him. "If I keep searching for
Noah, grief will come of it," he said.

Then he and the boy walked out amid jeers and catcalls.

•　　•　　•

"I can't believe it!" Cody McGraw was livid.

"What?"

"That you wouldn't fight!"

"Why should I fight? We were in no danger. There were too many witnesses for them to jump me."

"But what will all those people think of you?"

"That's no concern of mine."

"No concern!"

"Blister, I'm not responsible for what people think. I try to behave appropriately for a given situation. What people think of me is up to them."

"They prob'ly think you're a coward."

"But I'm not, so I can live with their thinking that. If I were, maybe I couldn't live with it."

"What if *I* think you're a coward?"

"Do you?"

Time out for pouting, then: "I don't know."

"Okay."

"But those guys . . ."

"What guys?"

"You *know* what guys. The three that were ready to whip your . . ."

"Fanny?"

"*Yeah!*"

"What about them?"

"What if *they* thought you were scared of them?"

"You think I should be concerned about those three jerks?"

"Well . . ."

"Do you care what they think of you?"

"No, but I didn't . . ."

"Back down?" Connor finished for him.

A confused, miserable nod from Blister.

"My young friend, I'm going to do something for you that I seldom do. I'm going to explain myself."

Blister was all ears.

"First, that was neither the time nor the place for a tussle; too many people. One on three takes lots of room, unless you want your head handed to you. Second, we now know that your dad's into something, or up to something, or hiding something. If not, why wouldn't Tate—and Ellie, for that matter—be forthcoming with information? We learned a thing or two, so the trip to the restaurant wasn't a total loss. Finally, if that trio of thugs does indeed believe that I was afraid of them, it might work to our advantage next time.''

"You think there'll be a next time?"

"Oh yes," was Connor's dour reply.

It was past midnight and Connor was reading Robert B. Parker's *Small Vices;* Spenser was still in California, recuperating with the help of Hawk and Susan Silverman. *That damn hill wears me out just reading about it,* Connor thought as he went to answer the phone.

"You home?" said Holmes Crenshaw.

"No. This is a recording."

"I'm coming over."

"Now?"

"Now."

"I'm busy."

"Bennie there?"

"Early class tomorrow."

"Then whatever you're busy with can wait."

"No, it can't. I'm waiting for Spenser to go back to Boston."

"You got the new Parker?"

"Yeah, Spenser's been shot, but—"

"*Don't tell me!* I haven't read it yet."

"Can I go now?"

"Fifteen minutes. Put on some coffee."

"In your dreams."

And they hung up.

"What kind of dog is that?" asked Holmes Crenshaw.

"A girlkin," answered Connor Gibbs.

"A what?"

"A girlkin."

"Never heard of it. Heard of a Boykin Spaniel."

"This one's female."

"I get it. So what's her name?"

"Zep."

"What kind of name is Zep?"

"As in 'Win one for the Zepper.' "

"That's *gipper*."

"Oh."

"You gonna change her name to Gip?"

"Her name's Zep. Want some camomile tea?"

"I'd sooner drink possum piss."

"You doubtless already had your daily quota."

"Is there no coffee around here?"

"You bet. I use it as mulch for the poinsettia."

"Decaf?"

"Regular. Plant's up all night anyway."

"Are you going to fix me some tea or not?"

"Would you like peppermint in yours?"

"Whatever, just so long as it's caffeinated."

And then they spoke of other things.

Johnston Thurgood was fairly salivating. He could just smell the barbecue, taste the Brunswick stew, hear the deep-fat fryer popping . . . in his mind, of course, since he was a quarter mile from Sizemore's Barbecue and the prevailing wind was against him. Ah, well; Thurgood was thirty pounds overweight, anyhow. His wife said more like forty, but what did she know, she who could eat four fruitcakes and not gain an ounce, still a size six like the day they were married, for Pete's sake, her chicken-necked papa standing there to give her away, him in a black suit better suited to a funeral, acting like he wore one every day instead of a carpenter's apron, all put-on airs, and Martha was worse, what with—

His reverie was interrupted as the last group of diners left the establishment, gabbing and laughing their way to their respective cars, one an Olds Cutlass, the other one of those nifty Nissan Z-cars, probably the turbo version, who gives a shit, it takes more than a neat car to . . .

Well, now.

Up came the binoculars, Nikon, good pair, as a man, coming to lock the front door, was briefly limned by interior lights. "Hello," Thurgood remarked, stretching out the word as a puerile grin split his fat face. "I got me five hundred clams, for Pete's sake," he commented gleefully, scratching one of his chins; then starting the motor, he eased in the clutch and slunk away in the dark. . . .

Johnston Thurgood sought the nearest pay phone—near the Cinema Twelve on Dellwood—and made two calls, smiling all the while. By ten the following morning, he was not five hundred but a thousand dollars richer. . . .

So he took his wife to the Olive Garden for lunch.

Holmes Crenshaw, comfortably nestled and now sipping tea, was saying: "You remember Billy Earl Scoggins? Used to snitch for Clark at the Bureau, did a few jobs for us in Honduras?"

"Do I ever. What's that cockalorum doing these days?"

"What the hell's a cockamacallit?"

"Look it up. What about Billy Earl?"

Crenshaw shook his head in exasperation, but continued. "He moved back to the States to open a Greek restaurant in Durham. He still keeps an ear to the ground, picks up an extra buck here and there."

Connor took a swig of tea. "And?"

"I asked him about Noah Sizemore. The story goes that Sizemore killed a guy in an automobile accident nearly seven years ago. Ran him off the road. Guy's car burned up with him in it. Some tourists from Iowa were passing by and saw the accident, then dialed 911. They claimed Sizemore ran the guy off the road on purpose. Our traffic boys and girls revisited the site and, bingo, no skid marks until well after the collision had taken place, and then only to avoid going over an embankment. After a day or two Sizemore was picked up for assault with a deadly weapon. That way the cops could hold him while they smoked things over.

"Then, the way Billy Earl tells it, the grand jury returns

a charge of vehicular manslaughter. Sizemore used to do business with Boz Fangelli—a little numbers, extortion—nothing big and nothing Noah got nailed for, until in 1988 Sizemore marries a schoolteacher and turns his back on crime.

"So when Sizemore gets his tail in a crack with this manslaughter beef, he turns to Boz for bail, one hundred fifty Gs. Sizemore coughs up fifteen percent to Boz and walks. Right out of town. Boz gets burned for the bond money, and is he pissed."

"Sizemore's been a fugitive from justice for seven years," Connor said.

"Listen, the plot thickens. Boz hires your best pal Jackson Slade to find Sizemore and bring him back, only Slade doesn't deliver. Sizemore's from a large mountain clan—six siblings at last count, and *beaucoup* aunts, uncles, and sundry—so he's well protected. He also had a $250,000 life-insurance policy on his wife, who was killed in a wreck two years before all this happens. Doubling it for accidental death, that's five hundred thou, nontaxable. When Sizemore vanished into the hills, he went heavy."

"Thus he wouldn't need to work, take a chance on showing up on some federal computer screen," Connor said.

"Correct. And speaking of computers, I can't figure how Sizemore didn't pop up on NCIC, since he's a fugitive. Can I have more tea?"

Connor fetched the teapot and poured for them both, then returned it to the kitchen, came back and sat down. "Let me get this straight. Noah Sizemore's into petty crime from his middle teens, then finds love and goes straight, but not too long after, his wife is killed in a car accident?"

"And I understood she died in childbirth," added Crenshaw.

"My God, she was heading to deliver the child and was killed en route?"

Holmes nodded. "By a drunk driver."

Absorbing this, Connor continued. "So Noah collects a lump of insurance money and dutifully rears his boy for a couple years. Then out of the blue he deliberately runs a guy off the road and kills him, gets arrested for assault, which is subsequently bumped to manslaughter, and cons Boz Fangelli into posting a hefty bond. After that he dumps the kid on his sister-in-law and scoots, with Jackson Slade in hot pursuit.''

"That covers it. This tea is great," Crenshaw commented, draining his cup. "And your dog just peed on the rug.''

"Not to worry, I've trained her to tinkle in exactly the same spot every time," Connor said, rising to get paper towels for blotting just as Crenshaw's pager sounded.

"Can I use your phone?" from the lawyer.

"No." Connor spoke from the kitchen.

"Thanks," said Crenshaw, and dialed the number displayed on the pager, saying "Holmes here" when it was answered on the other end.

He listened attentively for twenty seconds. "Where did you see him?" he said, then listened again.

"When?" he said, and listened some more.

"Don't try to hold me up. Of course I'll make it worth your while. How far are you from there?" More listening.

"Go back and keep an eye on things and it'll get you two bills.''

Mild dissension from the other end.

"Yes, in addition." He hung up. "Putz."

"Who?" Connor asked, kneeling and wicking up puppy pee. "Bad girl," he scolded. Zepper lay on her belly, feet sprawled fore and aft, and watched. She did not appear contrite.

"Hurry up," said Crenshaw as he shouldered into his suit coat.

"What's the hurry?"

"That was Johnston Thurgood."

"What'd he want, a dozen éclairs?" Connor kept dabbing.

"He's not far from Sizemore's Barbecue, where you had supper. Or at least waited in line for an hour."

"Thurgood was watching the place? Why?" Dab.

"Wouldn't say, but guess who else he saw there?"

"Cody Wainwright McGraw. With me." Squirt of Ly-
sol.

"Don't know about Cody, but he did spot his daddy."

Connor looked up. "Noah?"

"In the flesh. You ready yet?"

Connor was. They left.

SEVEN

Jackson Slade was plowing a fertile field when his phone rang at 12:28 ante meridiem. He stopped mid-stroke and barked, "Hello," then listened a spell, his *objet d'amour* rolling away to perform an excretory function. By the time she returned, Slade was partly dressed. She arched an inquisitive brow.

"Thurgood," he responded.

She arched the other.

"He spotted Noah Sizemore, out at his brother's dump," he informed.

"I like their barbecue," she countered.

"You would, Fatima," he said, and they continued to argue as he girded himself for battle.

Underneath baggy, pleated pants he secured a catcher's cup over his jockstrap; his scrotum was well protected. Soccer-type shin guards enclosed his former-soccer-playing shins and his biker boots had metal-reinforced toes; his lower limbs were well protected. He shouldered into a Second Chance Med Vest, a self-contained type of soft body armor designed for coverage front and rear; his torso was well protected.

Into a small-of-the-back holster, Slade snugged the

Czech CZ-52 his dad had brought back from Vietnam—an
ugly, bulky, relatively inefficient auto pistol that had two
things in its favor: very high muzzle velocity (for an au-
toloader) and commendable reliability. To his left forearm
Slade strapped an ASP, a collapsible steel tactical baton that
when extended to its full length measured twenty-one
inches. Atop his curly crown he set a blue hard-plastic
billed cap like professional baseball players wear when batting; around his neck went a strap of ballistic nylon, secured
with Velcro. Completing the accoutrements was a double-
edged boot knife sharp enough to shave a gnat.

"Think you're ready, Hummer?" Fatima queried with a
grin. She called him Hummer due to his predilection for
humming "The Battle Hymn of the Republic" as he neared
climax.

He grinned back, wolfine, conscienceless. "You wouldn't
want me to get hurt, would you? The Three Stooges are out
there tonight, and one of them bad boys weighs as much as a
draft horse."

"You could wear my nails, go for their jugular," she
prodded. No one alive could rib Jackson Q. Slade but Fatima.

"You reckon the glue'd stick?"

She grinned again, came over, cupped his cup in one tiny
palm. "Take care of the equipment," she advised. "You
may want to drill some more tonight."

"It's likely," he concurred. They kissed and he departed.

It was after one when Slade pulled off the blacktop and
onto the gravel outside Sizemore's Barbecue. He eased
around back, V-8 burbling, and scoped the employees'
parking lot. Near the back door squatted Tate's big Suburban, a tan thing too tall by half. *That hulk'd roll in a
tight S-curve at forty-five miles an hour,* he reflected. *Why
would anyone drive one of those things?* He switched off
his own sleek, low-slung conveyance to wait, while Ozzy
Osbourne wailed in his ear. He hummed in concert.

Not for long.

• • •

Sumo came out first, his three-hundred-pound mass making
the wooden back stairs creak as he descended. Spotting the
Camaro, he heeled-and-toed his greasy bulk over, humping
his shoulders like a constipated crab. "Who the fuck're
you?" was his nocturnal salutation.

"The tooth fairy. Any of yours loose?" Slade responded.

"Get outta the car and we'll see, candy ass."

Slade opened the door very suddenly, its leading edge
cracking into the larger man's kneecap, which HURT.
While Sumo was attending to his pained patella, Jackson
Slade was climbing out of his car; when Sumo stood to
thwart the threat, Slade kicked him on the very same knee,
in the very same place, which hurt A LOT. "Fuck!"
growled Sumo, reaching out a fat hand for Slade's shirt.
But the shirt was no longer there. It had shifted to port, and
from in front of it came an elbow, which impacted Sumo's
nose at a particularly vulnerable spot and showered them
both with blood. Sumo staggered back as Slade bored in,
fists pumping—left jab, left jab, right hook—Sumo's head
jerking at the force of each blow. Jab, jab, left hook, right
cross, and Sumo was down on one knee, the HURT knee,
which had had ENOUGH! He cried out in discomfort and
rage, but his bawl was cut short by an elbow that removed
three front teeth to deposit them down his throat.

Sumo was still choking when the fullback flew out the
door in a frenzy. Short-lived. As the gridironer stretched
out a threatening paw, Jackson Slade withdrew from his
long-sleeved shirt the ASP, bringing it across his body from
left to right, and on up over his right shoulder. The inertia
telescoped the retracted weapon to its full twenty-one lethal
inches. Then, striking forward and down as if hammering
a nail, he broke all the fingers on the fullback's right hand.
Rotating the baton swiftly to the right, Slade snapped his
opponent's left wrist, then swung the bar left again—using
the snapping power and speed of his own wrist—to break
the unfortunate man's ulna. The fullback, pain-racked and
demoralized, dropped his guard completely, so Slade
quickly executed a leg sweep, putting the fullback's rump

on the gravel, HARD, then applied the baton to his neck.
The big football star slumped to the side.

Red Tank Top appeared just as his buddy was biting the
dust, and couldn't contain his ferocity. He leaped from the
stoop—bypassing the steps altogether in his rampant male-
ness—and landed in a martial-arts stance, leading with his
left leg, bent at the knee, the right one to the rear and ready
to kick. As Slade advanced, obviously undaunted, Tank
Top launched a swinging back kick. Slowly. Slade de-
flected it easily with his left forearm, then cracked one of
Tank Top's ribs with the baton, whapped him behind the
ear to bring the fool to his knees, then the finisher, a back-
hand blow that pulped the scalp.

Abrupt silence, except for Slade's mildly labored
breathing . . .

. . . and the hammer coming back on a .357 Magnum
revolver.

Slade turned toward the sound, which had come from the
back door. In the doorway stood a thin pale man with a
long black handgun pointed at Jackson Slade, standing
there in his bulletproof vest.

Actually the gun was pointed at Slade's *cup,* which
would stop a rising knee, a darting boot, a swinging
club . . .

. . . but not a bullet.

Jackson Slade stood very, very still.

"Get into your sissy car and cart your slimy ass off my
property."

"I came for your brother, Tate."

"I know why you came. Also know you assaulted three
members of my staff, two with a deadly weapon."

"You're right. Go call the cops. Have 'em come arrest
me."

"You better leave, boy."

"Think I'll stay," Slade pushed, grinning wolfishly.

"You do, you'll be dead."

Slade thought that over. He had in fact assaulted two of
the meatballs with a deadly weapon, so Sizemore probably
could shoot him stone dead and walk away from it, espe-

cially since there were no witnesses except Tate's own employees.

Time to go.

"Next time I won't be alone," he said.

"You're never alone, Slade. Satan's always riding your backside."

Slade grinned again, demonically he hoped; he liked Tate's allusion. He went to his car, folded himself in, cranked up, leaned out the window. "You could be right," he said. "But what an ally."

At his rapid departure, gravel flew like brimstone.

A burgundy Camaro Z28 nearly ran Connor Gibbs and Holmes Crenshaw off the road about a half mile from Sizemore's Barbecue. Connor said, "Wasn't that our dear friend Jackson Q?"

"I believe it was," Holmes agreed. "That's the way he normally drives. But I thought his Zee was burgundy."

"That one was burgundy."

"Looked brown to me."

"Take off your shades."

"Did that, I wouldn't be cool."

They pulled onto Sizemore's graveled lot, where there were no cars in evidence. "Go around back," suggested Crenshaw.

They did.

Several cars there, and against the front tire of one leaned the very heavy man Gibbs thought of as Sumo. He was bleeding from several sources, most obviously his mouth; the stubby chin dripped crimson. Not far away, a teenage girl was attending to the man who resembled a football player, holding a sandwich Baggie filled with ice to his thick neck. The guy's right hand was bent, as if fingers had been broken, and held tightly against his side. Something appeared to be wrong with his other hand as well. Tate Sizemore knelt beside a fellow in a red tank top, who lay unmoving, facedown in the gravel. As Connor's vehicle approached the carnage, Tate stood and withdrew a long black revolver from his waistband.

Gibbs and Crenshaw got out of the van to confront Sizemore, who seemed even paler than he'd been earlier that
evening. The thin man was quivering with emotion. "You
two better leave right now. I'm about at the end of my
rope."

Connor said, "I think I passed Jackson Slade just down
the road. He do all this?"

Sizemore started to nod, but caught himself. "I said you
better go."

Holmes Crenshaw looked at Gibbs. "It appears Thurgood has been playing both ends against the middle."

"Looks like."

Sizemore said, "Who?"

"Johnston Thurgood, know him?"

Tate shook his head.

"Does gofer work for whoever pays. Obviously Slade
has been paying him to keep an eye on you."

"What for?"

"Looking for Noah, I suppose. Didn't he give Slade the
slip a few years back?"

Tate clammed up.

"Well, tonight," Connor continued, "Thurgood called
the good counselor here to say he'd spotted Noah. On these
premises. Must have called Slade as well, probably before
he phoned us."

Nothing from Tate.

"You going to call an ambulance for these boys?" asked
Connor.

"We'll take care of them," said Tate.

"He doesn't want cops involved," Crenshaw observed.

"That right?" asked Connor.

Tate said nothing again.

"Noah was here, wasn't he?"

More nothing.

"Look, I've got no beef with Noah. I work for his son,
who just wants to meet his daddy. Face-to-face. Noah man
enough to handle that?"

Tate simply glared, the long black revolver held at arm's
length beside his right leg.

Holmes said, "Guess Sizemore men don't amount to much. Dump their kids on their in-laws, then run off to the mountains and do the highland fling." He looked at Connor. "Inbreeding."

Suddenly the long black revolver was in his face, muzzle against his broad nose, the barrel trembling. "Shut up, you buck nig—"

Quick as the flick of a skink's tongue, Holmes brought up a big right hand, grasped the gun at the frame-cylinder juncture to prevent the cylinder's rotation, and jerked the piece from Tate Sizemore's diddering hand. Sizemore was no longer simply pale; he was *white*.

"Please, no racial slurs," Holmes insisted. "Oh, and if you ever point a gun at me again, you bloodless little man, I'll make you eat it."

A slim string of mucus trailed down Sizemore's philtrum as he stood there, tremulous, incensed, impotent. Holmes Crenshaw flipped open the cylinder, dumped the seven rounds into his right palm, snapped the cylinder back into battery, reached out, and stuffed the long black gun into Tate's waistband. He tossed the cartridges thirty feet away.

"Tate," Connor said, but Tate couldn't seem to take his rancor-filled eyes off Crenshaw. Connor was afraid the man was about to take a swing at Holmes—which would have been a major error—so he shouted, *"Tate!"*

Sizemore's head snapped around.

"You needn't be annoyed at my friend. He just spared your life. Last person I saw stick a gun in his face died, right then, right there. Holmes is being benevolent. Don't push it."

Tate smeared the snot with the back of a thin white hand and said nothing.

"Tell Noah his son wants to see him, God knows why. Either Daddy sets up a meet or I'll find him and he can explain to me why he didn't. And I'm not as easygoing as my pal, here. Get my drift?"

Tate just dribbled some more, the viscous fluid pale green in the glare from the streetlights.

"By the way, there'll be no cops involved in this situa-

tion. Whatever Noah's problems with the law, they have
nothing to do with me and Blister." There was naught left
for Connor to say but "Let's go, Holmes."

Tate Sizemore took five pills, washing them down with a
tepid cup of black coffee. The kitchen smelled of stale
grease and salad dressing. (One of the cooks had dropped
a gallon jar of thousand island.) Noah came in and sat beside him. "I'm sorry," he said.

Tate patted his arm, then mopped his own forehead with
a dishcloth. He reeked of perspiration and fatigue. "Not
your fault. You came to help me."

"I never should have gone to the door tonight, where I
could be seen. But I thought everybody'd given up on
catching me, it's been so long."

"Slade'll never give up. You made a monkey out of him.
Man like him won't never let that go. He'll be watching."

"So what do we do, big brother?"

Tate smiled at the familiar title and patted Noah's arm
again. "I don't know, boy. I surely don't."

Connor's cellular squealed as he and Holmes tooled homeward. "It is I," he said.

"And it is me," she said.

"What can I do for you, love?"

"Ring my chimes."

"Again?"

"Been since Tuesday."

"Oh, Horny, thy name is Woman."

"I believe that's 'Vanity.' "

"Not in your case."

"How about: Oh, Horny, thy name is Benella?"

"The ring of truth."

"So I can bathe? And shave?"

His breath snagged on the inhale. "Don't. It drives me
wild."

"I know," she whispered, and was gone.

"Bennie?" Crenshaw verified as Connor put down his
instrument.

"In the flesh."

"Ample, may I opine."

"But lean."

"No question. You're a very lucky man," Holmes remarked, then chuckled. "Why are you accelerating?"

"Shut up," Connor said priapically, and they motored on. Faster.

EIGHT

Benella Mae Sweet moved languidly, inadvertently brushing a bare flank against one of Connor's tender parts, turgid at the moment though he lay sleeping. "Again?" she murmured sweetly. When he failed to answer, she glanced back over a velvet shoulder. *Even as he slumbers,* she thought. *Amazing.*

She woke him.

An hour later they lay entwined, accumulation of fluids be damned, and enjoyed the afterglow. "Sigh," she said contentedly.

"And well you might."

"Was it good for you, too, Pegasus?"

He whinnied theatrically, then they giggled like truants skinny-dipping in a mill pond. After a spell of halfhearted groping and fishing, they rolled apart to cool spread-eagle.

After a moment, reluctantly she ventured: "The Jeep's dying," and felt his gaze upon her. She was embarrassed. "I'm sorry," she said.

"Your graduation gift."

"Eleven good years," she admitted, eyes glistening.

"Almost two hundred thousand miles and doesn't use a quart between changes."

"Want another one?"

"You offering?"

He kissed her, because they were not only lovers but very much alike.

She was, for a woman, as imposing as he—just over six feet and not far under 180 pounds. She owned a health club, taught aerobics and martial arts, captained a softball team, and volunteered at Habitat for Humanity; she had a soul mate, a wedded lady, whom she loved unabashedly but who wished to remain in the marriage in order to have children—not to mention the benefits of her husband's money and sphere of influence.

Benella had feelings for only one man, in fact allowed no adult male ever to touch her, except one: Connor Gibbs—lover, benefactor, savior, friend. Her *best* friend, and she his.

"Thanks, sugar pie, but I can afford to buy my own now."

"Of course you can," he said, nipping at her regal neck. "I'd just like to—"

"I know," she cut him off. "You're the most generous human I've ever met, and I love it about you, along with various other aspects of your person." She fondled one of those aspects as she spoke, gaining its enlargement. "Don't you ever get enough?" she purred, and lifted a lengthy limb to place over his.

"Of you? Never."

But he tried.

"So what are you getting?" he asked later, breath still laboring from exertion.

"A Stinger."

"What the hell's a Stinger?"

"New job, built in Puerto Rico with an aluminum skin, so it isn't very heavy and won't rust. I ordered it with leather seats, a bright yellow four-by-four with an onboard inflator for my bicycle tires. And two tops, one detachable, the other folds up like on my CJ-7.''

"It shouldn't require much engine to lug it around."

"A little 1.3-liter four-banger, supposed to get fifty miles per gallon and do a hundred and ten on the straights.''

"Where do you buy these things?''

"I'm getting mine through a client who does business in the Islands. Knows a guy in Nevis says he can get him as many as he wants.''

"Can I buy one?''

"Hell no.'' She bit him on a deltoid. "This gives me the one-up on you. For a change.''

"Hoyden.''

"Ha!'' She bit him again, harder. "I gave up politics.''

"That's not the definition I had in mind.'' He lipped her in defense, but in a more sensitive, protuberant neighborhood.

"Don't I know it!'' She chortled, then launched her supple body at him. Grappling and giggling, they fell off the bed, over four hundred pounds of golden humanity, her dominating at first, until he slipped inside and she arched her back and they winged off together in search of satiety.

In late May of 1988, District Attorney Taryl Drexler was fit to be tied. Able Johnson—a murderer as far as the DA was concerned, pure and simple—could not even be charged with DWI, let alone manslaughter. The reason? Because the asshole had not been arrested at the scene of the fatal collision he'd caused, but a half hour later, in the bathroom of a convenience store across the street, guzzling beer, with but a minor cut on his forehead and deep repentance in his soul. Oh, how Able had groveled and blubbered, vomited and pissed himself, begging for forgiveness for his horrible transgression . . .

. . . leaving the scene of an accident.

LEAVING THE SCENE OF AN ACCIDENT!

The sorry son of a bitch had known that the woman was badly hurt, maybe dying (which she ultimately had), and he'd still sashayed right on across the street—all contrite, of course—simply to drown his sorrow. . . .

Yeah, right.

Able Johnson had known that he couldn't be charged with drunk driving if he wasn't caught until after the fact, and imbibing alcohol at the time.

"Shit!" yelled Drexler, slamming a handball-hardened

fist down on his desk. He was a moral man, a man who'd fought drunk drivers with uncompromising zeal ever since the afternoon his own twelve-year-old daughter had been mangled by one as she walked the two blocks home from school. . . .

TWO BLOCKS!

DWI offenders were now his crusade, and he was their nemesis. Sometimes he and the law prevailed, sometimes not, but . . .

THIS SITUATION WAS A FUCKING TRAVESTY!

He gulped down his blood-pressure medication. And a Valium. He felt like he needed THREE . . . or a gun . . .

TO BLOW THE SORRY SON OF A BITCH AWAY!

He paced and fumed, then repeated, head throbbing.

Finally he called Martha, his wife of sixteen years, who could always calm him down. And she did, though it took her forty-seven minutes and two Tranxene to do so. After the ordeal she lay down for an hour to recuperate.

And thus did District Attorney Taryl Drexler manage to get through the rest of his day . . .

. . . as Able Johnson walked—minus five hundred dollars and his driver's license, to be sure, but he walked just the same, smirking triumphantly—to hail a cab.

After all, Able had spent more years of his life without a license than with one, so it presented no problem.

He drove anyway.

NINE

By 9:07, Connor Gibbs was showered, shaved, shampooed, and slicing cantaloupes—two big ones—and a half watermelon, tossing the seeds into the sink, garbage-disposal side. There was citrus in the blender, for juice, and pumpernickel for toasting, stacked on a plate. Skim milk, fresh-cut flowers, the morning paper. "Elysium," he greeted his partner as she descended damp and demanding.

"Not to me, bucko," she demurred. "Coffee, coffee, coffee."

"Yonder it steeps." Connor pointed. She beelined for the indicated carafe.

"That's not all you're going to have, is it?" he questioned as she slurped her first heated sip.

"For now. I'll have an Ensure after I dry my hair."

"Bennie—"

"*Connor.*" She mimicked his tone, then smiled at his perplexity. "I weighed 175 pounds this morning. That's two too many. Need to shed 'em."

He popped a cantaloupe wedge into his mouth and chewed, speaking around the juicy obstruction. "You're skipping breakfast over two pounds?"

"At my size, two pounds makes me look like an amazon.

Four pounds makes me look like Jabba the Hutt.''

"My dear," said Connor in Groucho mode, "you *are* an amazon.''

She grinned and spun with her cup to head back upstairs just as the doorbell tolled. "Oh crap," she expleted en route to the door. Two boys—one short, one shorter—stood on the stoop, all decked out in karate gis, yellow and white. "Come in, guys," Benella invited, opening wider. In they trooped. At the sight of Connor they stopped, milled hesitantly, then sat cross-legged in the foyer.

"Hey, fellas, I don't bite," from Connor. "Want some cantaloupe?" They elevated and came over, still a tad uncertain, and Benella performed the introduction. "Mr. Gibbs, this is Paul," she said; and Connor shook hands with the taller boy, who was about seven.

"And I," said the younger child, "am William. I'll be five in Septender.''

Connor suppressed a smile at the mispronunciation. "And I'll be thirty-five the very same month," he said, extending a hand. The boy shook gravely, *mano a mano*.

"I suppose you two are here for aikido lessons.''

The pair nodded in unison as Connor handed them chunks of melon. "How did you know?" asked William. Paul, older and wiser, rolled his eyes. William took a bite and waited for an answer.

"Lucky guess, I guess." Connor smiled. He was so much taller than they, it was like peering down at a pair of mushrooms dressed in martial-arts garb.

William chewed thoughtfully in response.

"Hair time," said Benella. "Excuse me, gents. Connor, will you chaperon until I get back?''

"Sure.''

And while all this was going on, across town Boz Fangelli was having a sour morning.

"Oh, that's fine. Just friggin' fine." Boz was hollering into a cell phone while gripping it so tightly his knuckles were white. He stood in his backyard with a prospective buyer from Nadnook, Pennsylvania, who was currently bending over to peer into a pen large enough for a Doberman.

"Nice bird," said the prospective purchaser. "What kindzit?"

"Araucana frizzle hen, lays blue eggs. No, not *you*," Boz yelled into the phone. "I'm tryin' to do some friggin' business here, y'know! Do you think he's still hangin' at that redneck eatery?"

"The hell's a frizzle hen?" from the prospective patron.

"Means her feathers curl up. Put the word out, Slade, a thousand to the guy that fingers him! Bastard cost me plenty! No, *more* than plenty! I'll hand you twenty Gs when you bring me his ass!"

The prospective customer grew apprehensive at the conversational drift. "Maybe I should check with Kelly in Wilmington," he speculated, edging toward his car.

"No friggin' mick up in Delaware's got what I got. Here, lemme show you somethin'. Slade, *find* the motherfucker, y'know!" He punched off the phone with a sausagelike digit and, beckoning to the prospect, waddled toward his barn.

Boz Fangelli was about five-feet-five, weighed about 270 pounds, and always wore leisure suits to "look nice." No ties, of course; too thick of neck. His black hair was larded with mousse, parted just above his left ear, from there combed over the top to cover thinly a spreading baldness. The shoulders of his navy jacket—not to mention the bulk of his hair—was littered with dandruff though he bathed twice weekly, even when not in dire need. He wore no socks under his wing tips, suffered from gout, and bet on the Cincinnati Reds. Often. (He lost a lot.)

Upon reaching the barn, Fangelli opened the door with a theatrical flourish and said, "Lookee there."

The chicken shopper did, at two small birds in a mesh cage. "Pretty. What the hell are they?"

"White-crested Polish blues. Bantams. They're full grown."

"Not very big."

"You wanna friggin' emu, there's a ranch down the road. These ain't for eatin', y'know."

"How they got room for all them feathers on their heads?"

"They got a lump of bone on their skulls, crests sprout from there. You can tell the sex by the feathers, rooster's come to a point at the end."

The man from Nadnook was sold, so they talked deal and money changed hands.

Jackson Slade hung up the phone carefully.

"What?" from Fatima.

"He yelled a lot," said Jackson, smiling.

"So why're you grinning like a canary-eating calico?"

"He bumped the purse to twenty."

Now she was grinning. "And how much from the insurance company?"

"Twenty percent of two hundred thou."

"That's sixty grand all told," she summed.

His grin widened. "Yeah."

"So"—she snuggled up to his chest—"you gonna find him?"

"Oh, yeah."

After three rings, Vera said "McGraw residence" into her mouthpiece.

"This is Connor Gibbs," said Connor Gibbs at his end. "I wonder if we might have a word."

Ambivalent pause, then: "Why?"

"Noah Sizemore's in town. He was seen last night at Sizemore's Barbecue."

"Whoopee-do."

"Ms. McGraw, this is important to Blister."

"I told you not to call him Blister!"

"Sorry. This is important to Cody."

"So he thinks," she grumbled.

"And you don't?"

Another pause. "Look, Gibbs, I gave you a lead on his sister, and even allowed you to take Cody out to that restaurant." She emphasized "restaurant" uncomplimentarily. "What more do you want?"

"Answers."

"I'm fresh out."

"May I come by and discuss things with you before you decide?"

Pause again, then a reluctant, "I suppose. But the house is a mess."

"I'll close my eyes."

She snorted and hung up.

TEN

"Come in," Vera said.

He did, looking around. "You call this a mess?"

The living room was spotless. From his vantage point, part of the dining-room table was visible. On it was the morning paper, strewn about as if someone had been recently reading; a coffee cup and saucer, no steam rising; an egg-stained plate.

"Is to me."

"Oh."

"Have a seat."

Connor went over to the couch and sat, crossing his legs.

"Do you always wear shorts?" she said, settling opposite him.

"Only when I'm stalking."

"Ha," she said. "Ha."

Bounding down the stairs came Cody McGraw, frequently called Blister. He skidded to a halt upon spying Connor, produced a toothy smile, and said, "Howdy, Mr. Gibbs."

"Thought you waren't no cowboy."

"Folks other'n cowboys say 'howdy.' "

They grinned like a pair of raccoons on a garbage can.

"What is it with you two?" Vera said.

"It's a guy thing, little lady," Connor replied John Wayne style.

Blister chuckled.

"I'd offer tea, but I'm out," Vera said.

"Hey, spud, you know Easy's Fresh Market down at the corner?"

"I reckon I do," said Blister.

"S'pose you could mosey on down there and rustle me up some tea? Any kind'll do."

"I'd be right proud."

Connor gave the boy a five-spot and he left.

"You should have asked me first," Vera admonished.

"I apologize. I wanted him out of earshot."

She nodded her understanding. "So you saw Noah last night?"

"Not I. A quasi–private eye claims he saw him."

"What's a quasi–private eye?"

"One too unsavory and disreputable to get a license."

"And you plan to check it out?"

"Already tried. They wouldn't let me in the place."

"Didn't you and Cody have supper there last night?"

"He wasn't there then, or at least we didn't see him before being asked to leave."

"You and Cody were thrown out of Sizemore's? I thought they'd let Timothy McVeigh eat there."

"Probably would. Unless he was looking for Noah. They appear to be uncommonly protective."

"They should be," she said grimly.

"What more can you tell me about Noah? Or Christy? Or both?"

"I could tell you a lot, but I won't. I will tell you this: The police have been searching—off and on—for Noah Sizemore for nearly seven years, and they haven't found him yet. A devil-dog bounty hunter by the name of Jackson Slade has also been sniffing around, to no avail. Out of curiosity, I once hired an investigator of my own to root Noah out, but he turned up zilch. Noah's family covers him like an impenetrable fog. No one is going to find that man unless he wants to be found, and no one but his family will ever get within fifty feet of him,'' was her conclusion.

But she was wrong.

She was reed thin but bosomy, wore mauve-colored nails, her sloth-brown hair up in a bun, an apron over painter's pants, an Atlanta Braves T-shirt, and said, ''What's that?''

He was average height, average weight, had black hair and yellowed teeth, wore handcuffs and a Beretta 9mm automatic, and he said, ''It's a warrant for Noah Barry Sizemore. Gives us the right to search the premises. Stand aside, please.'' He brushed past her with nothing more than a flash of his yellowed teeth. More uniformed men followed, and one plainclothes detective.

The dick said, ''Where's the owner?'' and Hair Bun said, ''In the kitchen,'' and the dick said, ''Go get him,'' and Hair Bun said, ''Get him yourself, peckerhead,'' and walked away.

''Want me to get her back?'' asked one of the uniforms.

''Naw, might catch something. Let's find the kitchen.''

Through the tremendous dining area (seventy tables at least, each covered with a red-and-white-checked tablecloth, a cheap vase with several artificial flowers, salt and pepper, sugar dispenser, and a bottle of Texas Pete's) they went, the smell of roasting pork in the air, and overcooked bacon, grits, java. In the kitchen now; there by the wall sat Tate Sizemore, thin and pale and sipping iced tea. ''You Sizemore?'' said the detective.

''There's lotsa Sizemores,'' Tate said between sips.

The dick looked down at the warrant. ''*Tate* Sizemore.'' Sip. ''That's me.''

''You know Noah Barry Sizemore?''

''I do.''

''He your brother?''

''We grew up together, in the same house, so it seems likely.''

''Is he here?''

Sip. ''You see him?''

''We're going to look around. We have a warrant.''

"I suspect so."

"You suspect so *what*?"

"That you got a warrant. Otherwise I'd toss your nasty ass out."

The dick glared at the thin, pale man seated before him. "Yeah?"

Tate's straw made a sucking sound, since there was no more liquid in the glass. "Yeah."

"I'd kind of like to see that, but since I got a warrant, I guess I won't."

"Guess not."

"I could come back later, though. Off duty. You could do it then."

"Come back and I will," said Tate, uncowed.

"We're going to start searching now."

Tate made another loud sucking sound with the straw.

The dick and his minions circumnavigated the large kitchen, took in the enormous pantry, three coolers, the freezer, the four huge cast-iron stoves bolted to the floor. One of the cops noted a wheelchair between the stand-up freezer and the wall. "Whose wheelchair?" he asked Sizemore.

"None of your damn business," was Tate's reply.

"Is there an attic?" asked the dick.

"You see a ladder leading up?"

"A basement?"

"You seen any stairs going down?"

The dick stared at the thin pale surly man a moment. "Let's go, guys. Noah's not here," he concluded.

But he was wrong.

"Maybe I can get closer to Noah than fifty feet if you'll help me," Connor Gibbs said to Vera McGraw.

"Frankly, Mr. Gibbs, I don't want you to find Noah. It'd just upset Cody."

"Why?"

"Because Noah's a sorry bastard!" The venom fairly dripped.

"Tell me how."

"Do you know where he was the night Cody was born?"

Connor shook his head, displacing a lock that curled down over his forehead.

"At the bowling alley. The *bowling alley*! Boozing it up with his friends, going for a seven-ten split, or whatever they do at one o'clock in the morning. My sister was driving herself to the hospital to have a baby and her no-good husband was bowling!" Tears now. "She was hit by a drunk driver, and hurt badly, so she had the baby right there beside her ruined car, on the asphalt, Gibbs! Delivered it herself as she lay there bleeding to death!" Torential tears, remembering the loss, the sacrifice. Vera buried her face in her hands.

Connor didn't know what to do, so he sat quietly and rode out the storm.

Directly she excused herself to mop up, returning with a box of tissues in case of future need. "Christy might not have died that night if her husband had been there to drive her to the hospital."

"I'm sorry," was Connor's lame offering. What else could he say?

"Well, I'm sorry, too. For Christy. And Cody. And me. Christy was special, you know? She'd have been a great mother."

"You seem to have been a fine mother in her stead."

Up came the head, the penetrating glare searching for patronizing or pretense. She saw none. Her look softened. "Thanks for that. But I'm not Christy. I never wanted kids, mostly because a husband goes with them, traditionally anyway. Christy, on the other hand, always wanted children. She had one a year before Cody. Stillborn. It nearly killed her."

Connor nodded sympathetically. "How did Noah take it?"

Her face closed up. "I do *not* want to talk about that sorry cocksucker."

He leaned back to wait her out.

After a minute she said, "Doesn't matter, anyway. Noah's safe in the mountains."

No he wasn't.

The dick crossed the graveled lot to where a burgundy Camaro squatted ominously. The June sun was high and hot, and his brow beaded as he walked. The Camaro's exhaust gurgled powerfully, its blacked-out windows keeping out the heat and harmful UV rays. As the dick drew near, the driver's window descended electrically and a narrow face appeared, stubbled and nether. "Well?" said the face.

"Nothing," said the detective.

"Your guys look around real good?"

"We know our business, Slade."

"Sure you do. Well, there goes my Crime Stoppers money."

"What's a thousand bucks to a high roller like you?"

Up came the window, motor purring it along, *zzzzzz.* "See you," Slade said as the gap closed.

The dick yelled, "We'll find him! He's likely scared shit-less!"

No he wasn't.

Blister bounced in, tea and change in hand, offering the latter to Connor, who told him to keep it for the trouble. The boy then popped a ceramic cup filled with water into the microwave, waited two minutes until the bell, plopped a bag into the heated liquid, then bore it to his large friend. Connor thanked him, then said, "Old folks talking here."

Disappointed but polite, the boy scurried up the stairs.

"What bowling alley?" Connor said.

No response.

"Please."

She sighed. "Bernard's Bowl-a-rama."

"Think anyone there will remember Noah?"

She nodded.

"Thanks."

She shook her head. "Won't do you any good, anyway. You'll never find him."

"All right if I take Cody?"

She shrugged. "What could it hurt?"

Little did she know.

Jackson and Johnston, sitting in a booth; Johnston squirming, fiddling with a tooth.

"You didn't have to whack my tooth," Johnston whined.

"Quit griping, I just thumped it with a forefinger. Next time I'll use a hammer," Slade promised.

"It's not my fault he wasn't there."

"Then whose was it?"

"He could've just left."

"And he could have been spirited away to Roswell, New Mexico, to hobnob with aliens, but I don't think so."

"I'll keep watching the place. He has to be close by," reasoned Thurgood.

Little did he know.

ELEVEN

Bernard's Bowl-a-rama was in its thirty-seventh year in Wendover. Originally it had been in Pilot Mountain, but pin pickings had been slim, so the owner, J. Busby Nussbaum, had moved to the larger city and never looked back. More than one three-hundred game had been rolled within its hallowed confines; more than one beer had been consumed, hot dog devoured, french fry digested into artery-clogging LDL. Part of a TV documentary had been filmed there in 1979, and once a notorious heavyweight fighter—later renowned for rape and pillage and ear biting—had tried to kiss the part-time shoe-rental clerk. Twice.

"What for you?" asked J. Busby himself at the approach of Connor and his young companion.

Connor tried tact. "I've never been before, but a friend of mine used to bowl here. Wrote me all about it."

J. Busby extended a hand for shaking. "Lots of people have bowled here since we opened in 1960. We got the hottest lanes in town."

Connor shook the proffered mitt and allowed, "That's what my friend said. Are you the manager?"

"Owner, manager, general factotum."

Connor smiled. "Then you're Bernard himself?"

"There ain't no Bernard, never has been."

Connor raised a quizzical brow. "Then why—"

"Who the hell'd come to a place named *Busby's* Bowl-a-rama?"

Connor nodded his understanding.

"But I did want a B-word, to go with Bowl-a-rama," Nussbaum explained. "Bernard's as good as any. Want to bowl a few frames for free?"

Connor tried ambivalence, rubbing his chin uncertainly. "I don't know . . . let me think about it. By the way, I wonder if you might remember my friend."

J. Busby's smile was as eager to please as a new puppy's. "What's the name?"

"Noah Sizemore."

J. Busby's smile went out like a doused match. "Never heard of him," he vowed, darting a look at a pair of men lounging nearby; within seconds they joined the small group at the counter. One of them had the largest eyes Connor had ever encountered on a man; they seemed ready to leap from his swarthy face. The other man had a wart on the end of his chin and a profusion of ear hair. Neither was especially handsome, bright, or gregarious.

Connor tried lugubriousness. "I didn't mean to upset anyone. I'm just looking for a friend."

Bug Eye said, "Who's the kid, big 'un?"

Connor looked down at Blister. "That's Mickey Rooney when he was a child star."

"That ain't no Mickey Rooney! Besides, he'd be growed now, anyways."

Connor turned to Blister and said, "Have you been lying to me?" and winked.

Cody said of the gentleman with the prominent orbs, "He ain't no rocket scientist, is he?"

Connor looked thoughtfully at Bug Eye. "Now that you mention it . . ."

J. Busby said, "I believe it's time for you fellows to go."

"You mean you're withdrawing your invitation for us to bowl?" from Connor.

Bug Eye erupted. "Listen, you starry-eyed sack of seal

shit. I don't care how big you are, if you don't leave right now, me'n Milton here're gonna ream you a new one!"

Connor switched his focal point to Ear Hair. "Milton?"

Milton shrugged his thick shoulders.

Connor looked at Blister. "Milton?"

Blister shrugged his thin shoulders.

Connor swung his gaze back to J. Busby Nussbaum. "You hired an intimidator named *Milton*?"

J. Busby shrugged, too.

To Milton, Connor said, "You should consider choosing a nickname, you know? Something tough like Rocky or Thor or Lurch . . . no, that last one would just make folks think you were a drunk."

Milton, obviously unflappable, said, "My daddy liked Milton. Reckon I'll stick with it."

Connor shrugged his own shoulders. "Just trying to help."

Bug Eye stepped forward angrily and got in Connor's face, so to speak—the man was ten inches shorter. But doing his best, considering that he was standing on tiptoe, he hissed, "Move it, you giant gob of goose guts."

Connor looked at Blister again. "He may not be much on manners, and he's not Marilyn Vos Savant, but he's pure hell with alliteration."

Bug Eye puffed up like a banty rooster, but J. Busby touched his arm appeasingly. "Mack," he said to Connor Gibbs, "if your great big self's not walking out that door in five seconds, I'm calling John Law. Be sure to take Mickey Rooney with you."

"What do you say, Mick?" Connor looked at Blister McGraw. "Shall we depart?"

"Might as well. We stay any longer, we could step in something."

So they left.

Without bowling a frame.

" 'We could step in something.' That was rich." Connor chuckled, back in the van now, with the air going and Blister beside him sulking. "You want a snack?"

Sulk.

"Well, I do. First enticing place I see, I'm wheeling in."

More sulk.

"What's the matter?"

Blurt: "What would it take to make you fight?"

"More of that old theme? What is it with you and violence, Blister?"

"But that guy with the monster eyes insulted you! Called you a sack of shit, and goose guts and stuff!"

"So?"

"So? *So!* What good's it to be big and strong and still have people be able to insult you?" He crossed his arms angrily.

"Blister."

Sulk.

"Blister?"

"What!"

"People can say pretty much whatever they want, by common practice and by law. So those lamebrains insulted us. How did that hurt us?"

"It hurt my *pride*!"

"Ah, well, your pride. Maybe I should have taken a jackhammer to them."

The boy just looked out the window in disgust.

"Your pride's not all that important in the grand scheme of things, my young friend, and certainly not worth hurting someone over. Mine isn't either. Besides, who got the maddest back there at the bowling alley?"

"Me!"

"Not until you were back in the van. Inside Bernard's you were pretty cool. At least you seemed to be."

No comment from the Blister.

"So, who got the maddest?"

Blister replayed the scene in his head. "The guy with the big eyes."

"Bingo. So if he got mad—so mad his blood pressure shot up and his eyes protruded even more—then who won the confrontation?"

"Us?"

"Right. Whenever you keep your cool while your opponents are losing theirs—not to mention face—then you win."

"What's face?"

"Self-respect."

Blister smiled despite himself. "We did sort of get old Pop Eye's goat, didn't we?"

"You bet."

"What about that other one, the big guy with the thing on his chin?"

"He was the more dangerous of the two. He wouldn't let himself be baited, he didn't get perturbed, and he showed no fear. His pal was a blowhard. Not so with the bigger guy, he was genuine. I don't know how tough he was, but he had the mental game under control, or appeared to, and that's half as good."

Blister, feeling a bit better, said, "That other guy really did have some peepers, didn't he?"

"Mm-hm."

"Why didn't you call him Bug Eyes or something, get him back?"

"That's against the rules."

"What rules."

"My rules. It would have been ridicule, not the requisite male posturing. His calling me a sack of shit was simply pissing on my turf. If I'd responded by singling out an obvious handicap, that would have been ridicule, and not nice."

Cody Wainwright McGraw thought about it for a while, then said, "Well, he did have big eyes."

Connor nodded as he pulled into a Dunkin' Donuts. "Biggest I ever saw. On a human."

"What animal do you suppose has the biggest eyes?"

"No contest."

"You know which one?"

"Sure."

"Which?"

"Think about it, see if you can figure it out by the process of elimination. Then later let me know which one

you've settled on. If you get it right, I'll take you to a
movie.''

Then they went in and bought seven blueberry muffins.
Mickey Rooney ate one.

That night, before Cody McGraw said his prayers, he lay
on the floor with his feet up on the bed and reflected, with
Stevie Nicks crooning softly in the background. Mr. Gibbs
sure enough had some pretty good reasons for not whippin'
those guys at the alley. And he'd seemed very reasonable—
and unafraid—last night at the barbecue place. Still, something nagged at his confidence in his giant new friend.

Had Mr. Gibbs actually, no matter how logically he'd
explained it, been . . .

Afraid?

Was Connor Gibbs, tall as a goalpost and half as wide,
strong as a bison . . .

Telling it straight?

Did he really believe what he said?

Or was he just a big, strong . . .

Coward?

TWELVE

Connor Gibbs visited Holmes Crenshaw's law office first thing Monday morning; the good solicitor was prone on the floor doing push-ups as Gibbs came through the door with Zep trotting along beside him.

"Do you have to take that mutt everywhere?" groused Holmes in mock umbrage. "I'll need to have the office fumigated." He jumped to his feet, breathing easily, and slipped a madras sport coat over his pale blue Gant broadcloth and yellow cravat.

Gibbs gave him a look. "Fumigate? With your clientele?"

"Good point, but at least they don't have fleas."

"Braxton Chiles had head lice. That's worse."

Holmes Crenshaw grimaced in genuine, not mock, distaste. "That Chiles . . ." He shook his head. "So what can I do for you today, as if I care?"

"May I sit down?" asked Connor.

"Sure. Find a spot on the floor there."

Connor settled into a blue leather wing chair, crossing one lengthy lower limb over the other. The dog lay at his feet.

"That pooch sure looks better clean and fattened up," Holmes said.

"So do you."

"What exact color is her coat, anyway?"

"Liver."

"Looks more like chocolate to me."

"Then why'd you ask?"

"You think she's the color of a slice of liver?"

"What difference does it make? To me she's just brown, like you."

"I'm black, I'll have you know."

"Only by race."

Holmes stared at the skin on the back of his hand. "I don't look black to you?"

"Mahogany."

"Well, don't let on to the brothers. Any progress since Friday night?"

Connor shook his head disgustedly. "I can't figure this case out. In less than two days I've been thrown out of a tanning salon, a barbecue restaurant, and a bowling alley. Not only thrown out, but threatened and intimidated and spoken to in a rude and inflexible manner."

"You just need a good cry," suggested Crenshaw.

"I would, but the dog hates to see it. Throws her off her feed."

"You shouldn't spoil her, *sufi*. You feel like crying, go ahead."

"I promise. So what new and interesting Sizemore trivia have you run across?"

Crenshaw told him. It took a while. Zep slept through most of it.

Back in his van, Connor's cell phone chimed; it was a collect call; he underwent the electronic operator's instructions, then heard, "Daddy?" His heart soared.

"Hi, sweetheart. How are you?"

"I'm okay," said his son.

"Great."

"She went to the store a minute."

"And left you alone?"

"No big deal. I'm nearly ten."

"Nearer nine and a half. So how'd school go?"

"Okay. I made all A's, except one B."

"Dat's my boy," in Jimmy Durante tonals.

"And I got superior at my last two recitals. So I got a trophy. Nicer than my soccer ones."

"I'd love to see it." Memories tugged at his heart. "Are you two getting along better?"

"Sure," his son lied.

"Cameron?"

"We really are," Cameron Layton Gibbs lied again, from nearly three thousand miles away. "She stays home more than she used to. At night I mean. And sometimes even on weekends."

Connor, caught by a red light, closed his eyes.

His son went on, "Consuelo's really nice."

Connor nodded. He couldn't speak right then.

"Daddy?"

"I'm here, babe," huskily.

"Consuelo took me to the dollar theater to see *Michael*. With John Travolta, from *Broken Arrow*? Have you seen it?"

"Which one?"

"*Michael.*"

"Yes."

"Wasn't it great, 'cept when the dog died. That reminded me of Butchie. I cried a little."

"Me, too."

"Anyway, you know how that lady in the movie wrote the song about pie, and the one when they were sitting by the road with that flat tire?"

"I remember."

"Well, I wrote a song. This morning, I went out to my fort and just wrote it. Want to hear it?"

"You bet I do."

So Cameron Gibbs began to sing:

Sittin' in the middle of nowhere,
Buyin' some ti-ii-me.
My wife said I didn't love her,
I tried to prove her wro-oo-ng;
But she didn't understand,
And she didn't even try-yy.
So she divorced me away and took
My one and only kid away from me,
And never to see him ever aga-aa-in.
So . . .
Sittin' in the middle of nowhere,
At the edge of the stre-ee-et.
Who'd want to stay in this cruel, cruel world?
Well, gonna be me, as you can see
Right no-oo-ow.
But there's nothing for me up or down;
Sittin' in the middle of the road,
Buyin' some ti-ii-ime.
Just sittin' in the middle of nowhere,
Buyin' some ti-ii-ime.

"That's it. What do you think?"

Connor didn't quite know what to think, so he said, "Amazing. I sure never wrote a song when I was nine. One thing, though, son. You and I will see each other again, I promise."

At the other end, his son beamed.

Connor went on, "I'm working on a case involving a nine-year-old boy who likes to be called Blister."

"Why's he like to be called that?"

"I have no idea."

"Is he pretty nice?"

"Yes. Not you, but pretty nice. I'm trying to help him find his dad. Hasn't seen him since he was two."

"He doesn't know where he is?"

"No. Neither do I, and I'm getting nowhere fast trying to find out."

"You'll find him. You always do. Don't you?"

"Yes."

"Wait. . . ." A rustling sound, then silence for fifteen seconds. More rustling sounds and Cameron was back, breathless. "That's Mom's car. I better go. She'd kill me."

Connor gritted his teeth, but said, "You need anything?"

"No, but thank you for asking. I'll call when I can. Love you, very much."

"And I love you."

But his son was gone.

Still.

It was twelve after twelve noon, with Connor sitting at his big oak office desk and Blister scurrying around the room, broom in hand, tidying up, when a shadow fell across the open doorway. Gibbs said, "Mr. Furter. Come take a load off."

"Name's Frank Murphy," said the hole at the bottom of the shaved head. "Don't know no Furter."

"Well sit down anyway. Want me to send the boy for a Coke?"

"I'm a RC man."

"Sorry. None in the building. Maybe even the city, for that matter. What can I do for you?"

"My wife . . . Ellie?"

"Met her last week. Fine lady."

"She ain't so fine right now. Since you come by she's been frettin' fit to kill. Makes me worry, I don't mind tellin' you."

"I'm sorry," Connor averred as Blister propped his broom in a corner and circled the room in full kibitz.

"So sorry you'll stop askin' after Noah?"

"Not that sorry."

The big thoroughly shaven man stood, flexing thick callused fingers, making them crack in the tenseness like walnuts. "Then I guess I'll have to make you."

Connor laced his fingers across his flat belly and tilted back his chair. "How?"

"Gonna whup you, right now. Hate to, though, in front of the boy. He can leave if you want."

"Thanks, but he'll stay. I'm not going to fight you."

"You don't think so?"

Connor shook his head.

Frank started to come around the desk, until Connor said, "I don't want to fight you, Mr. Murphy," looking him dead in the eye.

Frank was a good-sized man, work-conditioned, a scraper, bar fighter, head knocker, and he was genuinely concerned about his wife, who did not know where he was at the moment. "You scared of me?" he said.

"If I admit to it, will you leave?"

The shiny dome bobbed once in affirmation.

"Mr. Murphy, sir, I'm afraid that if you come around that desk to fight me, someone will get hurt. I'd rather it not be me."

"You quittin' on Noah?"

Connor shook his head again.

"Well, you better, you know what's good for you," Murphy warned, and left.

Connor unlaced his hands and eased his chair forward. Cody looked at him, eyes ovals of disappointment. When he opened his mouth to speak, Connor cut him off with, "Don't start."

So the child ran out the office door and slammed it behind him.

After waiting five minutes for the boy's rancor to settle, Connor sought Blister in the men's room, finding him sitting on the counter awash but livid.

"You all right?" said Connor.

"*No!*"

Gibbs shook his head in concern. "When are you going to understand?"

"Understand what? That you're a *chicken*!"

Connor turned on his heels and quit the room.

Thirty minutes later Gibbs was just finishing mopping when a subdued Cody McGraw made his presence known by clearing his throat from the doorway.

"You want to dust?" Connor said.

Blister picked up a rag and some Endust and made a halfhearted attempt. Connor sat in the client's chair and watched. The boy said, "I just don't understand."

"I'm not going to explain it anymore."

The dustrag stopped mid-swirl. "Why not?"

"I've tried twice, but you're too caught up in macho to grasp it. Which means you'll have to come to terms with it on your own."

Blister dropped his head.

"But that's normal," Connor continued.

Up came the head. "It is?"

"Sure. One of the major drawbacks of human nature is failing to learn from others' mistakes. Done it myself from time to time."

Blister dusted some more. "Did your dad ever fight?"

"He was in the Korean War."

"I didn't mean that."

"I know," said Connor, sighing. "Yes, he was in a scrap or two."

"You ever see him in a fight?"

Another sigh. "Once."

"Did your daddy win?"

Connor nodded sadly. "Yes. And afterward I never again looked at him quite the same."

Three hours later, high tea. English sweet biscuits, many. Milk for Cody W.

"Do you always eat a lot?" asked Blister.

"More than a hummingbird, but not proportionally."

"What's 'proportionally'?"

"In relation to size."

They munched awhile; sipped; munched some more. Then from the boy: "Why does everyone want to beat you up?"

Connor feigned offense. "Not everyone. Aunt Vera doesn't."

Blister hooted, "Yet."

"Isn't that the truth. Well, what can I say—is it my personality or my deodorant?"

"Both?" Blister charged, crumbs flying.

"That hurts. Seriously, fans, I've been wondering just why it is that everyone I meet who's ever been involved with your poppa either wants to strike me, warn me, diss me, or make me stand in line for my supper. Why might that be?"

Blister shrugged. "You reckon my daddy's not a nice man?"

"Now, now. Let's assume he is until we know otherwise."

Blister nodded in agreement while wiping away a milk mustache with his sleeve.

"Anyway," Connor went on, "it could be worse."

"How?"

"At least nobody's shot at me."

THIRTEEN

When the first bullet came through the window, Connor was walking past a framed portrait of his mother; the slug shattered the glass, perforated the photo, lodged in the wall behind. Connor dodged up the stairwell as the second bullet pierced the drywall where he had been only a second before. Slug number three took out an antique lamp; number four nicked the front cover of Michael Malone's *Handling Sin*—a rare first edition—as it lay on the cherry end table. Number five must have encountered a stud; it never made it through the wall. The sixth—and final—bullet finished off the picture window, then burrowed into the back of a leather recliner.

A moment later, when Connor hotfooted it back down-stairs better protected, he heard the squawling tires and V-8 growl of retreat. He went back up momentarily, then called the police.

The plainclothes detective examined the bullet a forensics technician had recovered from the leather chair. It was small, uncommonly light, and jacketed. "A .22 Magnum," said the dick, slipping it into a plastic bag. "Guy probably used a carbine of some description."

"A revolver, most likely," Connor disagreed. "One with a two- or three-inch barrel. Charter Arms maybe, or a Smith."

"How do you know it wasn't a rifle?"

"The report wasn't right for a rifle, especially with that load."

"How the hell do you know what load it was?"

"Only Federal Cartridge Company made a fifty-grain .22 Magnum cartridge, and the bullet in that bag is too long to weigh forty grains, like most .22 Mag bullets."

"You a gun expert?" said the detective sarcastically.

"I don't know a thing about them," Connor replied.

"Don't believe that. He knows *everything* about them," a cop said from the doorway.

"Hi, Estelle," Connor greeted. "You get any prettier and you'll have to wear a veil."

Estelle Lawson was prim, pert, and professional. And—very rare—a good cop. She was also not difficult to look at.

"Hi, Connor," she said, walking across the room with lots of hip flexion, most male eyes in the room following her progress. With a casual toss of her mane, she queried, "You okay?"

"Not since *he* got here." Gibbs indicated the male dick with a tilt of his head.

"Hey," objected said detective.

"Is for horses," Connor and Estelle said simultaneously, then broke up laughing. The dick left in a swivet.

"Tell me about it," said Estelle.

"Nothing to tell. I'd just come in from a run, hadn't been in the house three minutes. Bang,. bang, bang. Nothing serious."

"Nothing serious? Your living room is shot to hell."

"It's why I have homeowner's."

"Who have you been irritating? Lately?" she said, settling onto an ottoman.

"*Moi?*"

"You suppose this has anything to do with your search for Noah Sizemore?"

"Mmmm . . . could be," doing Mel Blanc doing Bugs Bunny.

"Oh, do Daffy, do Daffy."

They both grinned. Connor had been an excellent mimic since grade school.

"Let's discuss this seriously a moment, studly," Estelle insisted.

"No need."

"How can you say that? Someone tried to hit you to-night, and—"

"No they didn't."

"What?"

"Estelle, if it was a hit, they'd have done it outside. I told you, I wasn't home three minutes. Anyone who really wanted me dead would simply have popped me before I came in the door, or tried to. They were in the yard when they fired. I must have walked right past them."

She absorbed that, and his calm demeanor.

"Aren't you even scared?"

"It's why I'm sitting down. My legs're too shaky to stand."

She smiled in commiseration, patted his heavy arm, and went to confer with her colleagues.

The phone sounded two hours later, a breathless Blister. "Mr. Gibbs! Are you okay?"

"No. I'm trying to watch myself on TV and everyone keeps calling."

"Oh, sorry, I was just worried that—"

"I'm kidding, pal. Eveything's fine."

"You sure were lucky."

"Luck had nothing to do with it. Whoever did the shooting had no intention of hitting me. It was done to scare me off."

"You think so?"

"You bet. Makes me mad, though. The schmuck put a bullet hole in my momma's picture. Someday I'll speak to him about that."

Blister inhaled sharply. "You know who did it?"

"No, but chances are I will before all this is over."

"What'll you do to the guy when you find him?"

"Ask him to get me a new picture."

"Aw, Mr. Gibbs!"

Connor chuckled. "We'll have to wait and see, kiddo. What a bloodthirsty little guy you are. Probably watch too much Mel Gibson."

"I like Bruce Willis better. But Batman's my favorite fiction hero."

"Lee Chong is mine. See you tomorrow."

"Who's Lee Chong?"

"He owns a store."

"Where?"

"Cannery Row."

"What do you buy there?"

"Stuff."

Short pause as the wheels turned, futilely. "Mr. Gibbs, if I live to be eleven, I'll never understand what you're talking about half the time."

"Why should you be different?" Connor said, and switched off the TV.

Benella's sweet voice purred through the line. "Have you done your kata?"

"And brushed my teeth and said my prayers."

"How long?"

"I don't know. I started with 'Now I lay me down to sleep,' then went directly to the Twenty-third Psalm: 'The Lord is my—' "

"I meant the kata."

"Oh. An hour."

"Tired?"

"After an hour kata? Please."

"Can I come, then?"

"Often." He hung up and took a shower.

Though she was the approximate heft and temperament of a jaguar, Benella was putty in Connor's hands. And he in hers. After two hours of lustful laboring, they lay quietly, side by side beneath the ceiling fan, holding hands.

She rubbed one of his toes with hers. "I'm glad they didn't shoot you, bunny lamb."

"Bunny lamb?"

"I think I tend to overuse sugar pie."

"I like pie."

"Me, too. What's in the fridge?"

They went naked together and looked.   ·

The doorbell compelled them to dress. He rushed to the training room, chicken leg between his teeth, and stepped into the lower half of a gi; she slipped on one of his T-shirts, size XXL. Connor opened the door. There on the stoop stood a harried Holmes Crenshaw, head damp with rain. "Yo, Holmie," said Gibbs.

"That's 'Homey,' and you're not funny. I just got the word. Are you okay?" Crenshaw said, stepping inside to shake loose the water, taking in the defunct picture window, the puckered leather chair, the pockmarked wallboard. "Shit," he said, stretching the word out into two lengthy syllables.

"Nah, nothing to this," Connor dissented.

"Don't give me that. A drive-by's no joke, *sufi.*"

Connor made a dismissing sound. "This was no drive-by. A *walk*-by, maybe."

"That's only your op—oh, hi, Bennie." Crenshaw's eyes opened wide. "Is that a breast I see?"

Benella nodded. "Got two. Want one?"

"You have one without a bite taken out of it?"

The trio repaired to the kitchen with Colonel Sanders.

"So what's next?" from Crenshaw.

"Sleep."

"I mean tomorrow, smart-ass."

Connor was placing dishes in the dishwasher; he stared at the machine for maybe twenty seconds.

"What?" said Benella.

"You think I should put soap in there?"

Benella laughed.

Crenshaw said, "You're disgusting."

"Well, I did run water over them, and—"

Holmes came over, opened a cabinet, withdrew a green box of powdered soap, poured a modicum into the proper receptacle, replaced the box, closed the dishwasher. He gave Connor a look of exasperation and resat.

"The big dope's just clowning to distract you," opined Benella. "He has no idea what he's going to do tomorrow."

"That so?" Holmes asked of his friend.

"No, it is not. I plan to interview . . . excuse me, *interrogate* . . . that guy you told me about, Elmo Somebody."

"Noah's buddy from yon larcenous days," Crenshaw clarified.

"That's him."

"And what," Benella pressed, "if Elmo Somebody fails to provide a lead?"

"Then I'll wing it."

Benella looked at Holmes. "Novel approach," she said.

But she needn't have been concerned.

Elmo Somebody would definitely provide a lead.

FOURTEEN

Aptly enough, given his name, Elmo Scribner worked at a bookseller's, downtown amid a paucity of parking that didn't seem to hurt business any. The place was all leather and walnut and baize and indirect lighting. Money changed hands there, often and in quantity. Rich smells abounded: coffees and paper pulp and expensive perfume. The temperature was held meticulously to seventy-one degrees, regardless of season, and the air was discreetly humidified to mollify books and patrons. Full carpeting to hush footfalls; only Serious Reading allowed.

After two minutes taking the measure of the place, Connor Gibbs blew his nose. Loudly. (He'd practiced long as a teenager for just such occasions, and he could honk with the best.) Faces turned, lips curled into contumelious sneers. He put his handkerchief away and grinned happily. "Blister?" he said.

"Yes?"

"There's nothing like irreverence. Come, lad, let us browse."

They were standing in the juvenile section, with Blister perusing number five in the Animorphs series, when a voice said into Connor's ear, from *above:* "Mr. Gibbs?"

Connor turned to face one of the tallest men he'd ever met; he looked like Jeff Goldblum. "Yes, I'm Gibbs."

"Will you join me in the break room?"

"Sure." Connor turned to Blister. "You want that book?"

"Gosh, yeah . . . yes."

"Bring it." They followed the very tall man to the break room.

With the three of them seated in relative seclusion, Connor began: "What can you tell me about Noah Sizemore?"

Elbows on a tabletop, Scribner steepled his fingers. "We served time in reform school together, grand theft auto. We went for a joyride and got caught. Later we were nabbed for receiving stolen goods. The DA couldn't prove anything on him, but I was sent away for a year. I did eight months and never went back. Don't plan to."

Connor nodded encouragingly.

"I went to UNCC after that," Scribner continued. "B.A. in English, master's in journalism. I whored for the paper awhile, mostly book reviews. Always loved to read. That's how I wound up here."

"And Noah?"

Elmo shook his curly head. "We were a strange combo. Noah was not bookish at all, in fact had trouble staying in school because he wouldn't study. I helped him some, and he had a girlfriend who did also."

"What was her name?" asked Connor.

Shaking his head again, Scribner said, "I don't remember. Anyway, after prison, Noah and I sort of lost contact. I did see him once, after his marriage to Christy, and he was ebullient. She'd really turned him around, it seemed."

"What do you know about the manslaughter charge he skipped on?"

"Very little. I heard it involved an automobile accident. Someone was killed and Noah was charged and that was that. I can't recall the details. Sorry."

Connor smiled encouragingly.

Scribner went on. "I understand that Noah jumped bail—

which didn't make Boz Fangelli very happy, I'm sure—
then disappeared into a bosky westward glen. That would
have been very easy for him.''

"How so?''

"Noah had a very extended family. There were seven
siblings, plus at least six uncles and aunts, and goodness
knows how many cousins. And they're a clannish bunch. I
have little doubt that if Noah wanted to disappear, he could
have done so readily enough. And stayed disappeared.''

"Do you have any idea where he might have been for
most of these seven years?''

Scribner shook his head.

"He was seen at the edge of town recently, at his
brother's restaurant,'' Gibbs pursued. "Anywhere else he
might go here in town? Or close by?''

Scribner pursed his lips in thought, then shook his head
again. "Not that I can think of.''

"Do you have a copy of your high-school yearbook?''

Scribner nodded.

"Might you recognize his girlfriend if you looked
through it?''

"Maybe. She was a year behind, I think. I'll dig it out
tonight, give it a shot,'' he added helpfully.

"Thanks.''

"Oh, one other thing,'' Scribner concluded. "Noah
could not tolerate injustice. He constantly rooted for the
underdog, the downtrodden. He was always fighting in
school, weighing in to defend some nerd who was being
bullied. It caused him no end of trouble. He just couldn't
help it.''

Elmo Scribner looked at Blister closely for the first time.
"Are you related to Noah?''

Blister said yes.

"Well, you certainly look like him,'' was Scribner's
opinion.

Blister grinned all over.

After the bookstore, the newspaper offices; much scrolling
and squinting at microfilm, digging into history with the

ambience nothing like that at the bookseller's. Here, controlled chaos and clutter. Gibbs didn't need to blow his nose; if he did no one would notice.

He read several accounts of the wreck; they occupied considerable space in the local-news section for weeks after the fact. A man had died, been burned to death in fact. Witnesses stated that he'd been run off the road, deliberately. Noah Sizemore had been arrested and charged with assault with a motor vehicle. Less than a week later that was upgraded to manslaughter. Connor read where Sizemore was jailed, posted bond, disappeared. He also read that the charge was once again upgraded, this time to second-degree murder.

That stopped him. Murder Two. Wow; no wonder Noah was still in hiding. According to the news accounts, the case was pretty cut-and-dried; further evidence of guilt was Noah's flight to avoid prosecution.

There was a piece about the dead man's widow, Mildred Johnson, Route 2, Box 435, Stokesdale. Her husband had been insured for two hundred thousand, term life, double indemnity. The insurance company had paid off quickly, at proof of death, in this case dental records since the remains consisted mostly of bones and chum.

And that was all. Perhaps it was time to talk to the widow.

It took a while to find Mildred Johnson, since she had moved, remarried, divorced, and died. But Connor lucked up. A former neighbor pointed him at Mildred's daughter, who lived in Clemmons.

Off to Clemmons, with Blister beside him engrossed in fictional morphing.

He knocked at the door of a small, brick home standing on a small fenced lot with several large weeping willows and a birdbath. A woman came to the door. He could tell it was a woman because he could see some of her face and a portion of her colossal bosom. He could see only part of these anatomical features because the woman more than filled the doorway.

"Mrs. Adams?"

"Whaddya want?"

"Are you Molly Adams?"

"Who wants to know?"

"Are you Mildred Johnson's daughter?"

"Why do you ask?"

"This isn't getting us far."

The very large person before him threw back her head and cackled. "By golly, you're right. C'mon in," she said, and fortuitously backed away. (Otherwise he could not have *come* in.) She reclined her breadth on a creaky love seat—breathing heavily through her porcine nose from the exertion of crossing the room—and lit a Camel.

"You knew my ma?" she exhaled.

"No, ma'am," he said, holding his breath against a plethora of foul odors, the least of which from Joe Camel.

"Then whatcha doing here? You ain't from the 'surance company, are you? Naw, you're too damned big and good-looking. All them 'surance guys is weasly little weenies. And ugleeee, I never." She paused to hawk something from her throat. Once it was dislodged, she took a drag from the cigarette.

Connor felt like he was about to pass out. Thank God Blister had stayed in the van.

"Are you having difficulty with the insurance company over your mother's death?" he asked.

"Hell no," Molly croaked. "Her pissant little policy wasn't hardly enough to bury her. Them 'surance folks're wanting half their money back for my *daddy*. They say he wasn't no accident. Say it was murder. Want something to drink? Got root beer, Dr Pepper—"

"No, thank you. But the original charge against your father's alleged killer wasn't murder, it was assault with a motor vehicle."

"Not even that was proved, 'cause that Sizemore feller up and took off." She smiled and scratched herself, the sound of it loud in the room. Connor nearly gagged.

" 'Less they was to catch him," she elaborated, "them 'surance boys got no case."

Connor thought about it—as clearly as he could under the circumstances—and she was right. For nearly seven years Noah Sizemore had been merely an alleged murderer, not a convicted one. He just *bet* the insurance company was miffed.

"Want to watch some TV?" invited Molly. "I got some Eskimo Pies in the Frigidaire."

"Thanks for the offer, but I'm trying to quit."

"Trying to quit what, the Pies or watching TV?"

"Either. Both. I appreciate all your help. I'll let myself out."

He did, and stood in the yard for thirty seconds, hands on knees, sucking in huge drafts of fresh air.

"Was she nice?" queried Blister when Connor reboarded the van.

"Redolent."

The boy looked puzzled. "Is that good?"

"Depends on your point of view."

The lad wrinkled his nose. "Did her house smell like cigarette smoke."

"Unfortunately that's not all it smelled like."

Blister, brow furrowed from frustration, tried another tack. "Did you find out anything?"

"Yeah. I need to swear off Eskimo Pies."

Blister gave up, curled up, and went to sleep. When Connor reached the McGraw home, he pressed the bell; when Vera answered its summons, Connor carried the boy—still asleep—up to bed. Vera watched the big man gently tuck the child in.

"He's beginning to idolize you," she whispered as Gibbs turned to leave.

"See how astute he is? I make an excellent idol."

Tolerant smile. "You do?"

"Of course. I'm loyal, winsome, liberal-arts-educated, and fairly well house-trained. I have a full collection of *Mad* magazine, a gigantic poster of Stevie Nicks, and I know a guy who used to play for the Bengals. Who better than me as a role model?''

''Dennis Rodman?''

''Other than him.''

She actually laughed.

FIFTEEN

Connor Gibbs sat down at his hundred-and-twenty-year-old secretary and slid out a yellow pad. Bic. Reading glasses. This was an old habit, to help him keep things straight in his head. On the pad he wrote: "Things I know about N. Sizemore." Under the head he wrote: "DOB 6-26-61."

Thursday's his birthday. Happy birthday to you; happy birthday to you; happy birthday, dear Noah; I'm going to find you, he sang cerebrally.

Following the date of birth, he wrote:

"He has eluded fuzz 7 yrs (resourceful); marriage to Christy (deceased) resulted in son, Cody, now nine; abandoned (?) son at age 2, dumping child on sister-in-law (has he sent her $ over the yrs? *Ask Vera*); comes from large mountain family; local brother Tate, sister Ellie (I'm probably not on their Christmas card list)."

The phone interrupted his thought processes, so he answered it. Without preamble, Blister said, "A elephant?"

"Good afternoon to you, too."

"Good afternoon. Is it a elephant?"

"*An* elephant."

"Is it *an* elephant?"

"Not even close."

"Crap!"

"It's not Marty Feldman, either."

"Who?"

"You've never seen *Young Frankenstein*?"

"No."

"Then you've been culturally deprived. You should call social services."

"Does it live on land?"

"Uh-uh."

"In the water?"

"Where else is there?"

"The air."

"It would get awfully tired."

"Can I think about it some more?" the boy pleaded.

"Please do," Connor said, and rang off.

Back to his legal pad: "has been seen by reliable (?) source at BBQ recently; no one's reported seeing him since; my visit to sis may have elicited call (to whom?); visit to BBQ drew a bum's rush; possible lead—HS girlfriend (romance, or platonic?); into petty crime until marriage turned him around; deliberately (alleged) hit Able Johnson's car, causing Johnson's death (Was the death intentional? If not, why hit Able's car to begin with? What did Able ever do to Noah?)."

His thoughts branched out to include others:

"Slade's involved, in fact put Thurgood to surveiling Sizemore's BBQ; what's in it for Slade? Fangelli offering a reward? Why, his bond $ is irretrievable? Has the Johnson family offered a reward? (Molly doesn't seem the type— she'd kill Noah herself.) Maybe her insurance weenies put a recovery fee up for grabs; if Noah's nabbed, they could squeeze Molly for 200 G. Twenty percent of *that* would get Slade's attention."

"Okay," Connor said to Zep, a-snooze at his feet, "Shall we list things chronologically?" Zep did not respond. Connor made the list anyway. It went so:

Noah barely manages to get through high school, and runs counter to the law.

He goes to court a few times, then meets and weds
  Christy, who straightens him out.
Christy becomes pregnant with Cody.
Christy dies in an auto accident, but gives birth to Cody
  in the process (WOW!)
Noah rears the child two years, then deliberately runs
  Able Johnson off the road, killing him.
Noah is arrested, jumps bond, abandons his child in order
  to escape a manslaughter charge.
Seven years later Noah is spotted at Sizemore's BBQ by
  a man Slade has hired to watch for him.
THE BIG QUESTION: Why did Noah come out of hid-
  ing, take a serious risk of getting caught, not only by
  Slade but the police???

Connor wrote a new list, headed "What I don't know
about Noah":

Where he is
Why he crashed Able Johnson, if he did
Why he cared for his son for two yrs, then skipped
Whether he still has all or a portion of the half-million
  insurance money
If he does, will he give me some
Whether he still has contact with HS sweetie

"So why don't you go find out?" he said to himself,
since Zepper wasn't talking.
The phone sounded again. This time it was Cameron,
crying.
"Daddy?"
"What's the matter, babe?"
"I just got stung by a bee!"
"Where's your mom?"
"Jogging down the street somewhere with Mrs. Mabley.
It hurts!"
"Calm down and listen to me. Are there any onions in
the house?"
"I don't know! *It hurts!*"

"Cameron?"

"What?"

"Listen to me. Try to ignore the pain and just listen. It won't be easy, but concentrate on what I'm saying. The sting won't kill you."

A snuffy "okay."

"Are you in the kitchen?"

"No."

"Are you on a cordless?"

"Yes."

"Take it with you and go to the kitchen."

"Okay." A few seconds passed, then: "I'm in the kitchen."

"Look in the refrigerator for an onion." Connor heard the door being opened, drawers being pulled and shut.

"There's a big one with brown skin. It looks old."

"That doesn't matter. Now—"

"It *hurts*, Daddy!"

"Cameron, listen to my voice. Focus on what I'm saying, not on the sting. All right?"

"Okay." Soggy, but game.

"Now, find a fairly sharp knife and slice the onion in half. Be very careful, we don't want to add a cut to your problems. Hold the onion firmly on the countertop so it won't turn or spin. Then the knife might slip."

He heard sounds of activity at the other end, then Cameron said, "Okay, I cut it in half."

"Rub one of the halves against the sting, putting the place where you cut against your skin."

"*Ow!* It hurts too much!"

"Cameron?"

"I'm doing it, Daddy. But it seems to make it worse."

"That's mostly from friction, so don't rub too hard. Keep doing it for about ten minutes. That should pretty much make the pain go away."

"Can I put the phone down to do it? This is hard."

"Just hang up, sit down and try to relax, and keep the cut end of the onion against the sting. Call me back in ten minutes. Can you see a clock?"

"Yes. Thanks. I love you."

"I love you, too."

No sooner had Connor recradled the phone than it buzzed again. "Yeah, babe?" he said into it.

"Who's babe?"

"Mr. Scribner?"

"At your service. The girl's name was Lorie Kassinjure."

"Was?"

"She changed it."

"To?"

"You ready for this?"

"I'm trying to be."

"Mantra Marat."

"Good grief."

"It gets better. That's her third."

"Name?"

"You got it, and she's never tied the nuptial knot."

"What was monniker number two?"

"Autumn Dawn."

"I need to lie down."

He laughed. "You mean you need to lay Dawn."

"What a wag. This gets worse, doesn't it?"

"She was too young for the free-love sixties, but not for the me-first eighties. She ran a bar—hooking a little on the side until she got busted, no conviction—then she turned to Amway. After that didn't go over, she operated a chimney-sweep service and peddled reefers to the local college crowd. Then off to California for a while, to check out est. Alas, the coast was not for her. Wings back to good old Wendover in '89, then she was a topless palm reader for a couple years."

"A topless palmist?"

"You got an eyeful with your reading, and at no extra charge. What could be a better deal? She was receptioning at a local car dealership last I heard."

"Which one?"

Scribner told him; Connor thanked him; they bid each

other adieu, neither knowing that a key had just been delivered.

Connor got up to whiz, but had barely unzipped when the phone beckoned once more. "Hello."

"You told him to put an *onion* on a bee sting?" said a voice as cold as a Minnesota gravestone.

"Did it work?"

"An onion, Warren?" She'd called him Warren since the divorce; she knew it rankled him.

"Did it *work,* Felicia?"

He heard a hollow click on the line, then: "Daddy?"

"Yeah, babe."

"It feels lots better, hardly stings at all."

"Get off the phone, Cameron!" said Felicia Rawling-Gibbs, nearly three thousand miles away.

"But, Mom, he'd be worried about me if I didn't—"

"Get off the phone!"

"Bye, Daddy," Cameron said, and hung up.

"If I catch him calling again, I'll take away his photos of you," she promised, and slammed down the phone.

Connor stomped to his training room in a funk, to kick and punch the heavy bag, pump iron, jump rope, and grit his teeth for two nonstop hours. Then he ran eight miles. Afterward he felt better.

But not much.

Wacky Mavens, enjoying his third Long Island iced tea, was most mellow. Before him sat Rex Jobie—hitherto referred to as Sumo—who was not mellow; he was still sore from his dance with Jackson Slade. The pair was conferencing in Mavens's fleabag motel room.

Mavens, in response to a question from Rex, said, "Sure, I heard of Connor Gibbs, sumbitch the size of a cement truck."

"That's the guy."

"What about him?"

"He's been snooping around, looking for Noah."

"That who knocked your teeth out, and lumped up your mug—Gibbs?"

Jobie shook his head once, very fast, as if trying to dispel water from an ear.

"Who, then?" Mavens pressed, lips to the tall cold glass, Adam's apple bobbing like a toy monkey on a stick.

"None of your fucking business."

"Cool. So what you want me to do?"

Jobie told him.

"No problemo," was Mavens's view, and he punctuated it with another drink. He did not offer Rex Jobie one.

"You need to make Gibbs pay for the information, like you're ratting Noah out, otherwise he might not buy your story. Keep whatever you get from him, because it's all you're gonna see," added Jobie, then the big ball of suet climbed to his feet from the lotus position, modified somewhat on account of his bulk.

"No problemo, I owe Noah. For a lot. Tell him I'll be glad to do it."

"Noah don't know nothing about this. The word came from Tate."

Mavens guzzled some more. "Gibbs is not going to be happy with me."

"So? Don't let him find you. Either way, you got no choice," insisted Jobie.

Mavens looked up at him. "There's always a choice."

"You saying you won't—"

"I'm going to do it, Rex. Just don't tell me I don't have a choice. I don't work for the Sizemores anymore."

Jobie made a threatening move until Mavens opened his left hand, which he'd kept closed throughout the discussion. In it was a Beretta Tomcat .32. Jobie resumed a less aggressive posture.

"We understand one another?" Mavens asked.

"Sure. But you're gonna do it, right?"

"I said so, didn't I? Now beat it."

SIXTEEN

"How may I help you?"

The person before him was probably not Mantra Marat, but Connor said, "I was led to believe that a lady by the name of Marat was a receptionist here."

The person before him smiled pleasantly. "She was until December. I'm her replacement. Name's Nancy Fleming."

"Well, I'm Connor Gibbs, and I'll bet she was nowhere nearly as pretty as you."

Brown eyes sparkled. "Let me get my purse, that remark's worth at least five dollars." A kittenish five feet tall, Nancy was dressed in a red-and-white-striped cotton dress with Peter Pan collar and matching belt. White sling backs added a measure of height, but nothing was needed to embellish the personality; she was a seventy-year-old delight.

"Might you be able to give me a clue to Ms. Marat's current whereabouts?"

"Are you a relative?"

"No, ma'am."

"Bill collector?"

"Heaven forfend."

"A former beau, or aspirer to that position?"

"I've never even met her."

"Then why should I help you find her?"

"I'm with the Democratic National Committee. I need her to tell fortunes at a Washington fund-raiser."

The brown eyes waxed effervescent. "Will the president be there?"

"Without doubt."

"Then I'm sure she'd be delighted. Will you wait here a moment?"

"An hour's wait for you would be as nothing."

"Masher," she said, and poked him in the arm.

Around him the typical bustle of the automobile trade: salesmen plying, buyers buying, lookers kicking tires and twisting knobs, kids crawling in and out of backseats, the intercom system bidding the sales manager to answer line three.

In five minutes Nancy Fleming returned with a phone number, an address, and a wedge of homemade apple pie in a plastic airtight container. "You can drop off the Tupperware next time you come by."

"I can't take your pie, Nancy," he demurred through instant salivation.

"My niece made it, so I'd take it pretty hard if you turned it down."

"In that case."

"Besides." She winked. "If you're going to visit Mantra, you'll need your strength."

It was one of those three-story brick buildings built in the thirties, this one near downtown—on Fayetteville Street if you go looking for it—and moderately well maintained. The main entrance was at the center of the building; Mantra Marat's apartment number indicated third floor, so up Connor went. Upon reaching number 315, he discovered a note affixed to the door with masking tape:

Go to rear door.

Back through the long hall (smelling thickly of new green paint), down the stairs, around the east side of the building, up an outside staircase (desperately in need of paint, green or otherwise), to a tiled landing on which rested a gas grill and most of a bicycle. Evidence of an icebox on the right—a rectangular metal container going completely through the wall from the outside, with a latched door. An old-fashioned garbage chute clung precariously to the wooden railing at Connor's left, somewhat resembling an air-conditioning duct. The back door also bore instructions for the visitor:

> Don't ring the bell;
> It gives me a headache;
> Knock lightly or go away

Connor knocked lightly.

Ten seconds went by. Twenty. Thirty. He was about to knock again when a voice from inside said, "Don't do it!" and the door opened.

Before him swayed a woman of indeterminate height (she had on unlaced combat boots that had never seen polish) and undeterminable heft (she wore a caftan the color of river mud and lilacs). Her coiffure was in disarray, her skin splotchy from lying on it, her eyes misted from slumber.

"I'm sorry," Connor apologized, "were you asleep?"

"No, I was playing pinochle with Mick Jagger."

"Who was winning?"

"You want product, come back at six." She started to close the door.

"I want to talk. Fifty bucks' worth."

She stopped closing the door. "That'll buy you maybe ten minutes, unless you want a reading. That's a hundred, up front. And I don't flash my hefties anymore, not for the cost of a reading. You want tits, it's two hundred clams, and I don't take VISA."

"Clams? Are you a BC fan?"

"Ever since Calvin and Hobbs went south, I quit taking the paper. What'll it be?"

"Conversation."

She stuck out a hand. He put a fifty in it. "If we run over, I have more," he said.

"That's what I like to hear. Come," she said, and motioned him inside.

"It's none of my business," he said, "but do you sleep in a caftan?"

"*Au naturel,* but if I'd come to the door that way, I'd've had to charge you. Rest your cheeks in that rocker."

He did, introducing himself while she settled into an easy chair by the window. Harsh light filtering through the chintz highlighted her face; she'd lost some serious bouts with acne in her youth. "Clock's running," she informed.

"I understand you knew Noah Sizemore in school."

"Sure, and I once voted for Michael Dukakis. That and two dollars will get me a cup of Starbucks."

"Do you still have any contact with him?"

"Dukakis?"

He smiled at her wit. "Noah."

"Well, we don't swap spit anymore."

"But you once did?"

"Sure. Me and Barrymore were an item in our heyday. That's what I always called him, Barrymore. His middle name is Barry."

"How recently have you seen him?"

"Eleven-sixteen P.M., October ninth, 1979, a cold and blustery night . . . How the hell should I know when I saw him last? I think it was around Halloween the year we graduated, but who can be certain? Besides, I don't give a rat's ass. The creep owes me money."

"For what?"

"Product."

"Dope?"

"Weed."

"Noah Sizemore smoked marijuana?"

"No, he *mainlined* it. Sure he smoked it. Who didn't, besides my aunt Louise, and I'm not so sure about her."

"Did he do heavier stuff?"

"I have no idea. I didn't deal heavier stuff."

"What do you do for a living now, Ms. Marat?"

"I teach belly dancing at the old folks' home. What business is it of yours what I do?"

"For fifty dollars—"

"You get conversation, not my life story."

"Speaking of which, you mentioned a reading. Did you mean palm?"

"No, the lumps on your head. Sure I meant palm. I used to be a palmist. Only topless palmist in the state."

"Was it lucrative?"

"Are you kidding? I had such a great pair of boobs, guys'd line up for a reading. Some Saturday nights I had fifty, sixty customers, at a hundred clams apiece. Fellow I know opened a tattoo parlor right next door, to cash in on my popularity. He did a land-office business, since most of my clients were either drunk or stoned. Gave me twenty bucks a head to pull from my crowd. Lucrative? I was on easy street."

"Why'd you give it up?"

She hesitated so long, Connor thought she wasn't going to answer. "They didn't take my readings seriously."

"I beg your pardon."

"They spent so much time pawing or staring at my hooters, they didn't pay attention to my readings. And I did a good job, too. I had a gift, but nobody appreciated it." She looked quite melancholy.

"Perhaps they were more interested in your other, ah, gifts."

"Sure, but where's the pride in that, I inherited those. I *studied* to be a palmist. Like I said, I had a real gift, but none of those jerk-offs realized it."

"So why didn't you abandon the topless shtick and go"—he nearly choked—"ligit?"

"I did," she said in a small voice.

"And?"

"They stopped coming." She sank even deeper into melancholy.

"I'm sorry," Connor said. "I didn't mean to open a wound."

She perked up a little. "Why're you looking for Noah?"

"His son hired me to find him."

"Son?"

"The boy's nine."

"How about that. And he doesn't know where his daddy is?"

"Nobody seems to, except Noah's family."

"Did you talk to any of them?"

"Briefly. They were no help."

"I hope I was."

"At least you haven't hurt."

"A guy named Connor Gibbs just came by, asking about Noah," she said.

"What'd you tell him?"

"Nothing much."

"Good."

"Do we have anything to worry about?"

"Don't see how."

"If he finds Noah—"

"Don't worry, he won't. If Jackson Slade and four million cops can't find him, how you think that big lug can?"

"I don't know, there's something about him. I picked up some vibes."

"Don't start believing your own shit, Lorie."

"I told you to stop calling me Lorie. You just keep an eye on things. I'm sick of changing names and careers."

They rang off.

"Sur, Arthur, Cone, and Doyle."

"May I speak to Holmes Crenshaw, please?"

"I'm sorry, sir, he's in a meeting."

"It's very important. Won't take a second."

"May I ask who's calling, please?"

"Tell him Wacky's on the line."

"One minute, please."

Line hum, then Michael Jones pianoing in his ear. Forever.

Finally: "Hello."

"Attorney Crenshaw, I presume?"

"What is it, Wacky? I'm in a meeting."

"No you're not, you're talking to me."

"And now I'm hanging up."

"Get in touch with Gibbs."

"What about?"

"Tell him I know where Noah Sizemore's gonna be to-morrow."

"And?"

"It'll cost. Have Gibbs meet me. Five o'clock. Today."

"Where?"

Mavens gave the location and severed the connection.

Wacky Mavens wasn't much bigger than a bread box and was shaped similarly. He sat at the bar scraping his teeth with a plastic guitar pick as Connor Gibbs approached.

"Mr. Mavens?"

"Call me Wacky. Everybody else does."

"All right, Wacky. What have you got for me?" He leaned against the bar.

"I hear you're looking for Tate Sizemore's little brother."

"Noah, yes."

"What's it worth to find him?"

"What's the price?"

"Five thousand."

"Have a nice day," Connor said, and pushed away from the bar.

"Hold on, hold on," protested Wacky with a venal leer. "Just trying to make a living, here."

"No, you're trying to hold me up."

"How about a grand?"

Connor forked over a thin stack of Franklins.

Wacky counted them. "You know the area northwest of Wilkesboro?"

"Fairly well."

"Know where 16 intersects with 421 North?"

Connor nodded.

"Up 16, through Wilbar, nearly to Ashe County, just

before the parkway, there's a dump on the right called the Fat Brown Fox."

"Bikers' hangout, perched on an overlook facing almost due east."

"That's the dive. One of Noah's cousins is giving him a surprise birthday party, Thursday noon. Place is closed till two, so they'll have it all to themselves. Got some broad from Hendersonville coming over, gonna jump out of a cake and all. I hear she's a real looker, and can suck the brass off a doorknob."

"Wouldn't want to miss out on that."

"I figured as much."

"That all?"

"What else you need, an invitation?"

"This is straight, right?" said Connor.

"It better be. Cost me three hundred smackers, and I can find the guy if it ain't."

"Like I can find you."

"No problemo, cement man," Wacky said, and left.

SEVENTEEN

"That sounds exactly like the kind of party someone would throw for Noah, the sleazebag."

"Don't hold back, Ms. McGraw. Say what you really mean," Connor chided.

"You don't need to keep calling me *Miz* McGraw."

"It's out of deference to your ritual male bashing."

"All of you deserve it."

"I see no wings on you, Ms. McGraw, but our sparring is pointless. Are you going to let me take Cody to the mountains to see his father?"

"You don't like me much, do you?"

"That's irrelevant. I don't work for you, I work for Cody."

She arched her proud neck. "That's true. But here's one for you: what if I won't let him go?"

"Then I'll tell Noah that Cody wants to see him, and see what he might want to work out."

"I could keep you from seeing Cody."

"Not without a restraining order, which would be difficult to get since I pose no threat to either of you. Why not simply honor the boy's wish?"

She stood abruptly and circled the room, arms akimbo,

markedly agitated. "Because, Mr. Gibbs, if that piece of llama shit had been home with his wife nine years ago, *like he should have been,* my sister might not be dead now!"

"Or Noah might be dead, too. There's no guarantee he could have avoided the collision."

She spun around. "Oh, really? How do you think my sister could concentrate on driving *while she was having a baby!*"

"I don't know, I wasn't there. Neither were you. By the way, where were you that night?"

"You rotten—"

"Ms. McGraw, give me an answer. May Blister go or not?"

"*Yes!*" she screamed, and rushed from the room.

Connor and Blister left Wendover at 9:04 on a typical North Carolina early-summer morning: hot, humid, blue-skied. They stopped at a Quincy's in North Wilkesboro, where the yeast rolls were, if not to die for, at least worth becoming seriously ill. Blister devoured an ample portion but Connor ate uncharacteristically light. "Why?" Blister wondered. "You never know," Connor answered. "About what?" Blister insisted. "Nothing for you to worry about," Connor allowed.

Which was not strictly true.

Because Connor had a premonition . . .

When they were passing through Wilbar, which took twenty-three seconds, Blister said, "A whale shark."

"A what?"

"Whale shark. The biggest kind. They can get up to sixty feet long."

"You're making that up."

"Am not."

"Well, no, anyway."

"No what?"

"No, it's not a whale shark."

"Am I getting close?"

"You have the right milieu."

"The right what?"

Connor just smiled and headed northwest.

The squat building was gray-painted cinder block, had a red shingled roof, a paved parking area out front, and was less than fifty feet from the road. Out back was a steep drop-off, wooded though it might be. To the left rear corner of the building had been added a wooden deck; on the deck was a picnic table, though Connor could see only part of it because of an eight-foot privacy fence bordering the deck. There was a swinging gate leading onto the deck, a conventional door at the extreme left front of the building—painted red to match the roof—and another in the middle, also red. No windows except for a small pair of sliding ones to the right of the center door, which was obviously the main entrance. To the left of that door was a wooden sign measuring perhaps three feet by six, reading:

THE FAT BROWN FOX

It had been professionally painted. Near the top of the center door was a reversible sign that proclaimed:

SORRY—WE'RE CLOSED

There were no other signs or identifying markings. There were also no signs of patronization, unless you counted a blacked-out Chevy 4 × 4 parked beside a gleaming yellow Harley at the far left end of the parking area. Blister started to get out of the van, but Connor told him to hold up.

"Why?" said the boy.

"Let me check things out first. I'll motion to you when it's time to come. Lock the doors when I get out, and don't get out of this van unless I motion for you. Understand?"

Blister nodded, his throat suddenly dry. Why was Connor behaving so oddly?

Connor quit his side of the van, passing in front of it en route to the entrance door. A Nissan convertible whizzed by on the road behind him, the breeze from its passage stirring his hair. When he was thirty feet from the entrance, a man stepped through the door, a salty-looking customer in bib overalls and Nikes. His barrel chest was heavily thatched.

The pickup door opened and slammed, emitting a similar gritty specimen, taller but narrower, in jeans with no shirt, cowboy hat on top. Connor looked at each of them as they stood forty feet from each other, flanking him.

Well, now.

Through the open gate of the privacy fence spilled three more examples of testosterone gone awry, various sizes, all thickly necked and two with facial foliage. They must have been out back, on the deck.

Waiting.

To play.

"Howdy, gents," Connor greeted.

One of the foliated figures said, "Polite, ain't he?" to a mate. Everyone laughed. Except Connor.

"What's your intent?" Connor said to the overalled grub at his right front.

"Our intent?" The big man smiled hugely, displaying his crooked, tobacco-stained tusks. "We gon' bust you up some, then th'ow you off'n this little old mountaintop."

Connor turned toward the van, gave Blister a firm signal to stay put, then faced his adversaries again. "Well, don't be shy," he said. "Come do it."

EIGHTEEN

The cowboy from the pickup arrived first and, as soon as he was in range, threw a very fast right cross at Connor's chin. His aim was perfect. Unfortunately not only had his eyes betrayed his intentions, so had a slight dipping of his shoulder. Connor had plenty of time to bring up his own ham-sized right hand, snare the incoming fist in a viselike grip when it was still ten inches from his chin, lean back slightly, rotating his upper torso clockwise with the cowboy's fist still enclamped, pull the fist on past his face, and with the open palm of his left hand dislocate the hapless cowboy's right elbow with a sickening *crack!* Cowboy screamed, as well he should. One of the bearded baddies bounded to his aid, from Connor's right, dukes up. Connor, having held on to the cowboy's now useless hand while waiting until the second antagonist was within range, delivered a side snap kick to the man's leading kneecap, then—when the man yelped and stopped in his tracks—used the same right leg to roundhouse kick him in the temple with a sound like an ax going into a ripe melon. The guy dropped to both knees and was about to collapse forward when Connor applied another side snap kick, this one to the man's chin, and that was the ball game.

The second bearded man was coming now, from behind, quickly, so Connor jerked the woeful cowboy around—still retaining the man's right hand and hooking his own left thumb beneath the cowboy's right armpit, digging into the man's shoulder with four fingers—and so placed the pain-racked body between himself and the oncoming threat. When the bearded man paused to review his options, Connor released Cowboy's shoulder, jerked his own left fist back tightly against his chest, and snapped his left elbow forward very hard and very fast, impacting the point of Cowboy's jaw just behind his right ear, *crunch!* Lights out for two, now.

Bib Overalls danced in, weaving like a mongoose trying to intimidate a cobra, fists pistoning *zip-zip,* much faster than anyone might think a hefty man could move, so Connor skipped two lightning-quick side steps and delivered a spinning blade kick to Bib's exposed chin, right through his bobbing guard. Bib's head snapped back from the blow and he rubber-legged, so Connor urged, "Come on, girly-man," and moved in close, then tossed two forefist punches—both to the nose and both drawing grunts of appreciation—then looped a round punch into the side of Bib's neck, following with a forward-knuckle blow to the solar plexus, *Whap!* When Bib staggered again and reached out to grab him, Connor stepped close and forward-knuckle-punched his flagging opponent on the temple, *smack!* Bib hit the tarmac like a heap of compost, as the second bearded gent—with a spirited rebel yell—leaped onto Connor's broad back and began to pummel his head with clenched fists. In judo, there is a throw called *morote-seoi-otoshi.* Connor was very familiar with it. He used it now. Flexing his left knee to take the force of the throw, he extended his right leg to the rear, reached up and grabbed his assailant by the shirt, then pulled forward with both arms, bending at the waist and lowering his head toward his own left knee. Bearded Guy Number Two went sailing, then landed hard on his back, which drove the oxygen from his lungs. Connor dropped to his left knee—holding tightly onto the man's shirt with his left hand—

and popped him hard in the temple with an extended one-
knuckle fist, then twice more in the same spot, but palm-
heel strikes since he didn't want to kill him. No more
resistance. In fact, no more conciousness.

One to go, thought Connor, and there he was, charging,
a hammer raised high above his buzz-cut noggin, claw fore-
most to do the most damage. Connor waited until the fool
was almost upon him, then lashed out high with his right
foot, kicking the man over the heart to stop him. Then
Connor was up and shifting, taking the downward sweep
of the hammer on an outside forearm block, then smashing
forward a *jun-zuki*—snap punch—to the solar plexus, following with a reverse punch to the groin, then a plain old-
fashioned boxer's left hook to the jaw—rotating his fist
nicely at impact—which put the hammer wielder on the
pavement. An ax kick started five feet in the air and with
242 pounds behind it put him in la-la land.

Connor stood surveying the carnage, breathing deeply
through his nostrils. *Good fight,* he thought. *And a nice
morning for it. Love this mountain air.* He filled his huge
chest with some, then walked over to the main entrance
door of the Fat Brown Fox. Tried the knob. No dice. He'd
figured as much, so he started toward the van.

A Wilkes County sheriff's car pulled onto the lot. From
the north. He'd probably been watching, from a distance.
"What's the trouble here, hotshot?" the deputy said as he
exited the car.

"No trouble, unless you intend to arrest me."

"What happened to those fellers?"

"I was teaching them to Rollerblade. They're tired
now."

"Well, aren't you the big haw-haw."

Connor approached the law-enforcement officer, towered
over him, chest to face. He said, "We going to have a
problem, you and me?"

The deputy looked up at Connor's determined chin. Way
up.

"Not that I can see."

"Then good day to you, Deputy," Connor said, and turned toward his van.

"You do your Rollerblading in your own backyard from now on," the cop called after him.

Connor nodded assent as he walked.

"Wow!" Blister said.

Connor drove, sucking on his bruised knuckles.

"Wow!" Blister said again.

Connor drove and sucked.

"I can't believe I ever thought that you might—"

Connor glanced at him. "Be a coward?"

Blister looked sheepish.

Connor turned back to the road. "I told you that wasn't the case."

"But—"

"There was no way out back there, they had me boxed. I had to fight. Sometimes you do."

"You coulda run back to the van. I'd've had the doors unlocked by the time—"

Connor looked at him again. "No, I couldn't."

"Oh."

"By the way, I'm sorry."

Blister was startled. "About what?"

"That it was a setup. That your daddy wasn't there."

"That wasn't your fault."

"No, but I'm still sorry you didn't get to see him."

"That's okay, 'cause I got to see one helluva—"

"Blister."

"Yes?"

"Don't transfer to me your affection for your dad. He's your father, I'm just your friend."

Blister dropped his head. "Yeah, so where's he been for seven years?"

"When we find him, ask."

"Okay."

"It's still early, you want to go swimming?"

Excited again, like flipping a switch. "Where?"

"I know a place. Sandy beach, trees for shade, cold river water."

"I didn't bring a suit."

"We'll whip into West Jefferson and get you one."

"Okay."

So they did.

NINETEEN

"I need to get Wacky," Connor said into his cell phone as he and Blister tooled homeward on Highway 421 South.

"Okay," agreed Holmes Crenshaw. "This evening I'll pick up a couple of six-packs, and you and I can—"

"Mavens."

"Oh yeah? What did he do?"

"Noah Sizemore wasn't at the Fat Brown Fox."

"No kidding. Was the comely vacuum-oriented cake crasher there?"

"I didn't see her."

"Pity. I was hoping . . . well, never mind. So what happened?"

"Five men wanted to play king-of-the-mountain, and they wouldn't let me be king."

"Only five. Did you let them have their way?"

"No. I was in a bad mood, what with Noah not there and all."

"That's no reason to be spiteful."

"Well, they bruised my knuckles."

"With their chins?"

"It varied."

"I'll bet. So Wacky set us up."

"Us? You were sitting there in air-conditioned comfort, dictating a pleading, or scribing a memorandum, while I, a manly man, was nearly getting the shit kicked—"

"Did you take Blister swimming?"

"Of course."

"Where we used to go?"

"Of course."

"I hope you wore a suit."

"Please. It was daytime."

"How soon should I find Wacky?"

"As soon as, or even sooner."

"I'll put Braxton Chiles on it."

"Does Chiles know Mavens?"

"Who cares, he can find him. Chiles can find any of his competitors, anytime, unless they've fled to Krakatoa. Can I go now, scribe a memorandum or something?"

"Please do," Connor said.

The phone rang. "Yo."

"It didn't go so well."

"Up in the mountains?" Wacky Mavens wanted clarification.

"You got it?"

"What happened?"

"The dumb bastards didn't use chain saws, that's what."

"How many were there?" Mavens asked.

"Five."

"Five! You had five redneck mountain hoppers jump Gibbs and he walked away!"

"Nobody laid a hand on him, unless you count Orville. He jumped on Gibbs's back and pounded on his head some, but Gibbs slammed him down and beat the grits out of him. One of Tate's nephews saw it from down the road. He's a county mounty."

"Why the hell didn't he arrest him after?"

"Arrest one guy for stomping five? Gimme a fucking break."

"I suppose I should leave town for a while," Wacky lamented.

"It's why I called. Tate figured it the same way."

"I'll need some traveling dough," Wacky tried.

"Forget it."

"Listen, if Gibbs gets hold of me, I'll have to—"

"What, Wacky? You'll have to what?"

"Nothing. I'll see you."

"Don't bet on it," said Rex Jobie, who very much resembled a sumo wrestler.

The phone rang. "I wish you wouldn't call when I'm trying to sleep, whoever the hell you are," she said.

"Mantra?"

"Oh, hi." She yawned into the phone.

"I need about a suitcase full, and right damn now."

"Why?"

"Traveling expenses."

"Who's on your case?"

Mavens told her.

"Shit. I hope he doesn't backtrail to me when you turn up on vacation."

"Just get me the stuff."

"I don't have anywhere near that much. I'll have to call."

"How soon can you get it?"

"Couple days."

"Fuck me! Gibbs'll have pretzeled me by then. Can you bring it somewhere?"

"Where?"

Wacky thought a moment. "The beach place."

"At Holden's? Forget it. Takes too long to get to Holden's Beach and back."

"Mantra. I need help, here. We go way back, remember?"

Not far enough, she started to say. "Okay, okay, I'll see what I can do."

"Good girl. I owe you."

"You sure as hell do. And thanks for remembering to call me Mantra."

"I'll see you at the beach in two days."

No he wouldn't.

"Whatcha doing, my man?"

"Gasing up the fucking car, Chiles. What does it look like?" Wacky reached into his pocket for the Tomcat .32.

"Going somewhere?"

"You don't ever have to put gas into your own rocket, dickweed?" Wacky wrapped his fingers around the grip.

"It really hurts when you call me names, man."

"Go home and get your mother to blow on it." All Wacky had to do was yank the gun free if things went badly wrong.

Chiles lifted his right hand from where it had been hidden behind his leg. In his fist was a Colt Python .357 Magnum, with a six-inch barrel. It would open a hole the size of the Lincoln Tunnel. Mavens saw the gun and didn't like it. Chiles said, "If that hand doesn't come out of your pocket empty, I'm gonna spray-paint that pump with your balls."

Wacky's hand came out empty.

TWENTY

As he stood there, Braxton Chiles weighed about a hundred and ten pounds, and ten of that was shoes. He looked like a damp mop (all hair and bone), was five-feet-three, had an Adam's apple like a grape, and possessed the longest fingers you ever saw on anyone under, oh, five-eleven. Since he was not large, Chiles never fought with his fists. Or his feet. Or his teeth, elbows, or even a knife. Chiles was a gunny; he'd shot seventeen people—cosmopolitanly including several races, creeds, and sexual orientations—and one goat. He'd been collared for only two of the shootings, and released for lack of evidence. Savvy, mean, streetwise, vindictive, oddly honorable, he was additionally a very fine harpist. (Those long, delicate fingers.)

Alas, ablutions were not his wont. In fact, Chiles was so incredibly aromatic, his name was legend. Having grown up on an Arkansas farm not far from the Springs, the story went that Braxton's fifth-grade teacher had—in an extreme state of olfactory agitation—asked the youngster where he took a bath. "In the spring," Braxton answered, to which the frustrated schoolmarm curtly replied, "I said 'where,' young man, not when."

Connor Gibbs, thankfully downwind, addressed him
thus: "How are you, Mr. Chiles?"

"Fine as frog hair, my man. Thanks for asking, though.
You always were considerate."

The two of them were in the rental office of Chiles's
storage warehouse: metal stairs, mildew, wire mesh, an old
Naugahyde couch with stuffing leaking out, Braxton's Colt
Python lying on a littered desktop.

"Where's Mavens?"

"Number-two bin, downstairs. It's the rattiest I got." His
voice was high-pitched and grating, and his Adam's apple
bobbed as he spoke.

"Would you accompany me?"

"Sure, wouldn't want Wacky slapping you around."

They negotiated the stairs and Chiles unlocked bin two.
There was Wacky Mavens, tied to a lounge chair and
watching a black-and-white television with a screen the size
of a playing card. He blinked at them. "Chiles, you son of
a bitch! This tiny fucking TV is gonna roon my eyes."

"*Ruin*, Wacky," corrected Connor, "*Roo-in*, two syllables. A rune is a character in an ancient Germanic alphabet.
Also a poem or song."

Chiles chuckled; Mavens said nothing.

Connor knelt beside Wacky's fancy green-and-white
lounge chair. Wacky tried to lean away from him, but was
hindered by his fastenings. "Wacky?" Connor began.

"Huh?"

"Let us speak."

"I got nothing to say to you."

"Not long ago you had a lot to say, and for which I gave
you a lot of money."

"That was the skinny, Connor, I swear! That was just
the way I got it!"

"From whom?"

Mavens squirmed, turned his head.

"Wacky?"

Nothing in response.

Connor stood. "Okay, Mr. Chiles. Cut the power until
say . . . Monday. And nothing to drink."

"Hey!" cried Wacky Mavens. "There's rats in here. I hear 'em scurrying around!"

"Not to mention about ninety-nine degrees at midday," added Braxton Chiles. "Gonna get mighty thirstful, man."

"Wait a minute," Mavens said, then chewed his lip for a while. "I got the word from Rex Jobie."

Connor looked a question at Chiles.

"Big hard-fat dude, works for Tate Sizemore out at the restaurant. Oversees the parking lot, tosses brown-baggers, that kind of stuff. Thinks he's a badass. Last week Jackson Slade put a hurting on him."

"Does he look like a sumo wrestler?"

"That's the guy."

Connor thought for a moment, then: "Will you keep Wacky here for a few days? As my guest of course."

"Hey!" said Wacky.

"Cost you three bucks a day," from Braxton Chiles.

"You can feed him on three dollars a day?"

Chiles grinned happily. "Who said I was gonna feed him?"

"Hey!" Wacky protested, straining against his bonds.

Chiles went over, leaned forward, putting his long nose against Wacky's. "Mr. Gibbs didn't say I had to leave the lights on."

"Now, Chiles, let's talk about this. Chiles. Chiles? *Mister* Chiles!" Wacky screeched.

But Connor and Braxton had left, closing the door behind them. "Wacky always was a wuss," Chiles observed as he snapped the padlock.

Johnston Thurgood had just placed his binoculars in his lap to take a bite of meatball sandwich when an arm came through his open car window, encircled his flabby neck, and squeezed. Thurgood dropped the sandwich onto his steering wheel, reached into his waistband for a serrated Spyderco, opened it one-handed, and slashed the arm. The arm let go, but a second one came through the window to grasp his knife wrist and slam it into the wheel—once, twice, again—until he yelped and dropped the blade. Then the first arm was back, bleeding profusely but with a fist on the end of it that pounded his subereous face *bapbap-bap!* in rapid succession. Thurgood tried to fend off the attack, but there was insufficient room, what with his big belly wedged against the steering wheel. Finally managing to kick himself sideways, he scrambled toward the passenger side, arriving there only to have the door jerked open and his body be hauled out into the muggy night air. Boots then conscientiously applied to his head, his back, his shoulders, his thighs, his groin. He begged for respite, but the arms soon joined the boots in punishing him. Just before losing consciousness, he heard the boots say to the arms, "Leave him go. You're killing him."

"That's what I mean to do! Motherfucker cut me good!"

"But those weren't our orders. We were to rough him up, give him a message, and send him off."

"Well, do it, then!" roared the arms, stamping off in high dudgeon.

The boots got in Thurgood's face as he lay there pained and panting. "Can you hear me?"

Thurgood tried to speak but couldn't. He nodded instead.

"My boss man told me to tell you that if he catches you out here spying again, he's going to tie you to a truck bumper and drag you halfway to Burgaw, and I believe him. Do you?"

Thurgood nodded, then spat some blood.

"Good. Have a nice night," said the boots, then one of them kicked him in the side of the head and he passed out.

When he awoke, he was alone. He dragged himself to his car, heaved his aching body inside, cranked up, and drove away. And never came within two miles of Sizemore's Barbecue again.

As Johnston Thurgood was getting his head handed to him, Connor Gibbs was walking past a long line of would-be diners outside Sizemore's.

"Of all the nerve," one woman said.

"Hey, where you think you're go—" a man began, but squelched it when Connor looked at him unaffectionately.

Rex Jobie was near the door as Connor came through it. He headed for the office as soon as Connor spotted him, with Gibbs hard on his heels. The two burst through the office door almost simultaneously. Gibbs grabbed Jobie by the back of his collar, slung the three-hundred-pound body around like a burlap sack filled with feathers, and crossed the man's eyes with an overhand right, turning his hips with the punch for extra zest. Jobie hit the floor so hard, a plastic cup filled with pencils fell off the desk and scattered its contents on the linoleum. Jobie lay still, listening to the tweety birds sing.

Across the room sitting in a Kennedy rocker was one of the men who'd hastened Connor's departure Friday night. Instead of a red tank top, he now wore a yellow one. And a bandage on his head. He started to get up until Connor said, "Stay where you are or you'll need more bandages." The man stayed in the rocker.

Tate Sizemore, behind his desk in a wheelchair, reached toward a drawer. In two long-legged strides Gibbs was beside him, one hand gripping Tate's thin, pale wrist. "Forget the gun."

Tate tried to resist, but he was as weak as a ten-year-old. He gave it up. "Let go the arm."

Connor did, but pushed the chair away from the drawer, which he then opened to remove Tate's long black revolver. He stuck the gun in his belt.

"You're trespassing, guilty of two assaults—"

"Sizemore?"

"—possibly breaking and entering, and—"

"Sizemore!"

"—I intend to call the police if—"

Connor jerked the phone around, stuck it under Tate's nose. "Go ahead. Call them."

"—you don't leave immediately." Tate's ashen fingers trembled.

"Sizemore?"

Finally Tate focused.

"I don't so much mind being set up, but what would have happened to Blister if those boys had whipped me?"

"Blister?" Tate's eyes were red-rimmed.

"Cody. Your nephew."

"Nothing would have happened to him. They were told to leave immediately after. I didn't even know Cody was going to be there."

"If they'd left, Cody would have had a two-mile trek to get help, unless he'd thought to use my cell phone. What if somebody'd come along and grabbed him while he was walking up the road?"

Through pale, quivering lips: "I said I didn't know he would be there!"

"Why won't Noah meet with his son?"

"He'd be. arrested!"

"I'm not interested in past transgressions. Neither is Blister. He's looking to the future, and he wants his daddy to be part of it."

Tate Sizemore closed his eyes so tightly the lids flickered. When he opened them, he said, "That's not possible."

"What's not?"

"For his daddy to be in his future, not unless Cody were to leave that *woman*, and . . . no, it'd never work. Cody is exactly where he should be. So is Noah."

"Why? I'll meet Noah anywhere he says, with Cody. No cops."

Tate shook his thin pale head: left, right, once each way.

"Why not!"

"You don't understand . . . it just wouldn't work. Cody is where he must remain under the circumstances."

"What circumstances? The Murder Two rap? That was seven years ago. I have a friend who's a crackerjack defense attorney. He'll ask for a—"

"You don't understand."

"Explain it to me."

Tate shook his head: left, right.

Connor took a deep breath. "Then you leave me no choice but to find Noah on my own, no matter how I have to do it. He owes his son an explanation, even if the two of you don't seem to think so."

Tate continued to shake his head.

"I will find him. Count on it," Connor said, and left.

As soon as Connor was gone, Tate Sizemore turned to the man with the bandaged head. "Get some smelling salts, bring him around," he said, indicating the bulbous chump on the floor. "Then call Frank. Tell him no more warnings; they don't work. Tell him next time to put 'em where they'll do the most good, permanent."

"Tate."

"Tell him!" Tate yelled, then went into a coughing fit that lasted ten minutes.

TWENTY-ONE

Vera McGraw was pacing. The attic. Beset with ambivalence. She paused by the old steamer trunk, heat and guilt overburdening her, there near the eaves. Opening the trunk's lid, she stared into its accusing confines, torn by what she saw, then slammed it shut and retreated down the ladder, praying for release.

It was nearly ten when Connor's phone rang: Estelle Lawson.

"Hello, my dear," he greeted after she'd identified herself.

"Hello yourself, jelly bean."

"How's hubby?"

"How should I know? He's in Atlantic City."

"Then let's you and me go to a drive-in and neck."

"I'd take you up on it if you weren't so gosh-awful ugly."

"I'll wear a mask."

She laughed at last. "Thanks. I needed that. I have a bit of news."

"Lay it on me."

"Some of the boys in blue got a tip the other night, that

Noah Sizemore was seen at his brother's restaurant.''

"Old news, sweets.''

"Pay attention. One of our newer detectives dug up a warrant, went out to have a look. Took some uniforms along.''

"That I didn't know. So what'd they find?''

"Lots of nothing, unless you consider twenty-two gallons of coleslaw something. But they declared Tate Sizemore Mr. Uncongeniality.''

"Are you—and I mean 'you' collectively, of course—watching the place?''

"Half-assed, not around the clock. The word I get is that Jackson Slade put old Puff Belly to keeping an eye out, from the pecan grove on the hill.''

"Are you referring to Mr. Thurgood? How unkind. He's a fine figure of a man.''

"You a mean a fine figure of *two* men.''

Connor laughed. "Thanks for letting me know about the warrant, Estelle.''

"Anything for you, studly.''

Midnight now, Jay Leno in the background. Connor answered the phone groggily: Holmes Crenshaw.

"Don't you ever sleep?'' Gibbs groused.

Crenshaw said, "There I was, going over some briefs, when a little mouse whispered in my ear.''

"Was it the same one that hung around with Ben Franklin? Helped him invent electricity?''

"This little mouse told me that your role model was badly beaten tonight. So badly, he was in hospital, as my British cousins like to say.''

"You have no British cousins, and if you did, they wouldn't admit it. And who is my role model on this occasion?''

"Johnston Thurgood.''

"Somebody beat up Puff Bel—Thurgood? Who in the world?''

"My little mouse says Thurgood ain't doing much talking, but the drift is it was some*bodies*. Want to go see him? Take him some petunias?''

"He'd probably appreciate Mallow Cups more," Connor speculated.

And he was right.

"The porker's gone from the hill. You can slip out with the next crowd that leaves, but I think you're being foolish," Tate Sizemore told his brother.

"I'm going stir-crazy here. I haven't left in two weeks. It's like being in prison."

"There aren't any bars."

Noah smiled. "I know. And the food's good. But I need to check on some things, and stretch my legs. Enjoy some sunshine."

"Check on your business interests?"

Noah clouded over. "Please don't start, Tate. I don't want to argue with you."

Tate shook his head. "Neither do I. But it won't be much longer, and I want you here with me."

Noah put an arm around his brother's thin pale shoulders. "I know. It's why I came. But I need to check on some things. I'll be back in no time."

"The cops are watching."

"Only off and on. You've got men out sweeping the area. They'll spot anybody who's not coming here to feed his face."

"Maybe so, maybe not."

"Give me just two days."

Tate tried to smile his permission, but couldn't quite bring it off. He did manage to say okay.

But he didn't mean it.

Noah Sizemore walked out with a group of softball players from Reidsville. He'd borrowed one of their jerseys and a cap, so no one paid any attention to him—at least no one of any negative consequence—when he climbed into a Pontiac Grand Am with Rex Jobie behind the wheel.

• • •

Connor was home by 2:30, having received little information of value from Johnston Thurgood, except that Thurgood was quits on the Sizemore surveillance. As Gibbs was
brushing his teeth, Noah Sizemore was making a call from
a secure phone.

"Speak to me," a female voice said at the other end.

"I've missed you," Noah said.

He noted the quick inhalation of surprise, excitement.
"Me, too, baby."

"How's business?"

"Great, great." She sounded a little off-key.

"You're not high, are you?"

"I wish. By the way, Wacky called me for some quantity."

"How much?"

"He said however much I could get."

"Where's he now?"

"His place, I suppose."

"When did he call?"

"Yesterday."

"How'd you plan to get it to him?"

"He said he was going down to Holden. Wanted me to
send one of the regular mules."

He changed the subject. "Where's your man?"

"You're my man, baby. My only man."

"*I* wish."

"Don't be like that. You aren't able to see me that often,
and I need . . . you know. But it doesn't mean I love him.
I love you, honey."

Noah believed her, for the most part.

Back to business: "Who did you call Wacky's order in
to?"

"Nobody yet. I been watching *Independence Day* on
video. I was just planning to make the call."

"I'll handle it."

"Okay. You going by Wacky's place?"

"Uh-huh."

"Tell him hey for me."

He didn't.

• • •

Inside Wacky Maven's seedy motel room, the phone was ringing. Noah came through the door and picked it up and listened, saying nothing.

"Noah?" A female voice.

"Hi, Lorie."

"Mantra. Listen, do you know Braxton Chiles?"

"I met him once."

"Well, he's got Wacky down in that storage dump on Bleeker Street."

"What do you mean got him?"

"Has him locked up tight as a tick."

"Why?"

"I don't know."

Noah reflected; then: "Who told you about it?"

"One of my customers, nobody you'd know, fences some for Braxton time to time. Me, too, when I have to take stuff in trade."

"Is this guy reliable?"

"Always has been. Saved me from a bust more than once," she declared.

"What's that address on Bleeker?"

She told him; then: "You going to get him?"

"I'll smoke the situation over. Don't want to tangle with Braxton Chiles unless I have to. The son of a bitch is crazy."

"And pure poison with that big-ass Colt he totes around. Be careful."

"Lorie—"

"Please, call me Mantra."

"No offense, but screw Mantra. I've known you too long to switch. What I wanted to say was, unless you're seriously hurting for money, close up shop for right now. Things are about to bust loose, I can feel it."

She didn't speak for a while; then, as if in afterthought: "How's Tate?"

"How do you think?" Harsher than he intended.

"I was just asking."

"He's alive, Lorie. He's alive."

• • •

It was after four and the warehouse was dark. "We going in?" Rex Jobie said.

"Place could be wired, triple-locked, land-mined. How do we know? Chiles is nobody to fool with. I suppose it'd be best to wait until he shows in the morning, then go talk to him."

"I ain't afraid of that whistle neck," Jobie allowed.

"But you're not too awful smart either," said Noah.

"Shit, he ain't nothing without that gun."

"But he always has the gun, Rex. Always. I've even heard he has two, just alike. From the Colt custom shop, couple grand apiece."

"Little prick couldn't even *carry* two."

"You're probably right."

But they waited outside just the same.

Braxton Chiles approached his warehouse's front door at 7:15, carrying a bag of bagels. Blueberry. He slipped inside like a wraith. By the time Noah and Rex reached it, the door was closed and locked. So they banged on it. The door opened an inch. "Yes?" came a voice from within, high-pitched, nasal, and annoying.

"Braxton? I'd like to come in and talk with you."

"That you, Sizemore?"

"Yeah."

"What do you want to talk about, man?"

"Open the fucking door, you little scumbag," shouted Rex Jobie, shoving Noah aside to get at the door. A click stopped him. The click of a cocking hammer.

"Jobie?" said the high-pitched voice, especialy irritating this close. "The single-action pull on this Colt is two pounds, and I've taken up half that, which means there's only sixteen ounces of pressure separating you from glory. Catch my drift?"

Jobie swallowed. Hard. Twice. Then he couldn't any-more. He was out of spit.

He couldn't talk either, so he nodded, very slowly.

"Back up," ordered the high-pitched voice.

Jobie backed up.

"That your pony across the street?" asked the voice.

Jobie, still spitless, nodded.

"Go put your fat ass in the front seat. Now."

Jobie did.

"Okay, Sizemore," said Braxton Chiles, swinging wide the door. "Come on in."

Noah stepped in and Chiles closed and bolted the door.

"I hear that Wacky Mavens is a guest of yours," Noah said.

"Indeed he is."

"Can I see him?"

"Don't see why not. Gibbs didn't say he couldn't have visitors."

Wacky was sound asleep when they opened his cubicle. Noah had to kick his leg to wake him, and then it took a moment for Mavens to orient himself. "Noah!" he belched. "Get me out of here!"

Noah looked a question at Chiles.

Chiles said, "No way."

"Why not?"

"Because Connor Gibbs said to keep him here, man. And here he stays until Gibbs says different."

"What if I pay you?" Noah bargained.

"Wouldn't be ethical. Connor's already paying me."

"Three dollars a day!" Wacky screeched.

Noah was incredulous. "You're holding a man for three dollars a day?"

Chiles shook his head no. "I'm holding him because Connor Gibbs asked me to. The per diem is to allay expenses."

"What expenses?"

"Feeding him." Chiles pointed to Wacky with his chin.

"Know what he gives me? Cornflakes! Generic, not even Kellogg's! And fucking *skim* milk! I ask you."

Noah looked at Braxton Chiles.

Chiles shrugged. "Three dollars isn't much. Besides, cereal is pretty nutritious, and I give him all he wants."

"Ha!" Wacky spat. "After two or three bowls of that shit in a row, who'd want any more?"

"Bitch, bitch, bitch," said the high-pitched voice.

"Get me outta here, Noah."

"So there's no chance of working a deal." Sizemore made one last stab.

"No chance in the world, man. Until Connor Gibbs gives the word, Wacky Mavens stays right there in that chair, except to pee or take a dump. Twice a day on the former, once on the latter." He smiled benignly, like a barracuda.

Noah looked back at Wacky. "What'd you do to piss Gibbs off?"

Wacky sulked.

"Want me to tell him?" Chiles prodded.

"I sent him on a wild-goose chase, to the mountains, after you," Mavens admitted.

"And?"

More sulking.

"*And?*"

"Tate had five guys there, to beat him up. But Jobie put me up to it!" he whined.

Noah looked again at Braxton. "How's Connor's health?"

"Never laid a hand on him. Mussed his hair, maybe."

Noah closed his eyes. *Will this never end?* he thought. *No, it never will.*

He was pretty much right.

Back in the Pontiac Grand Am, with a subdued Rex Jobie at the wheel, Noah said, "Why'd Tate set Gibbs up?"

"I dunno."

"Bullshit. Wacky said Tate routed his orders through you." Noah stared at the pursy man as they tooled along.

Jobie was thinking, always an unpleasant experience for him. He tried a little lie: "Tate's just afraid Gibbs is gonna root you out, sooner or later."

"Why is Gibbs after me? He's not the reward-seeking type. Hell, he's richer than the potentate of North Bumfuck, Louisiana."

"I dunno," Jobie lied again.

"If I ever find out that you *did* know . . ."

Jobie turned his head. "Don't threaten me, Noah. You ain't got enough ass in your britches to make good on it."

Noah, despite more than sufficient ass in his britches, let it pass.

They motored quietly until Jobie said, "Is there really a North Bumfuck, Lou—"

"No. If there were, you'd be from there."

More motoring; then: "What's a potentate?"

Noah just shook his head.

TWENTY-TWO

"You should have seen it, Aunt Veer," Cody said. "Connor went through those men quicker than Jackie Chan!"

"Mmm," Vera mumbled, distracted. She'd hardly slept a wink, was burdened by PMS, and the contents of the steamer trunk were increasingly gnawing away at her. When this Let's Find Daddy business all started, she'd thought there wasn't a chance in the world of Connor Gibbs finding Noah. Now there seemed not only a chance, but a likelihood. Which would never do. What might happen if Cody met face-to-face with his daddy; would he choose to go live with him? The thought of losing Cody made Vera physically ill.

More unsettling yet was the probability of Noah asking Cody about—

"I was really scared," Cody was prattling on, "but he did it so fast. Biff, bang, boom, and it was all over but the bleeding. I'm not exaggerating, either. There was this one guy—"

"Go call him."

Cody looked up, milk on his top lip, grape jam on the lower. "What?"

"Call him."

"Connor?"

"Mr. Gibbs, yes. Tell him I want to see him as soon as possible."

Cody's face fell; he didn't like the sound of this.

"What for?"

"Just do what I ask for a change, will you?"

Unhappily: "Yes, ma'am."

He called Connor.

Immediately after Connor and Blister conferenced, Holmes rang. "So, *sufi*, tell me more about your brouhaha up in Wilkes County."

"Nothing left to tell." Connor was in his office opening mail when Holmes rang through. He tossed Ed McMahon in the trash. "Give it a rest." A plea from an insurance company went next, then the Disney Channel. Two VISA offers, and one for instant CA$H on his home equity. "What do you want, Holmie? I'm incredibly busy."

"Doing what?"

"Filing."

Crenshaw snorted. "You don't have a filing cabinet."

"I have a trash can."

"Ed McMahon came by your place, too?"

"Among others. Listen, Blister called and I have to run."

"I've been meaning to ask, why does he go by 'Blister'?"

"He hasn't taken me into his confidence."

"Strange choice, you have to admit."

"Anything else?"

"You question Wacky?"

"Yep. Claims Rex Jobie passed the word from Tate."

"Why is Tate so all-fired determined to keep you from talking to Noah?"

Connor thought about it. "Now that's a good question."

"You suppose Tate would explain his actions to you?"

"Ha," said Connor.

"Right. Now what?"

"I plan to do lunch with Mr. Jobie."

"Can I come?"

"You retired from the field, remember. You're a suit now, you can't go around doing a real man's work."

"Aw, let me come."

"Pick up the tab?"

And thus through graft was the deal consummated.

Cell phone this time, en route to the McGraw homestead before picking up Holmes: "I'm sure getting tired of the phone," Connor said into it.

"Then I apologize," came the high-pitched nasal twang. "What's stirring, Mr. Chiles?"

"Seemingly a lot. Noah Sizemore and his pet corpuscle were here asking to see Wacky."

"Did you let them?"

"Noah. I made Jobie sit in the car."

Gibbs grinned at the image. "So Noah's out and about. He want Wacky out and about with him?"

"He did."

"Did he leave a number?"

"He did not."

"What were they driving?"

Chiles gave him the year, make, color, body style, and plate number.

"Thanks, Braxton."

"No. Thank you."

"For what?"

"Not asking if I let Wacky go."

"Why would I ask? You said you'd hang on to him."

"Thanks for that, too," Chiles said, and hung up.

"Detective Lawson."

"Hi, cutie. I need a fix on a car. Right now."

"Goody. I was just sitting here trying to think up something to do."

Connor grinned at the phone, but Estelle probably didn't see it.

"Give me the data," she said.

He did.

"You want this going out over the band?"

"No, the guys in the Grand Am might be monitoring. Have them phone in to get it. And I want a location, not a stop."

"Who's in the vehicle?"

"I appreciate all your help, Estelle."

"Connor, I won't put any of my people at risk without knowing—"

"Just tell them not to stop and there won't be any risk."

She mulled it over. "Okay, but this better not turn sour."

"It won't if you do exactly as I said, and so do they."

She laughed sardonically. "How often does that happen?"

"Let's hope once. This once."

Connor hustled home. Parked the van. Trotted out of the garage the SVO Mustang: Five-speed; three-hundred-five horses; limited-slip differential; one-eighth tank of gas. Oops.

He fired her up, hustled to the nearest station, tanked up with ninety-three octane.

Now he was ready.

And more than a match for a Grand Am.

"I'm hungry," Rex declared.

"You're always hungry."

"So let's get a couple o' burgers."

"It's broad daylight, and lately I haven't exactly been low profile so far as the cops're concerned," Noah explained.

"So I'll drop you at Mantra's, get some grub, and come back and pick you up."

Noah considered it. As far as he knew, there was no recent connection between him and Lorie, not official anyway. It was probably safe; safer than floating around the city in a red Grand Am doing sixty in a thirty-five. Why the hell had Tate sent Jobie along, anyway? "Okay. Drop me at Lorie's."

"She'd really rather be called Mantra."

"Put a sock in it."

They headed for Lorie/Mantra's.

With that pain-in-the-ass Noah now safely tucked away, Rex Jobie intended to stuff his face properly. And unhurriedly. Hell, a man couldn't do a real job on the hash without he was given plenty of time, and Rex Jobie could do a real job on the hash. So he aimed his car down Creedmore Avenue and sought sustenance.

Connor was parked under a shade tree outside a Market Street deli eating hoagies with Holmes Crenshaw when his cell phone sounded. It had been two hours and nine minutes since he'd spoken to Estelle.

"You know Colgan's Choppery on Creedmore?"

"I do," he said, and drained his juice.

"Your car's there right now. Couple of vice guys spotted it on their way in."

"Getting doughnuts?" he said, handing the empty can to Crenshaw.

"That's so stale it's hackneyed."

" 'Stale,' I get it. It's a pastry joke, right?"

"The vice guys are baby-sitting the car, waiting till you get there. If it moves, they'll follow. What's your ETA?"

"It's about four miles. Say two and a half minutes."

"Connor, don't—"

"Thanks, 'Stelle."

The rubber streaks he left in the parking lot were twenty-seven feet long.

Rex Jobie was full of beans. Literally. Occasionally he siphoned off a measure of by-product (to the consternation of those around him), but he still felt bloated.

Hell, he *was* bloated.

He paid his bill and quit the joint, leaving a gaseous reminder of his passing in the entranceway (for diners to walk through), strolled nonchalantly to his carmine conveyance, and climbed aboard. His gastrointestinal emanations soon filled the car. As Jobie was just about to pull into traffic, he spotted Connor Gibbs.

And Gibbs spotted him.

The Grand Am lurched into the road directly in front of an aged Maverick, whose brakes were not up to par. Its hapless driver, confronted with swerve or strike, swerved. Into a black Nissan Pathfinder. The Pathfinder, running full tilt or a little faster, knocked the Maverick into a spin, slinging it toward Connor, who stabbed his brakes and jerked the steering wheel clockwise, bringing his tail around to absorb the crash. Which never came. Close, though. Leaving more rubber behind, he roared off after the Grand Am, which now had a half-mile lead down Creedmore.

Jobie checked his mirror for the tenth time. Though his tach was nearing redline in third, that fucking SVO Mustang was gaining. *"Shit!"* he said, pounding the steering wheel. But that didn't help; his Pontiac was simply no match for the Mustang.

Time for guile, something with which Jobie had only a nodding acquaintance. Nonetheless, he gave it his best shot.

Turner Avenue was coming up. At the light, he swung left, jumped the curb, nearly hit a city bus, and zoomed up Turner. . . .

The wrong way.

"The dumb bastard's cutting onto Turner!" Holmes Crenshaw said to Connor as he saw the Grand Am attack the one-way street. Panic-striken drivers dodged this way and that to avoid colliding, with one going through the front door of a Krispy Kreme that had too little distance separating its facade from the curb. Then the Pontiac zipped into an alley, scraping paint off on the corner of a Dumpster.

"Gotcha!" Gibbs said jubilantly.

Because he remembered where the alley came out . . .

And went there.

• • •

Jobie took out three garbage cans, a skateboard, and nearly one pedestrian during his alley passage, but he could see the opposite opening coming on fast. Suddenly said opening was filled with Mustang. *"Shiiiiit!"* he yelled, and stood on the brakes. The Pontiac's ABS system worked its magic, hauling the car to a stop inches from the Mustang's driver-side door. Jobie rammed the shifter into reverse.

Too late. Holmes was over the car's hood and reaching in the window, hands hooked into claws, to grip Jobie's shirt. Jobie tried to knock the hands away, so Crenshaw released the shirt with his right hand, made a fist, and applied it to the side of Jobie's strained, tight, thick neck, *fwap!*

Jobie's eyes bulged at the blow, and his digestive distress became even more acute. So acute, in fact, that he was afraid that if this ebony dervish struck him again, his next fart might have a lump in it.

"Hold up!" he squeaked (since his neck hurt), and threw up his hands in submission.

"Get out of the car!" Crenshaw boomed in his most impressive voice, his deepest bass, his preferred weapon of intimidation, usually reserved for cross-examination in a court of law.

It worked here, too. Jobie got out of the Pontiac.

"Whoa!" Holmes exclaimed, wrinkling his nose. "What you been doing, son? Filling your jeans?" He handed Jobie off to Connor and stepped twenty feet away.

Connor said, "Mr. Jobie, I know for a fact that it was you who sicced the quintet on me up in Wilkes County."

"What's a quintet?"

"And I am very unhappy about it. One of them rent a small aperture in my shirt."

"What's a aperture?"

"Further, I am incensed about your burning so much rubber off my tires."

"Me?"

"In conclusion, let me inform you that I feel compelled to bludgeon you repeatedly about the head and shoulders."

"What's bludgeon?"

"Have I made myself perfectly clear?"

"*No!*"

Holmes Crenshaw intervened. "Let me put it in street lingo. My friend here is seriously pissed, and he's going to beat the shit out of you if you don't tell him everything he wants to know, exactly when he wants to know it. *Comprende?*"

Jobie believed Crenshaw, and told them all he knew, which wasn't much.

Enough, though.

Mantra's phone rang. "It's daytime. I'm asleep," she answered. Then: "Just a minute." Hollering out into the kitchen to Noah: "Some gash. Says it's important."

Noah took it, but didn't say anything, just listened. The phone said, "You there, baby?"

"Why are you calling me here?"

"He just went out, in a big hurry. Heard from one of his cop friends that Connor Gibbs had corralled Rex."

"Well, shit."

"They'll be there soon, if I know Rex."

"Thanks, hon. I'm gone."

So was she.

Noah turned to Mantra, who was digging into her purse. She tossed him her keys as he was saying, "You have the junk cached?"

"Sure. They'll have to take this place apart board by board. Don't worry, just hurry your hinder out to the car."

He did.

"Haven't seen him since '79, you said."

"Up yours."

"Owes you money, you said."

"Piss off."

"Where's your car, Mantra?"

"It was repossessed, spooge breath."

"I can have ten DEA cops here in twenty minutes."

"Wait, let me run get doughnuts."

"That's hackneyed."

"What?"

"Mantra?" Connor said.

"Call me Lorie."

"How about Autumn?"

She shrugged. "Whatever."

"Mantra/Lorie/Autumn—"

"Wrong order."

He looked at her.

"What?" she said, worried now.

"I want to talk to Noah. *Talk,* you understand? Wherever he says, whenever he says. On the phone if that's his choice. I'll even give you the number to my DCS phone. It's secure."

"Okay, okay. I'll try to get in touch with him."

"Don't try. *Do.* I'll be right here waiting."

"Like hell you will."

"Me, or ten cops. Your doughnut bill would be out of sight."

"I can use your DCS to make all my calls?"

"You bet."

"Come the fuck in, then," she relented.

Connor turned and motioned to Holmes, who joined him and they both went in.

Connor used Mantra's phone to call Blister. Vera answered instead. She said, "I thought you were coming over."

"Something came up. May I speak to Cody?"

"Mm," she said, and handed off the phone.

"Mr. Gibbs?"

"Hey, pal. Listen, I may have a line on your dad. I've made contact with someone who will get a message to him. If he calls me, I'll try to set up a meet."

"Good."

"Good? Not great, or whoopee, or something?"

Sotto voce, Blister said, "She's not in a good mood."

"Your aunt?"

"Yes."

"Because I'm late?"

"I think that's part of it, but not all. She's been acting weird ever since yesterday."

"Tell her I'll come over as soon as I can. Got a pen?"

After various drawerly noises: "Got one."

"Write these down." Connor gave Cody his cell-phone number, his DCS phone number, and Mantra's landline.

"I have to go now," the boy said, and hung up.

TWENTY-THREE

The letter, written in longhand, said in part:

Sometimes I lie here at night, looking up at the stars and remembering all the fun we had. Like at the park, and the beach that one time, out on the fishing pier. It was great, I held you so tight, but you were still afraid I might let you fall in as a joke, but I never would.

Maybe we can do that kind of thing again someday, if I don't get caught and go to jail. Maybe we can leave the country, go to Mexico maybe, and see a bullfight or something. There'll be plenty of money, don't you worry about that.

Always remember that I love you. I always have and always will, no matter what anyone tells you.

Then ''XO XO XO XO,'' and he had signed it, his personal way.

It was the last one.

She tore it to shreds.

TWENTY-FOUR

Rex Jobie'd had a bad day. A really bad day. He'd gotten about 116 traffic citations, had his car impounded, his license jerked by an asshole highway patrolman, and been tossed in jail. If it hadn't been for Boz Fangelli, he'd still be there.

He had a bad case of the mulligrubs as he inserted his key into the door. Things were about to get worse.

From where he sat by the end table, Jackson Slade heard the taxi arrive, heard Rex Jobie's heavy footfalls, heard the key going into the lock. He then heard the door swing open, one shoe hit the floor across the room—where Jobie had kicked it—and the other land not far from where Slade waited quietly. When Slade hit the light switch, Jobie reacted like a deer caught in a car's headlights: he opened his eyes very wide and stared. Unlike most deer, though, he did manage to get out a sincere ''What the fuck!''

''Evening, Rex.''

''You're the fucking guy!''

''I suppose I am.''

''The one knocked my teeth out!''

''Want me to do it again?''

"No!"

"Then sit down and shut up, except when I ask you to say something."

Jobie sat.

"Now, tell me about your day, starting from when Connor Gibbs chased you down Creedmore Avenue. And don't leave anything out, because I'll know it and be annoyed."

Jobie left nothing out.

After communing with Rex, Slade went directly to Mantra Marat's. (Or whatever she was going by at that moment.)

Yep, there's Gibbs's Mustang, Slade thought. *Maybe I should let the air out of his tires. Nah, too childish.*

He bent the antenna instead.

Then twenty minutes later he was outside the McGraw domicile, sitting in his Camaro grooving to Marilyn Manson. He watched until dawn, hatching nefarious plots.

Connor's cell phone went off at 6:11: a sleep-deprived and thoroughly inflamed Vera McGraw. "Are you coming over or not?"

"I suppose I can if it's really important, but I'm working a lead here."

"Don't you ever check your messages?"

"I don't get all that many after midnight."

"Cody's still asleep. I'd like to talk to you in private, if you think you can manage."

"Hold on a minute." Connor woke Holmes, conferred briefly, then returned to Vera. "I'll be there in fifteen minutes."

She slammed the phone down.

Seventeen minutes later Vera said, "This is getting out of hand." She was wearing a pair of flannel pajamas under a pale yellow housecoat, was barefoot, and her hair had been recently and hurriedly combed.

"What is?" asked Connor.

"Sit down," Vera ordered, waving a hand vaguely.

He chose the wing chair by the fireplace.

She began, "I'm concerned about the fight Thursday. Up in the mountains."

"And?" he said.

"I don't think Cody should go places with you. It's too dangerous."

"He was in no danger. They weren't after him."

"How do you know that?"

"Why would they be after him?"

"With that sorry bunch of Sizemores, who knows?"

Connor was puzzled. "Have they tried to take him before, or get a court order effecting the same—"

"No! But who can predict what they might do now that Noah knows Cody wants to see him?"

"Didn't you adopt Cody?"

"Yes!"

"Then there's nothing they can do, legally. Besides, Noah is a fugitive from—"

"Yeah, and has been for seven years, but have they caught him!"

Connor was taken aback by her vehemence. "Has someone from Noah's family tried to get in touch—"

"No, and I wouldn't have talked to them if they had!"

"Then I'm a bit confused. What makes you think that—"

"I don't want Cody seeing his father! Ever!"

"Why not?" said Cody Wainwright Sizemore McGraw, from the bottom of the stairs.

Vera's face blanched, but she stood her ground. "Because!"

Cody advanced into the room. "You always told me 'because' was not a reason."

"Well, it is now!"

"You can't stop me."

"Oh yes I can! Don't you think for one minute—"

Cody, still calmer than she, said, "I'll run away."

"No you won't!"

"You can't watch me every second. I go to school, and to see my fr—"

"Then I'll home-school you!"

"You don't have enough money to quit work."

"*No, but* you *do!*" she screeched, then caught herself, hand flying to her mouth. She'd said too much.

Connor stood. "Have you had contact with Noah?"

"*No!*"

Cody came over to stand beside Connor.

"None?" Connor pressed.

"Define 'contact'!"

"You know, calls, letters, checks, faxes, E-mail, radio communication, smoke signals, notes in crayon on lined paper?" He was disturbed by Vera's histrionics.

She shook her head, side to side, over and over, nonstop.

"Because if I thought that the boy's father had been trying to—"

"*What!* Act like a father? It was too late then!"

"When?" said Connor.

"When *what!*" Her face was beet red.

"When was too late?"

"*When he went bowling!*"

Connor looked down at the emotion-torn face beside him, the tears tracking down. "Blister," he said gently.

The damp little eyes fixed on his. Connor knelt to make it easier. "I'll get you face-to-face with your daddy, one way or the other. I promise."

Thin arms snaked around his neck, clung there tightly.

"I promise," he said again.

"Get out!" Vera said.

Connor did.

Blister, undaunted, said, "What did you mean, I have money?"

"Go watch TV."

"What did you mean?"

"Nothing, leave me alone," Vera said.

"Did my daddy ever try to get in touch with me?"

Vera went to the kitchen table, sat, placed her arms on the table and her head on her arms, emotionally drained. She said nothing.

"Did he!" Blister pressed.

"Yes," barely audible.

Blister ran upstairs and slammed his door.

Getting up around the clock didn't bother him. Nor the feedings every four hours, the spitting up, the colicky periods, the ear-infection-induced crying, not even the poopy diapers. Noah nurtured his new son through the formula-to-solid-food transition; taught him his first word, "momma"; hovered protectively for that first step, and all subsequent ones, until the child was running, curly hair blowing in the breeze stirred by his own movement.

Noah's family offered help, of course. On occasion he even let them, when he was bone tired, needed a short break, or had business to attend to. But mostly he and little Cody Wainwright Sizemore were inseparable. At night Noah brushed the tiny teeth, knelt beside his child for bedtime prayers—always remembering Mommy in heaven—then read until innocent blue eyes grew heavy-lidded. It was no trial; rather, a privilege. Cody, fruit of his mother's body, was a constant reminder of Christy, a connection for Noah that would not be severed.

No contact from the in-laws. They never called, never came by, even to see the child. They blamed Noah for Christy's death. In fact, Vera, after having stood thirty feet away during the interment, came over at its end to spit in his face. *"You sorry son of a bitch!"* she'd screamed, her mother trying to pull her away. *"She'd still be alive if it weren't for you!"* she'd screamed, with her father now at her side, his bilious eyes boring into Noah's.

Later he heard that the McGraw family believed he'd been drinking that night—drinking and bowling and funning with the boys. Which meant Christy hadn't told them. Well, that wasn't surprising. Not one of his in-laws ever had anything nice to say about him, instead constantly ragging his wife about marrying beneath herself, so why should she tell them about their money problems?

So he reared his son pretty much alone. And what an experience; the child was a pure, undiluted joy. Noah carefully recorded every new word, then every phrase, not to mention each new physical accomplishment—from rolling over to crawling to throwing a dirty sock like a major leaguer.

After only a few months the child was sleeping through the night. Noah wasn't. Guilt. What if he had been home that night? But such thinking wasn't productive; he and Christy had made that decision together. Besides, she would have called him if she felt it necessary.

No. That drunken Able Johnson was the cause: of his losing his wife; of his son losing a mother; of her solidifying presence being removed from their lives.

He'd seen Johnson several times after the funeral, and always the sight made him sick. He remembered the time that sickened him most, when Able had left the courthouse—a free man—to hail a cab. The look on Johnson's face as he did so etched itself permanently into Noah's mind. No sorrow, no remorse, not even embarrassment as he saw Noah sitting there, on the concrete bench, motherless son in his arms nursing a bottle . . .

Noah clawed at his head, trying to drive away the image of Johnson sneering . . . SNEERING! . . . as he sauntered past.

He could barely stand it.

After eighteen months he no longer could.

Something snapped.

TWENTY-FIVE

When Tate gave Frank Murphy orders, Frank jumped. He jumped into Ellie's Mazda, plucked the .22 Magnum from its place under the seat, then jumped into his truck. "Where you going?" Ellie asked. "Tate errand," Frank answered. And that was that.

So all Saturday night Frank had been tooling around looking for Connor Gibbs. No luck yet, and it was near to daylight. He rolled by Gibbs's place, the house all big and dark, four-car garage and lots of trees, situated in a cul-de-sac. Frank U-turned and stopped at the corner, looking left and right. Two blocks away was a four-way stop. He went there. On the side facing west—toward Gibbs's street— were several mimosa bushes large enough for sitting amongst. So he parked his pickup a block away, hoofed it back to the mimosas, and sat amongst them. Him and Messrs. Smith & Wesson.

The sun was peeping through the trees when he ate breakfast, two Slim Jims and a Twinky. A man needs his strength.

•   •   •

Connor had just crossed Mantra's threshold when Holmes
came through the doorway from the dining area. "Noah
called not an hour ago."

"He leave a number?"

Holmes handed it to him. "Which phone?" Connor queried.

"Didn't specify."

Connor used his cellular. On the second buzz, a man's
voice: "Y'ello?"

"I'd like to speak to Noah Sizemore, please. This is Connor Gibbs."

"Gimme your DCS number."

Connor did.

"He'll call right back," the voice said, and broke the
connection.

"The battery's nearly dead on the DCS phone," Holmes
warned.

"And my spare is at home."

The phone buzzed. "Hello."

"Gibbs?"

"Speaking."

"This is Noah Sizemore. Why—"

The phone beeped once, then went dead.

Connor called the number he'd just called. Same voice:
"Mm-hmm?"

"Gibbs again. Noah called back but my phone died."

"What you trying to pull, brother?"

"Nothing."

"You on cellular?"

"Yes."

"Gimme that number."

Connor did.

"Gibbs?" Noah said.

"Yes."

"What are you doing?"

"Nothing, my DCS phone went belly-up."

"Anyone could be listening on this line."

"True."

"Your home phone clean?"

"Unless the IRS is still after me."

Noah snorted. Just like Vera. "You listed?"

"Yeah."

"Go home, have a cup of coffee. I'll call you from a secure phone."

"Do I have to have coffee?"

"How long for you to get there?"

"Fifteen minutes or so."

"Rush."

It was nearly eight when Frank saw a white Mustang approaching. An SVO, hot ride, pipes that sounded like Louis Armstrong in full throat . . .

He sat up straight to scope the car as it came to a rolling halt. Connor Gibbs!

Frank pulled the ski mask (ITCHY!) on, to cover his pink face, then climbed to his feet and charged.

Connor Gibbs, still going maybe five miles an hour, eased the shifter into first, and prepared to give it the gas when suddenly a masked man leaped from the bushes to his right front and pointed a small-bore revolver at him.

At the first shot, Gibbs leaned to starboard while simultaneously gunning the engine, popping the clutch, and spinning the steering wheel counterclockwise. His windshied starred once, twice, thrice as the Mustang slewed, fighting for traction, and his right rear came around, hard, the fourth shot sounding now, taking out his inside rearview mirror, then the fifth coming through the passenger-side glass, *zing,* cracking the plastic just above his head, him keeping the throttle down, continuing the spin into a complete three-sixty, the masked maniac tossing his last round at him, *pop!,* through the windshield, and then the Mustang found the man's legs and bucked him high in the air.

By the time Connor got the car reined in so he could jump out, his assailant was back on his big feet and pulling a knife, so Gibbs grabbed the guy's wrist and wrenched it *hard,* drawing a surprised yell, then smashed the same wrist with a rock-hard knee, and the knife went spinning away to land with a soft *poink* in the curbside grass as the idiot would-be assassin further compounded his problems by taking a wild swing, which Connor sidestepped, then landed one of his own, ridge hand to the Adam's apple. The masked man said *ack!*—or something very like it—and grabbed his throat. Connor executed a solid hammer hand to the side of his head, and the dummy sagged to his knees, made some kind of unidentifiable wheezing sound, and fell over. In a hurry, so as not to involve the police just now, Gibbs grabbed the man by the belt and the nape and tossed him onto the passenger seat.

He then drove sedately home.

"You said fifteen minutes."

"Yeah, well you didn't tell me you had a surprise waiting. If I'd known, I'd have told you twenty. It usually takes me five minutes to kibosh a murder attempt."

"What are you talking about?" said Noah.

"Good old Frank Furter," Connor informed.

"Who?"

"Your brother-in-law, Frank. Drives a Ford pickup, has skin like a lobster, hair like a wiener, the brains of a scallop? You know. Frank."

Pause for it to sink in. "Frank tried to kill you?"

"I'd say so. Not a warning this time, the real thing. I know the difference."

"Where is he?"

"Right here on the floor."

"What'd you do to him?"

"Not as much as he tried to do to me."

"Can I speak to him?"

"He's asleep."

Pause again. "I did not set you up, Gibbs."

"Of course not. That's Tate's forte. Frank just has a thing for mimosas."

"What?"

"Never mind. What I don't understand is why you are so dead set against seeing your son."

"What's my son got to do with this?"

"That's why I've been trying . . . didn't Tate tell you your son wanted to see you?"

"No."

"Cody hired me to find you. Why else did you think I was on your trail?"

"The reward maybe?"

"Hey, I like money as well as the next guy, but a thousand bucks of Crime Stopper money isn't sufficient for me to—"

"There's insurance money as well, and Boz Fangelli offering twenty grand for my hide, broiled or smoked. At least that's what he offered Jackson Slade, as if Slade needs additional incentive."

"You and Slade aren't pals?"

"I'm the only guy who ever gave him the slip, and for seven years, in his own state. It's personal with him, though he wouldn't throw away the money."

"Well, I have nothing to do with all that. I'm doing this strictly for your son."

That put the conversation on hold again. "Is Cody having a problem with Vera?"

"Until this morning I would have denied it. Now I'm not so sure."

"What does that mean?"

"Let's discuss it face-to-face, with Blister."

"Who?"

"Blister. It's what Cody likes to be called."

"Why?"

"I don't know, I didn't pick it. So can we set up a meet?"

"Get your DCS battery recharged. I'll call you back with a time and place. Soon. What you going to do with Frank?"

"What the hell do you think?"

Another lull. "I guess I can't blame you"

"You know what they say: shoot at me once, shame on you; shoot at me twice, shame on me. Can't have all those

bullets flying around. One of them might hurt somebody.
Frank's beginning to stir. Want to say good-bye to him?''
   Noah didn't.

The cops came and cuffed Frank—still groggy from the
hammer hand well applied—then took Connor's statement,
postured like cops do, wanted to know why Connor had
brought Frank here, wanted to see the riddled Mustang,
wanted to know why Connor had no coffee, and other cop
stuff. Gibbs bore it well, considering. Directly they left.
   Estelle called as soon as they were gone. ''You okay?''
   ''I suffered more at the hands of your collegues than
Frank's.''
   ''Well, you didn't offer them food.''
   ''How do you know?''
   ''They headed straight for Shoney's.''
   ''Will they buy Frank something?''
   ''Cops never *buy* food, studly,'' she said, and hung up.

TWENTY-SIX

Jackson Slade had surveillance on his mind, and for that he needed another car; his Camaro was too . . . visible. He considered Fatima's red Talon, but decided it was too flashy. He needed something ugly, elderly, innocuous. He called Boz Fangelli.

Fangelli answered the phone himself. "It's pretty friggin' early."

"I need to borrow your El Camino."

"It's in the shop."

"What're you driving?"

"My wife's Olds."

"What year?" Slade asked.

Boz told him.

"What color?"

Boz told him.

"Any dents?"

"You kidding? I said it was my wife's car. Of course it's got dents."

"Perfect."

"What, you close on Sizemore?"

"So it appears."

"Come and get the friggin' thing."

• • •

Vera McGraw was up in the attic, sitting sweaty and cross-legged in front of the steamer trunk, face fissured from worry. She'd never looked so haggard.

The ax was about to fall.

"Connor?"

"Yes," Gibbs said into the phone.

"Come get him."

"Cody?"

Vera nodded, not registering that Connor couldn't see her.

"Vera?"

"Can you come?" she said.

"I'm waiting for Noah to call. Can you drop him off?"

She shook her head.

"Vera?"

"I'm not up to driving." She wiped the sweat from her face, but the strain remained.

Gibbs thought a moment. "Can I call you right back?"

She hung up.

Benella Mae answered on the fifth ring.

"What're you doing?" Connor asked.

"Working on the bag. Spinning blade kicks."

"Both legs?"

"Of course."

"Can you go over to the McGraws and pick up Blister, bring him to my place?"

"I have thirty minutes left, is that okay?"

"Vera sounded pretty strung out. I think you should go on over, before she changes her mind."

"I planned to do some wind sprints in Grantham Park."

"Take him with you. I doubt the meet with Noah is imminent."

"Two hours about right?"

"I'll tell Noah that his son's not here yet if he wants it earlier than that."

"Okay, but it'll cost you," she whispered in his ear.
She had no idea.

The Olds was spark-knocking so badly, Slade wondered at first if he could keep up with traffic, but once the old girl got to rolling she did okay. He just hoped Gibbs wasn't driving the Mustang today.

He parked a half block from the entrance to the cul-de-sac—within sight of Connor's house—and lit up.

Blister answered the door. Standing on his porch was the tallest, the most shapely, the most beautiful person he'd ever seen. He was awestruck.

"Are you Blister?" said the goddess, her smile a faceful of sunlight. He just gaped.

Benella continued to smile; she was used to having this effect on males, of all ages. "Excuse me?" she said.

Blister, speechless, nodded and motioned her in.

"Thank you," she purred, and brought her radiance inside.

Blister stared through the world's roundest eyes at the world's bluest. She winked one at him and he nearly fainted.

"Hello?" Vera said from the living room.

Benella turned toward the voice. "Hi. I'm Benella Sweet, a friend of Connor's. He asked me to pick up Blister."

"Cody."

"Okay."

Vera swung her gaze to Cody, standing smitten and agog. She frowned at his enrapture. "Do you know her?"

He tried to nod and shake his head at the same time, and thus moved it in an inconclusive circle.

The country lyrics "He'll never be the same. . . ." flowed unbidden through Vera's mind. *Good grief! He's nine!*

"Let me call Mr. Gibbs," Vera said.

"Of course."

Vera fetched the cordless and came back to the foyer to

punch in the numbers. Gibbs grabbed it on the first ring.

Vera said, "You sent a lady to get Cody?"

Connor must have affirmed, because Vera said, "Describe her."

Obviously he did. Vera rang off.

"Did he describe me?"

"Yeah. He said you were incredibly homely, five-feet-one, and weighed two hundred pounds."

Benella said, "That's me."

"I can see that." Vera looked at the boy, still enthralled by his Hellenistic visitor. "Cody, you want to go with her?"

This time his nod was unambivalent: up and down, briskly. He had a chance to go off with *her* and Aunt Veer wanted to know if he *wanted* to? He could die right after and it'd be okay.

So they left.

Vera went back to her attic.

⁂

"So why do they call you Blister?" Bennie asked when they were in the car and belting up.

A dash of cold water.

"I just like it," he avoided.

"Okay," she accepted, not one to push. "We'll run by Connor's for a minute, see if your dad's called. Then you can stay with him, or go to the park with me for a bit of running."

Blister thought, *No contest there.*

Jackson Slade was on his fifth cigarette when who should show up at the Gibbs residence but the voluptuous Sweet woman. And—surprise, surprise—little Cody Sizemore.

A new plan began to form in the reptilian part of his brain.

"No news," said Connor. "English muffin?"

"Thanks, no. Blister?"

"Huh? I mean, yes, ma'am?" His temperature was back to about 112 degrees centigrade. Connor, noticing the boy's adolescent ardor, swallowed a smile; he'd looked often at Benella that way himself.

"Would you like an English muffin?" Bennie said.

Who could eat in the same room with you? Cody thought, but said, "No thank you."

"Are you staying here, or going with me?"

What a question. "I'd like to go with you."

Benella said, "I'll have him back in an hour and fifteen minutes."

No she wouldn't.

TWENTY-SEVEN

The farm was out near Thomasville, rural as poison ivy, with a pond full of bass and bream and snapping turtles that gave the baby ducks hell. Trees abounded, and corn, and mongrel dogs to keep at bay the raccoons that had corn on their minds. No cats, though. The Murphys hated cats.

The sun was behind a cloud; on Ellie's face, too, as she watched her eldest brother being helped from the van by a guy wearing a head bandage and an aqua tank top. An argument ensued; obviously the tank top wanted Tate to get in a wheelchair and Tate would have none of it. Tate won; he walked slowly over to where Ellie sat on the swing, each feeble step a trial.

Ellie didn't give a shit. Her man was in jail because of brother Tate, standing now before her, swaying slightly as if he were about to fall over. *Let him fall,* she thought. *Be damned if I'd pick him up.* She pulled a draw on her fag, exhaled smoke through her nostrils, and flipped the butt at him. "Don't you wish you could have one of these?" she said, lips curled.

"Ellie!" Noah yelled from up at the house, a glass of tea in each hand as he descended the steps. "Leave him alone!"

"Kiss my ass, reefer man! Both of you! And you, too, peanut brain," she said to the guy in the aqua top. "And I don't give a shit if you do shop at Big and Tall. I got something here in my pocket'll trim you down to size. Who gave you that shirt, anyhow?"

Tate said, "Shut up, Ellie," low-voiced. "I'm sorry about Frank. I've got someone going down there now to post bond."

"And then what? It's attempted murder, Tate. With witnesses!" Ellie barked.

"Once he's out, he can skip like Noah did. He'll get along."

"But he shouldn't *have* to get along, Tate. He did exactly what you told him to, and got caught. Why'd you tell him to gun this Gibbs character, anyhow?"

Tate didn't answer, just took the iced tea that Noah handed him and sipped.

Noah said, "I want to know, too, big brother."

Impatiently: "Because he was getting too close to you, boy. I asked around about this Connor Gibbs. Word I got was he couldn't be bought and never quit once he was on a case. Mind you, nobody warned me that a handful of tough mountain boys couldn't whip him, and that bullets singing around his ears wouldn't scare him. So he had to be put on ice."

"You're talking about killing a man."

Tate Sizemore was disgusted. "That's right, just what got you into this whole mess to begin with."

"That was different. Able Johnson deserved what he got, pure and simple. For two years I tried to live with him coming and going big as you please, and my wife cold in the ground. The law fined him and took his license, and then he drove anyway. I tried hard, but I just couldn't take it anymore."

"Right," Tate agreed. "So you gave your baby to that McGraw woman and turned your back on a normal life. Was it worth it?"

Noah's eyes clouded. "I thought so then. Not so sure now."

"Well, as the saying goes, you made your bed. Now here comes this Gibbs fellow and suddenly you're in demand again. Cops showing up, Slade sniffing around, that slobby Thurgood up lurking under the pecan trees. It was just a matter of time and they'd have stumbled onto you once you left the place."

"So you sacrificed Frank," Ellie said.

"He ain't blood, sister. Blood's what counts," Tate said scornfully.

"If blood counts so much, Tate," Noah said, "then why didn't you tell me Cody was looking for me?"

"What good would it have done you to know that? You walked away from that boy. Better that he doesn't get to know his daddy, 'cause the two of you can't ever be together."

"Maybe we can," Noah disagreed.

"What, you taking the boy up to the mountains to help you grow dope?"

Noah ignored that. "Christy was insured, Tate. For a quarter million. Since her death was accidental, I got double that."

"So where is it?"

"Safe offshore, where it's been for seven years, earning ten percent. Probably up to a million by now. If Cody wanted to, he and I could go anywhere."

"You think he'd leave that woman?" Tate fleered.

"I don't know. Maybe. Maybe that's why he hired a private investigator to find me."

"And where'd that leave me, if you and the boy ran off to Antigua or someplace?"

"Is that what this is all about, Tate? You?" Noah said.

"You better believe it," Ellie said. "Frank's in jail and you and your little boy can't get together because big brother Tate is afraid to—"

"Don't say something you'll regret!" Tate sprayed angrily, spittle speckling his chin.

"Afraid to *die!*" she expelled. "All alone, like Daddy, who had nobody to give a shit because he'd been so fucking selfish all his petty little life, *just like you!*"

Tate slapped her, surprisingly fast and hard. Her head snapped back, and for a moment she was shocked into in-action, but then she attacked, nails extended, teeth bared, intending to destroy. Tate went to the ground with Ellie on top, scratching and clawing, but the aqua tank top grabbed her like a doll and flung her atop a pile of firewood left over from winter. She scrambled and sprawled, then got her stout legs under her and launched herself at Tank Top. He stiff-armed her face and was about to follow with a hard left when Noah picked up a hefty chunk of cordwood and said, "I wouldn't hit her if I were you."

Tank Top swung his head around, took in the stout piece of kindling, the cold-eyed expression. As he was deciding what to do about the situation—if anything—Ellie tried to kick him in the throat, by way of his scrotum. He doubled up, clutching the offended area, and sank to the ground.

To his brother, Noah said, "You get Frank out of jail, immediately. I'll set up a meeting with Gibbs and go see my boy. Then you and I will talk. I'm not going to desert you, like everyone did to Daddy, but you aren't running the show anymore, Tate."

"Because I'm frail, don't think you can give me orders, boy."

"I'm not giving you orders. I'm just telling you the way it is."

"And I *ain't* afraid of dying alone."

"I never said you were. That was Ellie, and she was mad. Forget it. You won't die alone," Noah promised.

But he was wrong.

TWENTY-EIGHT

Benella Mae was still fairly well lubed from her morning workout, but she had cooled down considerably and needed to stretch a bit before she ran. Clad in a white T-shirt, royal-blue running shorts with white piping, and running shoes, she went through a five-minute warm-up routine. Cody, less in awe than he was earlier, watched interestedly.

"Do you know what has the biggest eyes in the world?" he asked as she started a set of jumping jacks.

She grinned. "You mean other than you?"

He blushed. "Yes."

"Sure I do. I'll bet you do, too."

"I've been trying to think, but so far I've come up with squat."

She kept jumping. "You a movie fan?"

"Some."

"You like Disney movies? I mean the old ones, not stuff like the *The Lion King*."

"Most of them."

"Remember one with James Mason and Kirk Douglas?"

His brow knitted in thought.

She was stretching her hamstrings now. "It involved a submarine."

"Wait, don't tell me. The sub was the *Nautilus,* right?"

She nodded. "Remember what they had to fight, on the bottom of the ocean?"

"A giant squid!"

She smiled her approval. He felt it down to his sandals.

"Ha!" he said. "Wait till I see Mr. Gibbs again."

"You want to run with me, or just watch?"

"Watch." He knew he could never keep up. She was too big.

"I'm going to run wind sprints, from here to that water fountain, then back. It's about fifty yards, one way."

"Okay."

So she began.

"Aw, ain't that heartwarming. A domesticated amazon," Jackson Slade said to no one. He was watching Benella and Cody from the seclusion of a copse one hundred yards away.

"Well, lady," he spoke again, "I'm about to relieve you of your responsibility."

He checked his gun, stuck it back where it went, and strode forth.

Benella had completed her fourth sprint when Slade arrived. She stopped and stared at him, her breath coming easy. "How're y'all?" he greeted in his most affected Southern accent.

Cody instinctively moved closer to Benella. "What do you want?" she said.

"Well now, ain't you the friendly one." More Southern cornpone, the way he obviously thought it should sound, anyway. (Slade was from Sutton, Nebraska.)

"Blister," she said, "go get in the car." She handed him the keys. "And lock the doors."

As Blister took the keys, Slade stepped up to block his way to the parking area. "Naw, let the boy stay. He's going with me."

"The hell he is."

In less than a second Slade had the gun in his hand,

brandishing it threateningly without actually pointing it at
anyone. "Yeah, darlin', he is."

Blister inhaled and held it, terrified of this evil man.

Benella shifted to starboard, moving away from Blister.
"Kidnapping? Is that your style?"

"Naw, this ain't a kidnapping, is it, kid?" He smiled.
Then stopped smiling. "Here's the way it's gonna go down.
The boy goes with me, you get word to his daddy, his
daddy comes to get the boy, and I get Daddy." He smiled
again, sharklike. "That's all there is to it. Simple enough
for you to follow, or do I need to speak slower?"

"I think I got it." She took another careful step sideways. "But what happens when the boy and I talk to the
feds about you?"

"You won't."

"And why not?"

"Because once Noah Sizemore's in jail, he'll be within
my reach, all the time. It doesn't take much bread to have
someone bumped off, not in jail. A simple knife fight, you
know?" He looked down at Cody. "Or worse yet, have
him blinded. How'd you like that, having to lead your
pappy around by the hand when he gets out, with him helpless and all. Assuming I let him keep a hand for you to
lead him by."

Slade looked back at Benella. "I don't think the boy'll
rat on me, darlin'. And as long as he doesn't, then it's my
word against yours, and who'd take the word of a steroid
queen over an upstanding citizen like me."

Benella's blue eyes hardened into steel. "There's one
thing everyone would believe," she said.

"What's that, darlin'?"

"That a sissy boy like you would *need* a gun to take
him away from me."

The mirth drained from Slade's face. Abruptly he
dumped the pistol magazine into his palm and stuck it in a
pocket. Kicked the cartridge out of the chamber. Handed
the gun to Cody. "All right, darlin'. Have it your way."

Blister said, "Benella!"

"Stay back!" she growled, unintentionally harsh; she

was focused on Slade, who wasted no time on ceremony. He set his feet and started to launch a rear-leg front kick. Benella saw it coming, and, as soon as Slade began the move, stepped away from the kick. Since she was now out of range for a front kick, Slade launched a side kick with the opposite leg, to take her off guard. It almost worked. At the last minute she went under the leg and reverse-punched him in the groin, making him regret not wearing his cup.

But he'd been hit in the balls before; it hurt but it wasn't fatal. Or even disabling, if you worked through it. He did, dancing into a boxer's stance, where he was most comfortable; this karate shit was new to him—he'd been working on it only a year or so. Boxing was his forte. He advanced on her, jab, jab, his left fist darting in and out. She had an inch on him in height, but he was five pounds heavier, stronger in the upper body, and he was MALE. He'd show this bitch a thing or two about fighting.

He threw a combination at her—left jab, right hook, left hook—but she slipped or blocked each one, even followed the left hook with a right front kick to his stomach, stealing his breath in a whoosh. He danced back out of reach. When he'd restored his breathing, he said, "Come on: You kick like a girl."

His baiting seemed to have no effect; she remained expressionless as she moved in on him and began a spinning back kick. Slade saw it coming and stepped back in avoidance. But Benella saw Slade retreat as she was about to kick, so checked her back kick and leaped in to launch a rear-leg roundhouse to his solar plexus, once again robbing him of air. But not of resolve. As she was resetting, he took two quick forward steps and hooked a left to her jaw. The blow staggered her, but she spun away and reset in a left back stance, ready to execute a double knife-hand block if he pressed his attack. She shook her head to clear it, blood trickling from her mouth where she'd bitten the lining from the force of the blow.

"Gotta watch that left, darlin', it's a doozy," he taunted, and moved in again, aiming a right fist at her heart. She used an inside middle block with her left arm to deflect the blow, then stepped into him and snapped a wicked right knife-hand strike to the side of his neck just below the ear. He brought an elbow up to whack her chin, but she stepped out of reach and delivered a back fist to his nose that sprayed blood on her white shirt. But didn't stop him. On he came, punching at her face, which she took with an outside middle block on her right arm, then lifted her right leg to knee height and side-kicked him in the stomach. When he doubled over involuntarily, she moved in and struck a right back fist to his nose—drawing more blood— then, as he danced away, she jumped into the air off her left leg, spun completely around while keeping her right foot high, and locked it just before impact—straight out— impacting his face with the edge of her foot, right on the point of his jaw.

Slade hit the ground, but was up again almost as fast as he went down. As he stood erect, Benella shifted to a left front stance, jumped into the air by shooting her front leg forward, lifted her right foot to knee height, and while in the air shifted her weight and snapped her left leg into a front thrust kick—clunking his jaw again—then landed deftly on her left foot. If Slade's head had been a football, it would have soared. . . .

As it was, his mouth just filled with blood as he lay there on his stomach. "Well, sissy boy," she said. "Had enough?"

Like a striking adder, Slade's right leg lashed out, mule-like, catching her in the midriff and knocking her flat on her back, but she continued the movement—rolling her feet, legs, hips, and then the rest of her long body on over her head, coming back to her feet in one fluid movement, where she went into a tiger stance, a defensive posture useful for regrouping, buying time. She sucked air into her depleted lungs as Slade came foward; as he drew near, she shifted into a kicking stance.

He stopped, spat blood, pointed at her abdomen. "I know, I know. If you can have a baby, a little old kick like that barely hurts at all," he sneered. She faked a kick, then

lifted her leading foot while tucking in her right arm tightly
as her supple, powerful body twisted, gaining speed and
momentum, and she shot out the leading leg and snapped
her right fist forward, into his beleaguered nose yet again.
His head whipped backward from the blow, causing him to
stagger, off balance, two steps back, just enough room for
her to deliver a flying side kick. She did, and his bells
chimed.

Breathing hard, and still bleeding a little, Benella took the
loaded pistol magazine from Slade's pocket as he lay pros-
trate, replaced it into the butt of Slade's own gun—retrieved from Blister—and held it in her hand. "I've never
taken steroids, puke breath," she said, chest heaving.
"Maybe you should, though."

She removed his wallet, found three hundred seventy
dollars, removed that, and handed it to Blister. "To the
victors," she puffed. "Maybe he'll think twice next time."

"Or just use the gun," Blister said.

"Good point. Still, it goes against my nature to turn anyone in to the gendarmerie, even a devil like him."

"The what?"

"Come, let me enhance your vocabulary," and they
walked to the car, discussing cops and fights and sheltering
knights.

Like Connor.

She told Blister how she and Connor had met, in a bar,
when she was thirteen and a man was trying to slice off
one of her ears with a broken beer bottle. Connor, at the
bar to confer with an informant, had taken exception to the
unlicensed surgery and treated the man to a three-week hospital stay. Benella not only owed Connor an ear, but a lot
else, though the big goof didn't see it that way.

When she'd finished her tale, Cody waxed silent. Directly he said, "I'd like to tell you something I never told
anybody before, ever."

Respecting the confidence, she said, "And I'll never tell
a soul unless you say."

He nodded. "My daddy kept me when I was little. But then when I was two or so, he gave me to my aunt Vera. I don't know why."

"I'm sure he had a good reason."

"I don't know. Maybe he just didn't love me anymore. Or I was too much trouble."

A tear started down, silently, just one, all the way from his heart.

"I can't remember much about my daddy," he said, lips trembling as he spoke. For a while he couldn't go on.

Benella reached over, took his hand in hers, and squeezed. "It's okay."

He reached deep to continue, get it all out, just this once, to someone else. "I remember one thing, though."

More silence, more trying. "He used to hold me on his forearms, with my feet to his chest, and say, 'Why, son, you're no bigger than a blister.'"

They were silent then, for a long time. . . .

Until he said, very quietly, "You can tell Mr. Gibbs if you want."

TWENTY-NINE

Cody "Blister" McGraw had never seen Connor Gibbs grim. He did now. And the more Gibbs listened to Benella's story, the grimmer he got. After securing from the medicine chest tinctures and swabs and other necessaries for repairs on Bennie's face, Gibbs carefully dabbed and cleansed while she finished relating her tale. When the first aid was nearly completed, Holmes Crenshaw came in, took one look at Benella, and the incident had to be replayed. At the conclusion of the second recounting Gibbs was heading for the door. Holmes hastened to stop him.

"Whoa, *sufi*. Where you going?"

"To see Slade," Connor gritted.

"And do what?"

"Turn him into a soggy dog biscuit."

"Seems Bennie already did that," Holmes pointed out.

"Then I'll . . . have him arrested."

"The charge?"

"Assault!"

"Think about that for a second. She left *him* on the ground, not the other way around."

Connor adopted a slow burn. "Attempted kidnapping, then."

"His word against theirs, and he's the one showing most of the physical damage. And remember, she can't even make a weapons charge stick. There's no weapon."

"The gun might be in his name."

"So what? He'd just claim he lost it, or it was stolen. Besides, knowing Slade, the gun came to him indirectly, so there probably won't be a federal form 4473 on file at any gun shop, not with his name on it."

Benella brought her puffy lip over to where the two stood by the front door. "Connor."

"Hmm?"

"I did him up good; you don't need to defend my honor."

"Yeah, well . . ."

"Don't give me 'Yeah, well.' I even took his piece for a trophy."

"You should have tossed his sorry butt in your trunk. That would have been a better trophy."

The puffy lip tried to smile, but got caught on a canine tooth. "Then *I'd* be guilty of kidnapping."

"Cruelty to animals, maybe. No, I won't let this pass. He tried to kidnap Blister, and if he hadn't underestimated you—"

"I made him underestimate me."

"Okay, you outsmarted him. Fine. Nonetheless, his intention was to take the boy, and if he'd known you were a modern Artemis, he'd simply have used his gun. That seems to have been his original plan."

"But he didn't use the gun," she argued.

"Doesn't mean he won't the next time. Slade went over the line here, so he's being removed from the board."

"Connor," Holmes said. "We're not in Panama. There're laws here."

"And which one is applicable to Slade?"

"I know what you mean, but—"

"You can't play by one set of rules while your opponent goes by another. That's movie stuff, you yield too much of an advantage that way. If Bennie hadn't outmaneuvered him, Slade would have Blister right now. Then where would Noah be, not to mention Blister? No, Slade's getting crossed off.''

Crenshaw sighed theatrically. "Okay. How?''

"I'll think about that.''

"Mr. Gibbs?'' Blister said, now that the grown-ups were through arguing.

"Yo.''

"Did my daddy call you?''

"I'm sorry, I forgot in the heat of the moment. We're meeting him tonight.''

"Really! Where?''

"It's complicated, but you'll be there, don't worry.''

"Great!''

"Now, would you mind calling your aunt? Ask her to join us here? It's important,'' Connor said.

Cody did; Vera agreed to come; Connor went to the store for snacks, with Benella alongside; Holmes Crenshaw sat to read the newspaper. Blister wouldn't let him; sitting beside him on the sofa, the boy said, "What was that about Panama?''

So Holmes told him.

"Once upon a time, not long after General Torrijos died—''

"I'm nine years old, Mr. Crenshaw. You don't have to start off with 'once upon a time.' ''

"Who's telling this story? Anyway, this General Torrijos—who was the honcho of Panama and the chief of their defense forces, the PDF—negotiated a treaty with President Carter to give the Panama Canal back to the natives, but not for a few more years. Torrijos was a very brave man, but he was also a drunk. He died under mysterious circumstances, and a sleazeball dope dealer named Manuel Noriega took over the country. Noriega went from chief of G-2—that's the intelligence wing of the military—to being full commander of the PDF. Now, the CIA had used Noriega as a spook since—''

"What's a spook?''

"A spy. What's with all the interruptions? The CIA had

fed off good ol' Manuel since he was a military cadet. In fact, he had become known as 'rent-a-colonel,' due to his willingness to sell information to anyone, even Cuba and Libya, longtime foes of the United States. When a federal grand jury in Florida handed down indictments charging Noriega with narcotics trafficking, that turned him into a wanted man. Unfortunately there wasn't much the United States could do about it, since Noriega wasn't in Florida at the time.

"Then Panama had a presidential election and Noriega's handpicked candidate was getting his head handed to him at the polls, which piss—made Noriega mad. So the good general ordered the PDF and his own goon squads—called Dignity Battalions—to seize the ballot boxes, close the polls, and throw custard pies at everybody who wasn't supportive of their man." Blister snickered at that. "Then he declared the election null and void, so his man wouldn't lose."

"He sure was a poor sport. I remember this one time—"

"Can I get on with it, please? Now, following the elections, American military personnel and their families were harassed whenever they got caught off the American base. One time the PDF even attempted to tow away a school bus full of American children. They were stopped only by the arrival of the military police, and barely in the nick of time.

"Then the Panamanian government, having lost *all* their marbles, declared war on the United States, if you can believe it. The very next day an American marine lieutenant was killed, and an American married couple brutalized by the PDF."

"What's 'brutalized'?"

"Tortured. So the Pentagon decided that they had to do something about this pesky Noriega and his nasty followers. President Bush considered a plan to kidnap him, but the plan was 'officially' rejected; if it had failed—which was very likely—reprisals were certain."

"What are 'repri—' "

"Revenge. If you keep interrupting, we'll be here till Labor Day."

"Then use words I understand," Cody suggested.

"I'll try. Note that I said the plan was 'officially' rejected. Unofficially a team was sent in, sort of a target-of-opportunity squad you might say. Not military, but civilian. I can't say who sent us, but it wasn't Pee-Wee Herman."

"Who's us?"

"Connor, six others, and me. They needed some brains in the outfit. Anyway, after parachuting into the jungle at night—a real experience, I can tell you—we split into two groups of four each. Our own G-2 had learned that Noriega had a special girlfriend, one he kept in a village not far from El Chorillo, along with a major stash of dope and moolah. El Chorillo got pretty badly burned, by the way."

"How come?"

"Because we blew the sh—stuffing out of it, that's why, and by 'we' I mean the U.S. military. But all that came later.

"So Connor's group—including me, of course—drew the short straw and went in after the girl. Early the next—"

"Did you plan to kidnap her?"

"One of the guys wanted to, but Connor nixed it. He said that once we knew her exact position, we'd simply wait for Noriega to show. The other guy, whose name was Alders, didn't like that plan. His argument was that the girl might leave, and if we didn't have transportation—which we didn't, except our feet—we'd lose her. He had a point, but Connor is not into holding people against their will—most of the time—and he said that since the lady was bait, not the enemy, we had no right to intrude on her until Manuel arrived."

"How did Mr. Alders take that?" Cody asked.

"Like a dose of Epsom salts."

"I beg your pardon?"

"Not well. But he had to go along because *sufi* was in charge."

"What does *sufi* mean? I've heard you call Mr. Gibbs that before."

"An old man we knew used to call him that. Means 'wise one' or something."

"In what language?"

"Who knows? You want to hear the rest of this?"

"Sure."

"Early the next morning, say four or so, the other pair spelled us on guard and it was my and Connor's turn to sleep. When we woke up two hours later, our buddies were gone."

"I bet they went to get the girl."

"Who's telling this? They went to get the girl. There were two guards with her, and our compadres killed them. Then Alders went to work on the girl."

"He beat her?"

"Well, a little, but mainly he, um . . ."

"Raped her?"

"What do you know about rape?"

"I've heard talk about it in movies. Some guy grabs a girl and tries to kiss her and stuff. It's not very nice, I think, and I have no idea why anyone would want to do it in the first place."

"You're absolutely right. Well, when Connor and I arrived at the lady's house, Alders was sort of, ah . . . in progress, and Connor got really piss—angry. He yanked Alders up and rendered him *hors de combat,* especially so far as raping anybody else is concerned. Meanwhile the other guy went nuts. It turned out he was the one knifed the two guards, and now he pulled the knife on Connor."

"Did you help?"

"I'd have just gotten in his way. Besides, I was watching out for *other* guards; there were plenty outside, you know. So, in maybe ten seconds Connor had the guy's knife, and the guy had a broken arm, three cracked ribs, and was on the floor unconscious. He'd forgotten Rule Two."

"What's Rule Two?" said Blister.

"Never try to cut Connor Warren Gibbs. It just makes him mad."

Blister said, "What's Rule One?"

"Never, ever, *really* never, try to shoot him."

"I won't."

"Good boy. Anyway, Connor took care of the lady, who was very upset, as you might imagine. She said she had no allegiance to that *cabrón* Noriega, and since she'd heard that an American invasion was coming, could we take her with us? Connor said sure. So we went shank's mare to a prearranged LZ—that's landing zone—and waited for a chopper to come in. Then we left Panama behind."

"What about Alders and the other guy?"

"We left them."

Blister's eyebrows shot up. "You left your friends?"

"They had jeopardized the mission and put us all in danger, not to mention that one of them had assaulted a woman and the other had killed two men, perhaps unnecessarily. So, yeah, we left them. Had it been up to me, I'd have killed them both."

Blister's eyebrows stayed up. "Really?"

"Really. But it wasn't up to me, it was up to Connor. So we just left them. One of them eventually got out, I heard. Never learned which one."

Blister was shocked. The fact that this nice fellow—a close friend of Connor's—would willingly have killed two American men was more than he could accept. But then Benella's defeat of a powerful, *wicked* man like Jackson Slade had been pretty shocking as well.

Maybe Mr. Crenshaw is joking, he thought.

Crenshaw was not.

When Connor and Benella returned, Connor recounted to Blister his limited conversation with Noah, and how they planned to meet. He did not tell the boy where.

One never knew what Jackson Slade might have up his sleeve.

Vera McGraw arrived, accepted tea and a chair, and listened to an account of the day's events. She wasn't happy.

"So, thanks to you, Cody's in real danger," she directed at Connor.

Benella said, "Thanks to *him*?"

"None of this would have happened if he hadn't come into Cody's life."

"Uh, excuse me? Your nephew came to Connor, lady."

"Nevertheless—"

"There's no 'nevertheless' to it. Blister asked Connor to find his father, and Connor found him. Or at least is on the verge. Then, when Jackson Slade tries to kidnap your nephew, it's Connor's fault? Puleeze."

"All I know is—"

"Very little," Bennie growled.

"Ladies, ladies," Connor refereed. "Let's discuss our future plans, not past contingencies."

Vera nodded.

"Fine," agreed Benella Mae Sweet. "But you lay off Connor," she ordered Vera, then stomped off to the kitchen.

"She's very protective of me," Connor explained.

"Yeah, right. Maybe she should be kept in a cage, like any other wild an—"

Connor's face went dark. Vera noticed.

"Okay. A truce," she acquiesced.

And they made plans for that evening.

When Vera drove home an hour later, she was very upset. Life with Cody—at least as she'd known it—could come to an end tonight. She pulled over to the side of the road and wept.

What a thing to do . . . and to a child, one she dearly loved. Why had she done it?

Stupid question . . . she knew *exactly* why, and if that lowlife bastard had only done right by her sister . . .

But that bile had gone stale.

She had no one to blame but herself. . . .

And her vengeful nature.

THIRTY

Ice cream woke him. It dripped onto his forehead, then *plooped* onto his pointy, bloodied nose to follow the furrow leading from his nostril to the corner of his mouth. Out snaked his tongue: Strawberry. He liked strawberry. Better when his head wasn't killing him, though.

Slade opened an eye experimentally. Ach!—too bright, pinwheels of light, multicolored, kaleidoscopic, almost painful. Let's try a liiittle . . . *squint*. Ah! Better. Focus now, in stages, though the pain in his head—not to mention various elsewheres—did not diminish. Directly above him stood a child, a girl he was fairly sure, with an ice-cream cone, the contents of which mostly ran down her hand to cascade onto his face. He sat up, only to be sorry immediately; his head not only ached, it felt like the spin cycle of a washing machine. "Groan," he said, onomatopoeically.

"Are you all right?" the child asked in a lilting voice.

"Do I *look* all right, you stupid little wench?"

"I don't think you should call me stupid."

"Why the hell not?"

"This is why the hell not," she said, and plunged the ice-cream cone into his left eye.

It stung for quite a while.

"Good grief," Fatima exclaimed. "What happened to you?"

"I was jumped by a troop of Boy Scouts. What the hell do you think happened?" said a surly Slade.

"I thought for a moment you'd taken up bronc riding."

"Everyone's a comedian." He tossed his bloody shirt on the back of a chair. It slid off. "Shit," he said, picking it up and slinging it across the room.

"What's that in your hair?" Fatima asked.

He dabbed, transferred, looked at the transferred material. "Ice cream," was his declaration.

Doing her best to suppress a guffaw, Fatima said, "You probably shouldn't eat ice cream with your forehead, Hummer."

In a funk, he clumped his way to the shower. Fatima's smile after Slade left the room would have lit Broadway.

"Thurgood here."

"Yeah, and I want Thurgood *here*."

"That you Slade?"

"No, it's a Keebler elf."

"I don't feel too good, man."

"You'll feel a hell of a lot worse if you aren't here in forty-five minutes flat!" Slade yelled, and hung up.

It took Thurgood but thirty-seven minutes.

When Johnston Thurgood came in the door, Slade handed him a cup of instant coffee. "Damn! What happened to you?" Thurgood said.

"The other guy got the worst of it."

"Then he must look *really* bad."

"Let it go, Thurgood, and come into the kitchen. We've got things to do and damn little time."

"Fatima." Thurgood nodded upon entering the kitchen.

She said "Thurgood," and then the two of them deferred to Slade.

The plan was simple. Slade was convinced that by now Connor Gibbs and Noah Sizemore had liaised on the phone. That would mean a meet, and soon. Slade didn't have enough eyes he could trust, so he planned to use tracking devices. Fatima would plant one on Vera McGraw's car; Thurgood would cover Holmes Crenshaw and Benella Sweet (the bitch); and he—Slade—would sneak onto Connor's place and bug everything in sight but the riding mower. If he had time, he might go to Connor's parents' house and bug their vehicles as well.

Then he—Slade—would surveil the Gibbs place just in case Noah sent someone to pick them up. There were scenarios they couldn't plan for, but when you couldn't plan, you couldn't plan.

Everyone gathered their plunder and scattered.

Vera was still in emotional turmoil. She sat in front of the steamer trunk rocking back and forth, hugging herself. She fixed on the trunk's keyhole, staring, blinking seldom, the brass key leaving its impression on her sweaty palm.

No, she thought, over and over. *No, no, no, no, no . . .* Noah was *not* going to take Cody away from her.

Ever!

She climbed down from the attic, washed her face, changed into black jeans and a black sweatshirt, tied a navy scarf on her head like a babushka, penciled mascara streaks all over her face. Like soldiers in the movies. *(Hey, SEAL, is that Estée Lauder on your face? Ha-ha.)*

From the top shelf in the closet, she retrieved a metal box, locked. Unlocking it, she removed what was in it, stuck the item in her waistband, and went to her car.

She was driving away when Fatima turned onto her street.

Quick cell call. "What?"

"She left as I was driving up."

"You still see her?"

"Yes."

"Follow her."

"Roger dodger," said Fatima, enjoying the intrigue.

So far.

Vera McGraw went to a street intersecting the one Connor Gibbs lived on, parked her Taurus, and sat watching.

Fatima drove past, turned a corner, parked out of sight, walked to where she could see but probably not be seen. Out came the cell phone.

"What?" answered Jackson Slade again.

"Guess where I am?"

"I don't have time for bullshit games."

"About a block from Gibbs's house. She's watching it."

He thought a minute. "That means I'll now have to come in from behind his property, jump the fence, and see if there's a rear entrance to the garage. I'd better wait till dark. Hope they don't leave soon."

"Good luck."

"You watch that damned broad," he ordered, and hung up.

Zepper had finished her puppy chow, slurped a bellyful of water, and was in the backyard chasing her tail.

She wasn't much of a guard dog; too friendly.

She also did not know that Jackson Slade hated dogs.

She was about to find out.

It was dark as a hockey puck when Slade went over the fence into Connor's yard. Through one of the rear windows he could see Gibbs and . . . yes, Holmes Crenshaw. And there at the sink was Benella Sweet (the bitch). Good, no one out in the yard sniffing honeysuckle. Except maybe the kid; hey, wouldn't *that* be great.

On to the garage.

Zepper had abandoned her tail to bedevil a firefly. In raucous good humor she gave chase as, its abdomen flashing, the insect flew erratically.

Toward the garage.

• • •

Jackson Slade tripped over a root, causing him to stumble into a rosebush. *Son of a bitch!* he yelled in his head, and plucked a thorn. *It's too damned dark out here! I need more lightning bugs,* he thought wryly, *or I'm gonna break my neck. Hey, here comes one now.*

Zepper was closing in on the firefly when she caught sound, scent, and movement simultaneously. She stopped, nose working, head cocked, trying to pierce the gloom.

There! Smells human. Oh boy. She galloped toward the tall dark shape, intent on some licking and cuddling.

Which was not what she received.

The dog didn't bark—not once—just jumped up onto Slade's leg from out of nowhere, not the least threatening, but wanting to play. Slade didn't. He had little indication of how big the dog was, or whether it might bark warningly, and he didn't care. He drop-kicked it like a soccer ball, heard it sail into the rosebush and holler in pain.

Out came his knife. He headed for the last place he'd seen the dog.

Zepper was surprised, hurt, dismayed. But she was not stupid; she knew where her master was. And sought him.

"Listen." Connor Gibbs held up a hand. "That was Zep yelping." Then he was across the room and out the door.

Zepper was just a pup. She couldn't run like a grown dog, so when Jackson Slade spotted her small form moving across his range of view, he had little trouble catching her. Snatching her as he ran, he brought up the knife, intending to slit her throat in one smooth motion.

Holmes Crenshaw flipped the floodlights as Connor went through the back door. The result was instant, pervasive, blinding *light*. Light that reflected off Slade's knife as it came up, up, eager to slash. . . .

• • •

When Cameron Gibbs had been seven years old, he'd been smitten by his dad's physical-fitness bug. Daily, he did scores of push-ups, sit-ups, and jumping jacks. Chins, too.

The problem with chins was finding a bar low enough for Cameron to reach. Since his mother wouldn't let Cameron "roughhouse" inside, the chinning bar had been erected outside.

Near the garage, not far from the rosebushes . . .

Where Slade's head found it—the bridge of his nose, actually—and for a moment the stars in his head outshown the floodlights. He dropped the dog, the knife, and almost his supper, but he neither fell nor stopped completely, instead making for the fence like a drunken ferret. He soared over before Connor could reach him, and disappeared into the darkness of a neighboring yard.

Instead of following, Connor went to his dog.

There she was, a lump on the ground. He knelt beside her as Benella bounded up. "Is she okay?" she yelled.

"No," said Connor, jaw set.

"A couple of cracked ribs," said the vet. "She's bruised and hurting, but she'll be fine. Tough little gal."

Connor put a big hand on the vet's shoulder. "Thanks for coming so quickly."

"No problem at all." The man smiled. "Anything for an animal."

Connor paid, gathered up his bundle of bruises, and carried her into the living room.

Slade approached Fatima from the north, and she wasn't aware of his proximity until he touched her arm. She jumped about six feet. "Jeepers! You trying to . . . What in the hell happened to you?"

Both Slade's eyes were blackening and blood oozed from both nostrils. "I went hang gliding. Don't try it at home."

She pulled out a Kleenex and dabbed at his upper lip.

Batting her hand away, he said, "That hurts! Let it be,

I won't bleed to death. Haven't you ever had a fucking broken nose!"

"No. Sorry."

"You think I look bad now, wait till morning."

"Are you going to a doctor?"

"Later. I didn't get to his garage. We're gonna have to eyeball it. Where's your car?"

"Over there." She pointed to the driveway of an adjacent house.

"What were you going to do if they came home?"

"I took a chance. There's a half-dozen newpapers on the porch, and no lights."

He nodded his approval of her reasoning.

"Now what?" she asked.

"I go get my car, bring it around. We may have two vehicles to shadow."

They didn't.

Connor placed Zepper on the couch, sat beside her, and rubbed her coat, very gently. Crenshaw came over. "Broken ribs," Connor said. "She'll be okay."

Holmes handed Gibbs a knife. On the grip were the initials *J S*, in sterling sliver.

"But he won't," Connor snarled.

Holmes believed him.

"It's almost time," Bennie called from the other room.

Blister had come in, knelt beside Connor, was rubbing Zep's little nose. "You ready?" Connor asked him.

He nodded.

A long night had just begun.

THIRTY-ONE

At ten minutes to midnight Connor and cohorts cleared his garage of vehicles, parking them in the yard. Watching closely, Jackson Slade said, "Now what?"

"At the stroke of twelve, the cars will turn into pumpkins," Fatima postulated.

Slade shot her a look that would curdle yogurt.

"I'm kidding. Lighten up," she suggested.

He didn't, just rotated his aching head on his creaking neck.

At one minute to twelve, a pale green Mercury Topaz idled down the street, turned onto Connor's driveway, pulled into the garage. Then the garage door motored down, *ggzzzz*. Thirty seconds later the door elevated itself, *ggzzzz*. No one was visible, either in the garage or the Merc. The car backed out of the driveway, onto the street, and parked with its motor running. Immediately a second car—this one a Lincoln—purred down the street, onto the drive, into the garage to repeat the foregoing performance. Now there were two cars—their interiors invisible from outside— parked in front of Connor's house.

"Shit," said Slade, getting the idea now.

Fatima was singing "Crazy 'Bout a Mercury" under her breath.

As if on cue, here came the third vehicle, a big Dodge Ram pickup—diesel engine, six wheels, blackout windows, rear end like a dowager. It, too, disappeared into the confines of the garage; but on exit, it led the parade off down the street.

"Fuck me!" Slade gritted. "You stick with the pickup, I'll take one of the others," he instructed, running toward his car.

Fatima was singing *"Crazy* 'Bout a Mercury!" as she hotfooted it to her Honda.

Vera McGraw had spotted Fatima spying on her sometime earlier, so she'd angled her rearview mirror to spy back. When she saw Fatima hustle off to move the Honda, Vera slipped out of her own car and disappeared into the shadows of an adjacent house. She now watched Slade and Fatima from her aerie—a dogwood tree behind Connor's garage—and smiled to herself . . . because she knew which vehicle contained Gibbs and Cody.

In seconds she was running to her Taurus. A few seconds more and she'd kicked it over and was in hot pursuit.

Connor Gibbs and "Blister" Wainwright McGraw were in the Mercury and in phone contact with the Dodge Ram, who had already spotted tails. Two, maybe three. So, as planned, they headed for a predetermined cul-de-sac in the vicinity. After the Mercury turned onto the street, the Lincoln and the monster Ram did likewise, but parked nose to tail in the entrance to the street while the Merc hustled to drop its two passengers at the curb. Away they ran— through a yard, over a fence, through another yard, down a cobbled drive (*That cost some dough*, thought Connor), and into a waiting Mazda 626. The Mazda was speeding away just as Slade spotted the roadblock and kept on going, with Fatima in tandem; one of them was grinning, the other not.

Vera noted the logjam from a distance and took a side street. After a couple blocks of travel, she spotted a white Mazda quitting the scene in a hurry. Following her instincts, she followed the Mazda.

"That went pretty slick," Gibbs said to the Mazda driver, one of Noah Sizemore's more unsavory cousins, who didn't bother to answer. Cousin Unsavory wore a Cowboys cap backward, smoked a particularly malodorous cigar, and had the air conditioner up full blast as if to compensate.

"Where's the cab?" Connor asked.

"Corner of Fourth and Apex," the driver informed.

Connor turned to look behind them. At the moment, nothing. In five minutes, approaching the corner of Fourth and Avery, he checked again. One car, well back. Coincidence? He would see.

Vera was scared to death someone in the Mazda would spot her, so she stayed a half mile back. When the Mazda veered off Plymouth Street onto Fourth, she stayed straight for one block, then swung onto fifth, cut her lights, eased up almost to the Avery intersection, and peered around the corner of an all-night beanery. And there were Connor Gibbs and her nephew, departing the Mazda. Ha!

Connor leaned back in to thank Cousin Unsavory, but she merely blew cigar smoke at him and took off, the door slamming of its own weight. So he climbed in beside Blister, gave the cabbie instructions, and they left.

Slade was fit to be tied, but there was no help for it. He'd been hoodwinked. So he followed Fatima home and pounded her bones, though she didn't really feel like it. Ah, well, sometimes rough was good. Right before spending, she bit his neck hard, which instead of angering him as she thought it might, induced him to hum louder, until he was over the edge, sailing, lousy day forgotten—or at least in abeyance. She went along, though she often didn't, arching

against him, panting, pumping, pinching, nipples distended.
Because she *hadn't* had a bad day.

Yet.

The cab dropped Connor and his sidekick at the corner of
Wendover's most expansive public park: 142 acres of ball
diamond, swimming pool, putting greens . . . and woods. It
was into the woods they walked. And there—in a tiny glen
sheltered from prying eyes, illuminated by one feeble street
lamp—on a bench sat Noah Sizemore.

Waiting for his son.

THIRTY-TWO

As Blister came up the path beside Connor, he was trembling from excitement, trepidation, anticipation. He was about to see his *daddy,* for the first time in seven years. Would Noah be ashamed of him? After all, he wasn't very tall (even for his age), and his cowlick wouldn't lie flat (all the kids picked on him about it), and his feet were awful big, (which Aunt Vera said meant he'd grow into them, and even Connor had said it, too, about Zep's feet), and his grades weren't all that good, and he couldn't kick a football a lick. . . .

They entered the clearing and there he was, bigger than life, his *daddy,* right *there*—where he could run over and touch him, hug him, say (no, *yell!*) how much he had missed him all these years . . . missed hearing him sing "You Are My Sunshine," missed feeling him caress his cheek with a rough forefinger, the tickling on the living-room floor, Dr. Seuss at bedtime. . . .

But Cody was rooted to the spot, remembering. Remembering how his daddy—that man RIGHT OVER THERE— had not only given him away, but hadn't even loved him enough to send a card at Christmas, a birthday balloon, a photograph . . . something, *anything* . . . to let his own son

know that he was okay, that the police hadn't caught up
with him, tossed him in jail . . . that he wasn't sick, maybe
dying like momma had, that . . .

he just . . .

. . . loved him.

And then his father—tall and dark and ominous—was
on his feet, striding forward, towering, his shadowed face
a mask as he grew near, nearer, twigs crunching underfoot
in his haste, the dim ambient light blunting his features, so
that Blister couldn't see the eyes, read the *eyes,* know what
was there, as his father stopped to look down upon him,
the small boy with the cowlick who couldn't kick a football.

God, please make him love me. . . .

Suddenly Daddy scooped him up into big strong arms,
tossed him featherlike into the air, his broad honest face
filled with emotion and delight and fulfillment, and uncon-
ditional, undeniable, undiluted, clear-to-the-bottom . . .

Love.

And for a brief while Cody Wainwright McGraw, widely
known as Blister, was in heaven.

THIRTY-THREE

Vera McGraw watched Connor and her nephew ease up a path that threaded into a narrow patch of woods. *Now there's an ideal meeting spot,* she thought. *Secluded, out of sight, one primary entranceway, several likely exits once noise isn't a factor. Brilliant, Noah, you sneaky bastard.* She should go to a pay phone, "drop a dime," as the parlance went.

No.

He deserved worse.

Connor stood at clearing's edge, studiously examining his fingernails while Noah and his son—seated on the bench—talked. "Why did you leave me with Aunt Vera?" Blister was asking.

Noah hesitated before answering; just how much could a nine-year-old be expected to understand? "Because I did a very bad thing."

"What could be so bad that you gave your child away?" asked Blister.

Maybe this boy could understand a lot. "I killed a man," Noah said.

Blister didn't bat an eyelash. "You must have had a good reason."

"At the time I thought so. Now I'm not so sure."

"Why not?"

Noah thought some more, searching for cogency. "Killing the guy only made things much worse for you and me, and it didn't solve a thing. Well, one thing: that sorry so-and-so will never kill anybody again."

"Who'd he kill?" asked Blister, wanting to know, to understand, to forgive.

To Noah's eyes tears came, and accompanying them a constricting lump in his throat. But he managed to say: "Your momma."

Blister jumped to his feet. "But she died having me!"

"Yes, she died having you, but not *from* having you."

"I don't understand."

"The night you were born, your momma was driving herself to the hospital and was hit by a drunk driver. She was so badly hurt, she delivered you herself, right there beside the car, on the pavement, while the skunk who hit her went across the street to suck up another beer."

"Wasn't he arrested for drunk driving or something?"

"No, for leaving the scene of the accident. He didn't do five minutes in jail, not for killing your momma or anything else. After it happened, I tried to put it behind me, and nearly did for two years. But it was eating me up. I couldn't accept it that this guy could just kill your mother and get away scot-free. So I killed him."

Blister, overwhelmed, sat back down.

Noah continued, "I watched the guy for months, learning his habits, his hangouts, his routes to and from home. Then one night I laid for him, followed him, and ran him off the road."

"And it killed him?"

Noah hesitated again. "He died."

Connor heard all this. And so did Vera, crouched thirty yards away beneath a stunted spruce, in a patch of dark, ears burning, lips curled contemptuously. *You told him most of it,* she thought venomously. *So tell him the rest. Tell your little boy where you were the night his momma was killed, you no-good prick.*

Her right hand snaked toward her waistband.

Connor walked over to Blister and his dad. "It's none of my business, but I couldn't help overhearing. Given the mitigating circumstances, couldn't you turn yourself in, try for a deal, maybe get a reduction back to manslaughter? I know a very good trial lawyer."

"That black guy who's been with you while you been hunting me?" Noah said.

"Holmes Crenshaw is his name."

Noah shook his head. "No offense to your friend, but I've never had much success dealing with the law, from either side. I thought about it a lot before I decided to do what I did, and I just couldn't see any other way. I knew Cody would have a good home with Vera. Her family is kinda uppity, but they got money, and most of them have a college education. My family's pure country, good folks but not very refined, and half my cousins never finished high school. Hell, I almost didn't."

"But didn't you want to have a relationship with your son?"

"Sure. That's why I wrote all those letters. I figured—"

"What letters?" Blister interrupted.

Oh God, oh God, oh God, here it comes, here it comes....
And the gun slipped clear of Vera's waistband.

"What do you mean 'what letters'? The letters I sent you every week, along with the money. I knew when you were little that Vera'd have to read them—"

Blister was on his feet again. "I never got any letters!"

"Son, I've sent you a letter every single week since I left seven years ago—most of them several pages long—in an envelope along with two hundred-dollar bills. Tate had one of his employees deliver—"

A branch broke, the anhydrous *snap* resonating through the still dark night.

Vera McGraw's worst fear had been realized: Cody knew about the letters! *That son of a bitch Noah Sizemore, he kills my sister and now . . .*

She'd brought her revolver up to eye level, but couldn't see its sights; the light was too dim. And if she couldn't take dead aim, she might hit Cody.

So she had shifted her position . . .

And knelt on a long, thick branch that snapped under her weight.

Three heads snapped around in unison at the sounds of Vera bumbling from her hiding place. She staggered into full view, the gun also, pointing at Noah. Blister stepped in front of his daddy. "No!" he screamed.

Too late.

A bullet was on its way.

The bullet gouged a gash into the wooden bench and whipped off into the trees. No one moved except Connor Gibbs. He stepped in front of Blister, saying, "Put the gun down, Vera."

She wouldn't, just kept trying to get a clear sight picture, not really caring whom she shot as long as it wasn't Cody. Her eyes, burning intensely, showed expansive white. She thumbed back the hammer on the gun.

"Vera!" Connor said. "You don't want to shoot Blister!"

"I told you to call him *Cody!*" she screamed—the timbre indicating a human at loose ends—then moved to the side to get a better crack at Noah.

"Better shoot *me,* Vera. I'm coming for the gun. Now!" Connor broke into a weaving run.

At her.

Vera fired again, one last desperate attempt to excise Noah Sizemore for good. She couldn't be sure where the bullet went, but to her horror she saw Cody falling forward ...

... and then Gibbs was almost on her, his bulk looming, and she knew nothing could stop him. ...

So she put the muzzle to her temple and pulled the trigger.

THIRTY-FOUR

The stitches hurt like hell, but Vera McGraw was resilient. Distraught, disobliged, dismayed, and displumed . . . but resilient. Cody hovered, holding her hand as she lay there with the needle going in and out, guided by the knowing hand of a brusque man wearing metal-rimmed glasses, thin rubber gloves, and a scowl.

"Connor, Connor," he was saying as he sewed.

"I know, I know, I know. But we don't want this reported to the police. It'll draw a few thousand questions too many."

"I could be disbarred," the brusque man objected brusquely.

"You're a lawyer?" Vera said in a Valium-induced semieuphoria.

"Yes, but he was once a corpsman in the marines. I had to jump out of a plane—"

"Shh!" shushed the medic. "Classified."

"Still?" said Connor.

"So tell me again how she came to shoot off her eyebrow."

"Actually, she was trying to shoot off her left ear, from the other side, by going through the middle," Connor said.

Vera and the ex-corpsman each shot him a dark look, as in "That wasn't the least bit funny."

"I was almost on top of her at the time, but she already had the muzzle to her temple. I decided if I stiff-armed her face, the barrel might tilt forward and blow off several of my fingers. If I went for the gun itself, or the hand it was in, she might get the muzzle caught on her ear as it jerked backward. Then she'd simply blow out an eardrum and several ounces of gray matter."

Another pair of dark looks, and a bit of green around the gills from Blister.

"So I aimed for her chin and it worked, kind of. When I hit her, she collapsed, with her head flying backward and the gun moving forward. Unfortunately, when it fired, the muzzle wasn't entirely clear of her head. Sorry."

"No need to be sorry, you saved her life. Hear that, lady? You owe the Lithuanian Stag, here, your life, no doubt about it."

"The Litho-what?" from Vera.

"Never mind," from Connor.

The medic grinned, then said, "She doubtless squeezed her eyes shut just as she yanked the trigger, which protected her eyes from the muzzle blast. It's a good thing the slug didn't take out an eyeball or lobotomize her. Even I couldn't fix that. There. Done."

He packed up his paraphernalia and stood. "Nice to have met you, ma'am. Hope I see you again under better circumstances. Of course you know that's going to leave one serious scar."

She nodded bleakly.

The ex-corpsman shook with Connor. "You know this is going to cost you."

"How much?"

"Tickets for the rest of the Bats' season."

"With their record?"

"Hey, give 'em a break. They're young yet."

"Done," Connor agreed, and the lawyer/medic left.

Blister was obviously very concerned about his aunt. The feeling was reciprocated. She said, "I saw you fall after I fired the second shot. I thought I'd hit you in my rage. I couldn't have dealt with that."

From a doorway across the room, out of Vera's sight, a voice said, "I shoved him to the ground to get him out of the line of fire."

It was Noah Sizemore.

Vera closed her eyes tightly, but that hurt. She opened them again.

"What'd you do with my letters, Vera?" Noah said angrily.

Blister waited to hear.

Connor, too.

"I threw them away."

"All of them?" said Noah, incredulous.

She nodded. "Well, all but one. I found it a couple of days ago, stuck between the lid and the hinges of a big steamer trunk up in my attic. But I tore it up, too, and tossed it in the trash."

"Why would you do that?" Noah asked in bewilderment.

"Because, you rotten bastard, if you hadn't been out drinking and bowling and laughing it up that night, Christy might still be alive." There, she'd said it, just as if it could excuse the horrible thing she'd done.

Noah came over, knelt down beside her. "Veer, just for the record, I was not out drinking and bowling that night."

"Like hell you weren't. My dad knew someone on the force. He told us where they found you at 2:30 in the morning: Bernard's Bowl-a-rama."

"That's where I was, all right."

Her chin went up defiantly at the admission.

"But I wasn't bowling. I was working."

Her mouth dropped open. "Working!"

"I'd taken a second job, as cleanup man at Bernard's. Christy had decided to lay out of work her first semester, to spend time with the baby. We knew money was going to be a problem. Tate wasn't paying me much at the restaurant, certainly not enough to support a family on. So I asked Busby if I could have the close-down job at the alley to supplement—"

"Why didn't you ask the family for help?" Vera interjected.

"Christy wouldn't even consider it. I tried talking to her about it, but she wouldn't discuss it. She said that before we got married, her dad told her that was it, that she'd get zero financial help from anyone if she insisted on going through with it. All your family ever did was bad-mouth me, and Christy hated it. That's why she wouldn't come to Sunday dinner, Thanksgiving, Christmas—because she was forbidden to bring me. Hard as this might be for you to hear, Christy and I loved each other. So when I took the extra work, she didn't tell anybody. She was afraid it would just be more grist for the mill."

Not wanting to accept the blame, or any part of it, Vera said, "So why didn't *your* family jump right in? Why didn't Tate give you a raise?"

"He said I needed to learn how to get by on tight money, like he had, like all the Sizemores had. Said Christy had no business giving up half a year's pay anyway, not if it was going to make it go hard on us financially. He said there was day care, and to screw La Leche."

"So if you two hadn't needed money . . ." she began.

Noah's eyes filled. "Can you imagine how many nights I've laid awake thinking about that? About what might have happened if I'd been behind the wheel? Johnson hit the driver's side of the car; the passenger side was not even damaged. So I'd probably be the one dead, not her. You think I wouldn't trade places in a second!"

Vera was still not convinced. "You seemed to manage pretty well after Christy died, for someone under a financial burden. But then, I understand you got a bundle of insurance cash."

Noah was taken aback. "You think I'd have lived off that money? Money from my wife's *death*! What if something had happened to me? I doubt your family would have taken care of Cody, and my relatives had their own mouths to feed. Besides, I planned for Cody to go to college, the first Sizemore ever. Cody's education fund is brimful, I'll tell you that.

"When Cody was a baby, I took care of us the way I knew best. This guy I used to . . . be in business with in high school, looked me up a week after the funeral. Bills were piling up, so I checked things out a little, got my feet wet, then went in with him big time. I had the land, the workers, and the protection; he had the *guanxi* . . . the connections. Eventually we changed our relationship a little, and I pretty much took over," he concluded.

"Well, I . . ." Vera started to say, looking at Cody.

"You what, Aunt Veer?"

"Have a trunkful of hundred-dollar bills in my attic that belongs to you."

Vera had drifted off; Cody was asleep on a cot beside her; Connor Gibbs and Noah Sizemore were at the kitchen table. Noah nibbled on a BLT, wilted iceberg lettuce peeking between the bread slices, while Gibbs bit into a banana-and-peanut-butter on whole wheat, milk on the side. The house in which they rested belonged to one of Holmes Crenshaw's clients, currently sojourning at Tweetsie Railroad with the kids, all five of them.

"Now what?" asked Noah, a dollop of mayonnaise at the corner of his mouth. He blotted it with a napkin.

"Up to you. And Vera. And Blister."

"Why does he go by Blister?"

Connor smiled. "Ask him when he wakes up."

"You don't plan to turn me in?"

"You thought I might decide to turn you in and you still arranged a meet?"

"My kid wanted to see me."

Nothing else needed to be said, not as far as these two men were concerned.

"Where do you spend most of your time? Obviously you don't just walk the streets, at least not here in Wendover."

"I don't live here. I just came down a couple of weeks ago, for Tate."

"What about him?"

Eyes fixed on the middle distance, Noah said, "He's dying. Lung cancer. Too many years going steady with R. J. Reynolds."

"Sorry to hear it," Connor said.

"Me, too, but nobody made him smoke. The problem is, Tate's always been like a daddy to me. So when he called, I had to come. I do have a perfect hidey-hole, except it's boring. Safe as mice, though."

"So what are you going to do about the situation with Blister?"

"Situation?"

"Spending time with him, at least occasionally."

"I can't very well come visit, can I? Not to mention that Vera might not want me to see him. I wouldn't take him away from her, even if I were in the legal position to do it. She raised the boy, for cripe's sakes, and did a hell of a job, it appears to me."

"You're not the least bit angry about her trying to shoot you?"

"Pshaw. If I had thought she was responsible for Christy's death, I'd have done the same. Only sooner."

"There is that alleged tendency of yours. So what about Blister?"

"How should I know? I don't even know if I'm going to stay out of jail, what with Slade breathing down my neck. The wick has been turned up."

"Peddling grass doesn't help."

"Don't lecture me, I do what I have to. I can't very well get a normal job, and I won't live on the family dole; I like to earn my keep. Besides, I don't force anybody to buy from me."

"And the law's looking for you anyway?"

"Exactly."

"Can't say that in your shoes I might not do the same."

"I hope you're never in my shoes."

And on they talked till dawn.

Meanwhile, across town, Jackson Slade licked his wounds and colluded with the devil's minions, while in his bailiwick Tate Sizemore hacked and hurt and doped things out on his own.

"Packrat Storage Warehouse," said a squeaky voice.

"Is that you, Mr. Chiles?"

"Is that you, Mr. Gibbs?"

"It is us."

"I'm delighted, man."

"You may let Wacky go."

"Damn, just as I was beginning to relish his wry repartee?"

"There's a bad sign. You better let him go *quickly*."

"I won't tell him you said that. He's a man of delicate sensibilities."

"Maybe: Oh, I wouldn't give him his gun back."

"What gun?"

"Right. Thanks very much for your help."

"You'll get a bill. And Gibbs?"

"Still here."

"Slade is on the warpath. By the way, give Benella my warmest regards and a hearty 'Well done.' *Au revoir, mon grand ami.*"

"Easy for you to say, you're from Quebec."

And thus did they ring off and Wacky Mavens go free. Into the pit.

Noah Sizemore followed Able Johnson from bar to bar, watching the man get ever drunker. The last pub (Suds for Duds, obviously owned by a man with a sense of humor) tossed him out on his ear; he was too drunk by half. So Johnson swayed uncertainly in the parking lot, then tottered over to a beige Caddy to vent his bladder. Upon zipping, he snared a piece of shirttail, but was too drunk to pay much attention. Instead, at half-mast he sought his own vehicle (a dung-colored LTD), crawled in behind the wheel, and spun its tires leaving.

In a four-wheel-drive Suburban, Noah was right behind him.

The curve on Hawcourt's Road was notorious, having claimed the lives of five people over the years, three of them teens. The poorly maintained road was winding, single-laned, improperly banked, narrow-shouldered, potholed, and clung to a steep hillside. In a word: treacherous. Local residents had stumped for a guardrail for years. Finally a skimpy one had been erected, about right to prevent some-

*one who was traveling prudently from going over. In fact,
it had done so once.*

   Not tonight.

*Able Johnson—on the final bender of his life—took up
both lanes and some of each shoulder, though he wasn't
going very fast, not in his view anyway, and weren't
there a lot of white lines tonight, not a damned one
of them straight, and the fucking d.t.'s giving him the
shakes . . .*

   *Now who the hell was this coming up so fucking fast,
headlights blaring* "Get outta the way" *like he owned
the road? Able romped on the gas and stuck a fist out the
window—his middle finger poking skyward—and did his
best to keep the LTD between the verges . . . sixty, seventy, eighty . . . smoke from a badly needed ring job bil-
lowing,* BLINDING THAT MOTHERFUCKER, *like a
fog bank rolling in . . . eighty-five, ninety . . . about all that
old 351 Cleveland had, what with its missing on number
six and all . . . but* LOOKIT THAT FUCKING SMOKE,
surely the stupid bastard can't see a thing . . .

   And suddenly he was almost into the curve.

*Noah slammed on the brakes in the nick of time. But so
did Able Johnson. The rear end of the LTD slewed back
and forth like a crazed pendulum, smoke from tires and
brakes roiling, blending with that from the overused motor as Able fought the steering wheel, thinking once that
the old car was about to roll, but no, traction again, its
weight keeping it down, and the fishtailing came under
control . . . fifty-five, fifty . . . he was going to make it . . .
but suddenly out of a blue cloud behind him came the*
FUCKING LIGHTS, *ramming into his right front fender,
slamming the car sideways,* wham! *into the guardrail, its
flimsy supports sucked from soft sod—too much rain
lately—and Able Johnson was suddenly tilting, nose
down, going . . . over . . . down . . . rolling . . .*

   He never screamed.

• • •

When Noah was certain the LTD was unstoppable, he accelerated on through the curve, nearly hit an oncoming car, and roared off into the night.

THIRTY-FIVE

Where Vera's eyebrow wasn't hurt like hell. She needed a painkiller, but Tylenol 3 was all that was available, and it constipated her. So she sat in the strange living room and just hurt. For distraction, she turned on the TV: a talk show, with former-governor Weld as guest, still wanting a free ride to Mexico, or at least a confirmation hearing. Vera switched off and drifted off. A pale light was sifting through the curtains when Noah came in and sat beside her on the couch. He watched her sleep, quietly marveling at the striking resemblance to Christy. Vera woke with a start, turned onto her side—bumping him with a bare foot—and said, "I suppose you hate me."

He shook his head. "You look too much like Christy for me to hate. Besides, I've never hated anyone except Able Johnson. I pretty much figured your side of the family hated enough for everybody."

"You could have told us about your job," she defended.

He shook his head again. "You'd've thought I was just making an excuse. No, the McGraws've made a career out of bitching about Noah, and I never did a thing to any of them, except marry one. You ever read Shakespeare?"

"Don't patronize me, you ignorant—" She stopped, embarrassed.

"See? It's in your veins. Don't fight it, we're not going to the prom together."

She paused a moment, then said, "What about Cody?"

"He's officially yours. You raised him, and did a fine job, too. Besides, I'm always looking over one shoulder. There's no changing that."

"He can visit you, wherever you want. We'll arrange it so he can be sneaked out of town or something, and you can meet him. He could stay with you awhile this summer, and Thanksgiving, like that."

"You mean visitation? Like a divorce?"

She colored.

He patted her arm. "I'd like that, Veer, I really would. And I appreciate your offering. Can I call you Veer, by the way, since Christy did?"

She nodded. "I'm really sorry about the letters."

His turn to color, and to think carefully before speaking. "I lingered over those letters. Sometimes it took me days to write even one, and get it *just* so. Perfect, you know? I wrote him about things me and him did when he was little, and about his mom, things I remembered that we did that were special, like going to Niagara Falls. And how much I loved her, I told him over and over, hoping to keep her alive . . . in his mind. Do you remember that old song . . . how did it go?" He gazed toward the ceiling, closed his eyes, sang softly: " 'Faded photographs, covered now with lines and creases . . .' "

He looked back at Vera, eyes glistening. "I meant for her to be more than a photo to that baby. She gave her life for him, and all I could do was . . . write letters." He couldn't go on, overcome as he was by his loss.

For the thousandth time.

She took his hand. They remained that way through the dawning.

THIRTY-SIX

"Yippee!" shouted Blister, jumping onto Connor's lap.

"Well, yippee right back at you," Connor exclaimed. "What are we yippeeing about?"

"Aunt Veer is gonna let me spend the rest of the summer with Daddy!" The boy was glowing.

Connor looked downcast. "There goes my fun summer."

Blister hugged his big neck. "You can come, too, I bet."

From the doorway, Noah said, "Anytime."

"And by golly, I might just take you up on it," said Connor, standing to toss Blister into the air.

"What about me?" Crenshaw asked, coming in from the kitchen with a flagon of coffee in one mitt.

"No lawyers!" everyone yelled in unison. Holmes made a face and laughter reigned.

Premature laughter.

The day had just begun.

"Mantra, where's my product?" Wacky said over the phone.

"I'm thinking about going back to Autumn," she answered, ironing a shift. Flowers, cute little collar.

"I don't give an aardvark's ass what you go back to, where's my fucking stuff?"

"Noah said he'd take care of it," Lorie/Autumn/Mantra allowed.

"I tried all three of his numbers, and called Tate, too. Tate told me to kiss his grits and nobody answered Noah's numbers. I need to split before Connor Gibbs gets hold of my young self."

"You're not all that young, Wacky. I'll see if I can reach Noah, or get word to him. Give me a number."

Wacky read her the number off the pay phone and hung up.

Connor's DCS phone screeched. "Webster Hubbell," he said into it.

"Who?"

"Is that you, Ms. Marat?"

"Last I checked. Noah there?"

"And consuming pancakes at a prodigious rate."

"Wish I was. I had a bowl of oatmeal. Plain. Yuck. Can I speak with him?"

"One moment, please."

Connor handed the phone to Sizemore. "What can I do for you, Lorie? And don't tell me to call you something else."

He listened a moment, then said, "Wait a minute."

Holding the phone to his chest, he said to Connor, "You looking for Wacky?"

"Not anymore," Connor vowed.

"Tell Wacky there's no rush. Connor's forgiven him." Noah listened some more, then said, "Tell him I'm busy at the moment." More listening. "You got a thousand in the house?" Apparently she did. "Give it to him. I'll make it good." Some disgruntled chatter came over the line, then Noah said, "I don't have time for Wacky right now. I have to get back to Tate's, see if I can talk him into—" She must have interrupted. "Lorie, I—" Yak. "Lorie?" Yak, yak. "Lorie! I don't have time for this. Tell him you'll give him a thou, and for him to go to the beach and wait to hear from me.'' He rang off.

''Is Wacky upset?'' asked Holmes Crenshaw.

''It appears so,'' answered Noah. ''But that's nothing new, and it's no big deal.''

How wrong, how wrong.

''You said you were planning to talk to Tate. At the restaurant?'' asked Connor.

''No,'' from Noah. ''Too tough getting in and out. If I were planning to stay, as I originally was, then I might go back. Not now.''

''You have a good hidey-hole inside?'' said Crenshaw.

Noah smiled. ''The walk-in freezer has a false floor. Slide it aside and there's a ladder going down to a pretty decent room. Just a portable potty, though, and no TV, and I'm not that much into reading at long stretches. Solitaire gets boring.''

''You could've played poker with Rex Jobie and the guys,'' Holmes prodded.

''Right. There's not a pound of brains between all three of them boys put together.''

Vera came in and sat down, placed her aching head in her hands. Blister, taking time out from Sega, rubbed her back with his small hand; she reached back to pat his leg. ''Hurt bad, Aunt Veer?'' he asked, concerned.

''No worse than sticking my head in a garbage disposal.''

''Take something,'' Noah suggested.

''The strong stuff doesn't agree with me,'' she said. ''I'll live with it.''

Noah said, ''Wish you didn't have to. Well, I need to go see Tate. Make arrangements.''

''Can I go with you?'' Blister asked, excited.

Noah smiled at him. ''Too risky right now, son. Otherwise I'd be tickled to have you.''

''Risky how?'' Cody's disappointment was palpable.

''Jackson Slade is out there, just waiting, and I doubt the police are on vacation. But I'll set something up soon, I promise," Noah said, forgetting that folks shouldn't promise what they can't deliver.

But then, Noah probably thought he could.

Fatima said "hello," and Wacky said "Lemme speak to Slade," and Fatima said, "What about?" and Wacky said, "None of your fucking business" and Slade jerked the phone out of Fatima's hand and yelled, "Who the hell do you think you're talking to, asshole?" into the phone and Wacky told him things he didn't want to hear in return for a promise of lots of money.

When Slade put down the phone, he had a very strange look on his face. It worried Fatima.

Justifiably.

"So I get Vera?" Holmes said.

"If you can spare the time away from the office," Connor agreed.

"If I can't, I'll take her with me."

Vera looked up from her discomfort. "What did he mean, he 'gets' me?"

Connor was worried that she wouldn't take the situation seriously. "Vera, if Slade was willing to beat up a woman and try to kidnap a child, who knows what else he might do to get at Noah?"

"What woman did he beat up?"

"I said *willing* to beat up. Slade couldn't take Bennie on his best day, not in a stand-up fight. He is, however, not averse to cheating. Which is yet another reason I plan to deal harshly with him once we have a chance to bond."

"What are you going to do?" said Vera.

"My plan is still in the formulation stage."

Holmes said, "You could break all his legs, rip off an arm and stuff it up his nose, crack both his—"

"Those are viable options."

Vera snorted. It hurt her missing eyebrow.

"Say it isn't so."

"Say what isn't so?" said Fatima.

"What Wacky just told me."

Fatima was very nervous. "What did he tell you, Hummer?"

"Let's put it this way," Slade said, fingering his ASP. "I probably won't be humming again. Not with you, anyway."

Her intention was to make it to the front door.

She didn't.

Connor's DCS phone again. "Hello."

"Gibbs!"

"Yes?"

"Oh God, let me speak to Noah!"

"Mantra?"

"Quick!"

"He just left."

"Oh God!"

Connor, seriously alarmed, said, "What is it?"

"He found out!"

"Who found out?"

"Wacky told him!"

"Told *who,* Mantra?"

"He'll kill her!" she screamed, and hung up.

Ring! "Hello?" she said.

"Bennie!"

"What's wrong, sugar pie?"

"Are you okay?"

"Sure. I was just leaving for the gym. I have a class in—"

"Mantra Marat just phoned for Noah, hysterical. She said some guy—I don't know who—found out about something about a woman, and was going to kill her. I was afraid she might be referring to you."

"Why me? She asked for Noah."

"You're right. I just—"

"Thanks for the concern, babe. Can you get in touch with Noah?"

"No. Wait . . . maybe. I'll try Tate."

But he couldn't reach Tate either.

Noah answered his own DCS phone as he drove along Dawson Boulevard in Vera's Taurus. "Hello."

"You never shoulda fucked with me!"

"Fucked with you how, Wacky? I told Lorie to give you a thousand—"

"Fuck a thousand, and *fuck you*!"

"What's your problem?"

"No, what's *your* problem, dickweed? *That's* what you should be concerned with!"

Noah had a sudden chill. "What are you talking about?"

"Your fucking *bitch,* that's what I'm talking about! Slade'll fucking kill her, and *it's your fucking fault*! You shouldn't ignore your friends, asshole! When they need a little money, just a little, after all they've done for *you,* man, you *don't just fucking ignore them*!"

Noah slammed on the brakes, slewed to a stop in the middle of his lane. Horns honked. He was oblivious. "You told Slade about Fatima!"

"You're fucking right! You're gonna lose two, *two* women in one lifetime. *Fuck you!"*

The line went dead.

"Connor!" It was Noah.

"Noah, Mantra just called and—"

"Listen! Do you know where Slade lives?"

"Twain Place," Connor said.

"Right! You're closer, can you get over there, right now?"

"Sure, but—"

"You need to *go*! He'll kill her, or make her wish she was dead!"

"Who?"

"Slade!"

"No, who's he going to *kill*?"

"Fatima!"

"Why would he—"

"Just go!"
Connor went.

No one was at Slade's place when Connor arrived. He stood
not on subtleties, simply kicked the door in.
  No Slade.
  No Fatima.
  Blood on the floor, though.
  He phoned Noah.

Fatima was in pain. Slade had been venting his rage when
he'd suddenly realized that he could still use her. As he
smashed the third finger of her left hand—he'd already broken all those of her right hand, in a satanic paroxysm—he
seized upon the idea of using her as bait. After all, he had
few cards left to play in the Sizemore sweepstakes, so why
not use her. So, as she lay writhing in agony on the living-
room floor, he sat beside her fine-tuning his scheme. Every
once in a while, noticing that her pain had diminished, he'd
reach over to rap her knuckles with the ASP. This induced
screaming and more anguished writhing, which cheered
him and helped him to think.
  After a few minutes he grabbed her by her long hair,
dragged her from the house, tossed her in her own Honda,
and drove off.

Noah came sliding into Slade's driveway, tires protesting
mightily. Connor met him at the door with, "No one was
here when I arrived."
  Noah brushed past him, going straight to the blood-
stained carpet. He knelt beside the spot and rubbed his tem-
ples.
  Connor said, "Not much blood. It could have come from
a busted nose. Don't dwell on what you think *might* have
happened. Besides, why would Slade hurt his own girlfriend?"
  "She's not his. She's mine."
  Gibbs looked bewildered.
  "Fatima and I were . . . close, starting in junior high. Af-

ter I got married, she moved to Atlanta and got a job in a
bar. When she heard Christy had . . . well, she moved back
here. After I left Cody with Vera and took off to the mountains, Fatima sent a message saying she wanted to see me.
Sparks flew, as they say. But she hated the boondocks.
Jackson Slade was breathing down my neck. The cops
weren't traipsing after me, but he sure was.

"So Fatima had an idea. She'd go back to Wendover,
hang around Slade's haunts, and make a move on him.
She's a looker, there wasn't much chance he'd ignore her.
So they took up together, and she kept me posted on his
every move. She still does. She's saved my bacon more
than once, I'll guarantee."

"And it didn't bother you, her living with—"

"Of course it bothered me," Noah snapped. "But it was
practical. Besides, no matter how much she loved me, Fatima just couldn't stand country living. She's a city slicker,
a nighthawk, a party-hearty girl. And she likes sex. A lot."

"A workable relationship."

"Yeah. And I'll tell you this, Fatima loves me. If I'd
move to a big city, say Chicago or Denver, she'd go with
me in a heartbeat." He looked down at the floor, the blood.

"We better go," said Gibbs, and they went.

Holmes Crenshaw answered his cell phone: "Hello?"

"Don't give me that shit," Slade growled into the phone,
then laughed gleefully.

"You got something to say, Slade?"

"Yeah. Bibbiddy-bobbiddy-boo. And Fatima's mine,
too."

"Oh, great. Code."

"Here's the code, sunshine. I'll call Gibbs tonight at ten,
on the dot. I won't talk to you, I won't talk to Noah, and
I won't talk to John Fogerty. Connor Warren Gibbs, Es-
quire. You dig?"

"I think I got it."

"One more thing."

"Yeah?"

"Stay out of this one. It's gonna be a tsunami. Everyone but me's gonna get washed away."

"I'll keep it in mind."

"You do that, sunshine."

"Oh, and Slade?"

"Yeah?"

"Yo' mama likes sunshine."

THIRTY-SEVEN

Estelle Lawson was having brunch in the police annex cafeteria: egg substitute, whole-wheat toast, ersatz orange marmalade, skim milk, decaf coffee; nothing deadly, except to her taste buds. Two forensic medical examiners took the adjacent table, young guys, full of themselves and their lot. One of them was saying, "... guy had the worst case of toenail fungus I ever saw, but absolutely the cleanest ears. Spotless. Not a hint of earwax."

His buddy smirked, leaned over, and said, just loud enough for her to overhear, "I heard he was gay. Maybe his ears were so clean because his boyfriend was a needle dick."

"Eiuww, how disgusting," the first one said, falsetto, and they broke up laughing.

"Delightful," Estelle said, dropping her final forkful of Egg Beaters onto the plate. "You guys are a riot."

"Thanks, 'Stelle," one of them responded. "Tapioca?" He held out his dish.

She left them beating their fists on the table in mirth, and went back to her office. There she found a message to call Detective Lieutenant Bork. She did.

"Lieutenant Bork," he barked into the phone.

"Yeah, Charlie. This is Estelle Lawson. What ya got on—your mind?"

He grunted. "Ain't heard that since high school. Listen, I got an informant tells me that Jackson Slade has a line on some bail jumper named Noah Sizemore. Claims that Connor Gibbs has something to do with it all, and that we should stake out both Gibbs and Slade, and Sizemore's brother's barbecue lodge as well. Got any thoughts?"

"I've heard rumors, here and there. Probably wouldn't hurt to keep a watch on any or all of them, but I'll guarantee that if Gibbs has anything to do with it, it'll be to bring Sizemore in."

"No aiding and abetting, or obstruction?"

"Not Gibbs. He's straighter than a Kansas interstate. And if Slade's involved, it'll be to feather his own nest. Tate Sizemore's another story. He'll protect his brother no matter what."

"How about I put you on Gibbs for a couple days. Just to keep an eye out. Anything suspicious, you bring in backup, pronto. Don't be Joan of Arc."

"I'm in no danger from Connor Gibbs, Charlie."

"Listen, Estelle. There's them and there's us. Don't ever forget that. It might keep you alive."

She'd heard it a hundred times before. "I know, I know. I'll be as careful as a gazelle at the Lions Club."

"Hardee-har-har, as my great-great-grandaddy Edward Teach would have said."

"That wasn't really his name."

"So I've read. You get on Gibbs pronto. The word is this is happening real soon, maybe twenty-four hours."

"Aye-aye, Cap'n."

They shoved off.

Boz Fangelli's leisure suit today was hunter green, with white stitching. Avant-garde, except for a few chicken feathers clinging to a trouser cuff; as he walked, they flitted away. He was saying, "So what do you want from me?"

"Three guys," Slade said. "Good ones."

Fangelli stopped, turned to look Slade in the eye. "I *got* no friggin' good ones, Slade."

"Import some."

"From where?"

"Charlotte."

Fangelli spat in disgust, the dollop raising a small puff of dust. "Charlotte. Shit. Thought you said good."

"Atlanta, then."

Boz spat again, missing the first quid by mere inches. He was very accurate.

"Jersey City. It'll cost me fifteen grand, y'know. What am I getting in return?"

"Noah Sizemore," Slade said.

"Yeah, well, that'll make me feel real good and all, but where's the percentage?"

"You told me twenty thousand for him, eyes open or closed, you didn't care."

"Yeah, well, I was pissed. And I hear things are getting pretty hot around Sizemore. Wacky Maven's squealing to everybody, the little shit."

"Then Noah will go right back underground, like he always has," Slade speculated.

Fangelli resumed walking. "So how you gonna prevent that?"

Slade told him about Fatima.

"Where's the girl now?"

Slade pointed to the Honda. "In the trunk."

Fangelli stopped again. "You kidnapped a broad and brought her to my house?"

"I couldn't very well phone you about this."

"To my friggin' house! Where my babies live!"

"Don't cop an attitude on me, Boz."

"Or what, you petty gunsel?" Fangelli stepped close. Real close. So close that Slade could smell the anchovies from last night. "Now you listen to me, Jackson Friggin' Slade. I'll bring two guys down from Jersey in ten, twelve hours. And they'll take their marching orders from you, long as it's nothing, y'know, stupid. But for one day, that's all. Then they disappear into the friggin' sunset. You need another guy, you get him.''

Slade nodded his agreement.

"One more thing.''

"What?''

Nose to chin now. "You ever come to my home again, for any reason at all, and your friggin' fossil record will be incomplete. Know what I mean?''

Slade did.

Wacky Mavens was packing. For a long trip. He'd received five thousand dollars from Jackson Slade, still had most of the grand that Connor had given him for the bum steer, and he had sold his personal stash of weed for thirty-five hundred. Added to what he'd gotten for his TV and stereo, he had a little more than ten thousand, enough for a start elsewhere. Not a lavish start, but a start.

He took his bags to his car, threw them in the boot, slammed it shut, slogged back into the fleabag motel room for a final look around. Nothing left except an Elmore Leonard paperback and his Tomcat .32. He stuck the book in a back pocket, the pistol in his waistband, and left for good.

When the phone rang at his warehouse, Braxton Chiles was playing chess over line two with a cousin in Cedar City, Utah. "Queen to king's bishop five,'' he said, then, "Gotcha'' as he jerked up line one.

"Mr. Chiles?''

"Is playing chess long-distance,'' Braxton said curtly.

"This is Connor Gibbs.''

"I recognized your voice, but I'm losing. Can it wait?''

"Wacky Mavens has run amuck. He provided Jackson Slade with information that impelled him to kidnap his own girlfriend, or at least the lady he thought was his girlfriend, but who, it turns out, is actually Noah Sizemore's girlfriend.''

"This sounds more complicated than my chess game.''

"It gets worse. There was blood on Slade's living-room

floor, leading us to conclude that Fatima is hurt, perhaps badly.''

''Why would Slade kidnap his lady friend when he could simply beat the hell out of her then kick her out?''

''He phoned Holmes Crenshaw with a message. Said he wants to speak with me tonight at ten o'clock. I suspect he plans to trade Fatima for Noah.''

''So Fatima's probably okay.''

''Alive at least. Slade would realize I'd ask to speak to her. She could be in pretty bad shape, though.''

A pause while Chiles thought. Then: ''If you knew where Slade was, it might defuse the situation.''

''At least make it more tenable.''

''What would you like me to do?''

''Find Wacky. See if he'll play show-and-share.''

''Now?''

''Sooner.''

''This will cost you more than three dollars.''

''Whatever you think is fair.''

''It'll be pretty steep. I'll have to forfeit my game.''

''How serious can that be?''

''You don't understand. My cousin's never beaten me. In sixteen years. Never.''

''I apologize, sincerely.''

''No offense, but it doesn't help much.''

Chiles hung up line one, returned to line two, and said, ''Knock over my king.'' It made his cousin's day. Year, actually.

Connor had chauffeured Vera to his house; she was asleep in the upstairs guest room. Blister was lying beside her watching television when the doorbell sounded. Connor went to answer it.

''What's goin' on, jelly bean?'' said Estelle, standing there on Connor's stoop, all dressed in navy and yellow and right out of a *Vogue* ad. You couldn't see her gun. If you could, she'd never make *Vogue*.

''Come in,'' said Connor, mildly exasperated. ''The word is obviously on the street.''

"What word?"

"You tell me."

"Games, Connor? From you? Say it isn't so."

"We've got a serious situation, Estelle."

"So maybe I can help."

"Off the record?"

"You need to ask?"

"Okay. Come, take a chair." They went into his library.

"I love the smell of all these books," she commented, settling onto a mauve love seat.

"Tea?" he offered.

"No. Information."

He sat in a leather recliner and told her everything. (Which was perfectly safe; he didn't know where Noah was anyway.)

Her wise, laugh-wrinkled eyes stayed glued to his face, absorbing every nuance of the tale and the telling. "So you think the call tonight will be about a trade," she advanced.

"That's what I think."

"We can handle this better than you."

"Maybe. Maybe not. But it's Noah's choice, and he can hardly bring in the force, can he?"

"But you don't have to be involved."

"Yes I do. Noah is Blister's father, and Blister is my client. Besides, Noah has had more than his share of lousy breaks. One more is one too many."

"I could force this."

"And I could tell Slade that I'm covered and he'll have to make an end run."

"He might just give it up, go away."

"Not Slade. He's gone too far to quit. Besides, where would that leave Fatima?"

Estelle sighed. "I know. But I've got a bad feeling about this, galoot."

"You think I don't?"

Estelle got to her feet, walked over, put a hand on one of Connor's. "I've been told to follow you."

He nodded.

"But you'll make me, going through a yellow light or something."

He nodded again.

"Then you'll shake me."

Another nod.

"I could lose my job if this blows up."

"Fatima could lose her life. Noah too. Slade can't turn him in now, he's too far outside the law himself. So he'll kill him."

"You won't let him."

"I'll try not to."

"You got a plan?"

"Working on it. But it's Slade's move."

She squeezed his hand. "If I get canned, will you give me a job?"

He smiled up at her. "Sure. You can be my sex slave."

"Oh, goody. I'll work for free."

She let herself out.

Wacky Mavens was filling his tank at the BP on Salisbury Street when Braxton Chiles walked up and said, "Whatcha doing, my man?"

Wacky did an immediate double take. He recognized Braxton's voice, but it sure as hell wasn't Braxton standing there in front of him! At least it didn't *look* like Braxton. This bozo was taller, though it could have been the seventies-vintage disco shoes that made him appear so. And this guy was heavier, though it could have been the sofa cushion stuffed under his windbreaker that made him look that way. And this guy had on surgical gloves and a Groucho mustache and incredibly baggy pants and wire-rim glasses and a wide polka-dot tie and a glued-on picadilly weeper, not to mention the truly ridiculous bright yellow plastic fireman's hat.

"Going somewhere?" said the guy under the yellow hat.

"Yeah. And this time not with you," said Wacky as he palmed his Tomcat and cut loose.

•   •   •

Jackson Slade cruised the north side until he found a house
with a yardful of newspapers and a garage. He pulled into
the driveway, left the car running, walked up onto the
shaded porch, jimmied the lock, waited, no alarm, then
walked through the house into the garage, electrically elevated its door, got back into the Honda, and drove in. He
then lowered the garage door, removed a strangely silent
Fatima from the trunk—duct tape still firmly in place over
her mouth—and carried her into the house to toss her onto
a futon. He searched for something to eat—he was starv-
ing—then sat beside her still form with a cup of yogurt and
a teaspoon in hand.

"Hey," he said, licking goop from the spoon.

No response.

"Wake up," he demanded.

She didn't.

He shoved her leg roughly, then took another mouthful
of Cherry Delight.

She lay still.

He suddenly threw the half-empty cup on the carpet and
ripped the tape from her mouth, listened closely for
breathing, then checked her carotid for a pulse.

None.

She was dead.

"Shit!" he yelled, and hit her in the mouth, again and
again and again.

She didn't feel a thing.

Connor went upstairs to check on Vera. Still asleep. He
whispered to Blister, "Want to go on a little errand?"

"Will she be all right?" Cody whispered back.

"I think so, but you can stay if you want. Watch TV."

Blister thought about it. "No, I'll go with you. The TV
might wake her up anyway. Can we leave her a note?"

"You bet."

Blister carefully climbed off the big four-poster double
and sought pen and pad. Connor sought Crenshaw, sound
asnooze in the downstairs guest room. He was a light
sleeper, not only by temperament, but by training; when

Connor crossed the threshold, Holmes opened his eyes.

"Blister and I're making a run to Carolina Firearms. Want me to pick you up some fried chicken and greens on the way back?"

"Sure. Tiger's coming over. Beat it, Fuzzy."

Fuzzy beat it.

Estelle Lawson was parked two blocks from Connor's house when he pulled out of the drive. He waved as he drove past. She cranked up and took off in pursuit.

He didn't lose her. Or even try. Instead he stopped at Stamey's, hustled inside, leaving Blister waiting in the van, then came out with three peach cobblers to go. He detoured to her car, handed her one and a plastic spoon, blew her a kiss, and drove away.

Galoot, she thought in his wake, eating and steering. *You're gonna get me fired yet.*

Since Braxton started late, Wacky finished first, his little .32 automatic spitting twice, *pop!pop!*, sounding like firecrackers on the Fourth. Both wicked little Silver-tip hollow points punched through Chiles' sofa cushion, and coursed head-on into his Second Chance vest, where they expanded and stopped. Chiles was late, yes, but *his* gun didn't make a sissy little popping sound, but an ear-shredding *boom!* The bullet took Wacky Mavens on the left point of his clavicle, then dug deep into shoulder muscle and exited. Not fatal, but it sure hurt like hell. Wacky's little gun went *pop!* again, but merely blew a hole in his windshield, since Braxton's Magnum bullet had turned him half around. As he was trying to square off, get back into the fray, Chiles shot him again, *boom!* amidships, and *boom!* through the neck, and Wacky staggered, partly spinning again, sideways, and Chiles's next shot *boom!* took out a kidney.

Suddenly Mavens was falling, caroming off the fender of his car, onto his knees, then, spotting a haven—kind of—under his car, he scrambled for it, but Chiles had come around and was firing into his back, *boom!boom!* between the shoulder blades, and he couldn't make it. . . .

Because he was dead.

Next day, the police found in a Dumpster two blocks away a fake beard and mustache, a pair of patent-leather high-heel men's shoes (size seven), some eyeglass frames (no lenses), a sofa pillow (somewhat the worse for wear), a pair of baggy chartreuse trousers, a gray London Fog (damaged), and a bright yellow plastic fireman's hat.

Braxton had kept the wide polka-dot tie as a souvenir. It had a pair of bullet holes in it, and turned out to be a prime conversation starter at parties.

Connor's cell phone chirped. "Hello," he said into it.

"Mr. Gibbs?" A young voice, probably mid-teens.

"I confess."

"I'm Thornton Chiles. My brother asked me to tell you that through no real fault of his own, Wacky is perforated to hell and gone."

Connor paused, then said, "Is Braxton responsible?"

"Regrettably. It was a matter of survival imperatives. Mr. Mavens shot first. In fact, he shot my brother in the tie. Twice. It was one of his favorites, too."

"I'm sorry, both for the tie and not having a chance to commune with Wacky again. I trust your brother is okay."

"He's fine. He had the foresight to wear a vest."

"Glad to hear it. And how much do I owe him?"

"I called merely to express Braxton's apologies for his imprecision, and any additional hazard it might cause Ms. Fatima. There is no charge, of course."

"You speak well for a youngster. Where do you go to school?"

"I'm home-schooled, sir."

"By whom?"

Silence.

"An autodidact?" asked Gibbs.

"Guilty, sir."

"Well, I'll be. May I shake your hand someday?"

"If ever we meet." And they rang off.

THIRTY-EIGHT

Carolina Firearms was in Fayetteville, not far, and was the most complete source of firearms and related equipment within a thirty-mile radius. The co-owner was Glenn Barnes, a tall, affable, mustachioed gent who did Connor a favor now and again. When Gibbs and his young escort entered the building, Glenn was holding court at the pistol counter, his lofty self towering over a modest-sized man wearing cutoffs and a T-shirt with Dan Rostenkowski on the back. In drag. The Rostenkowski shirt was about five-eight and 165 pounds, with brown hair, gray-green eyes, and an unassuming manner. His name was Tyler Vance.

At Vance's side was a smaller version of himself, son Cullen, age six, same hair, same eyes, same cut of the jib. As Tyler and Glenn discoursed, the boy watched and listened, absorbed and cataloged. "Blister, I want you to meet some interesting people," Connor said.

Vance, a man who was constantly aware of everything around him, espied Gibbs on the approach and turned, offering a callused hand for gripping and a wide smile of greeting. Cullen extended his own small hand to Connor, the epitome of polite behavior; Connor shook it as the boy said, "Nice seeing you again." Connor then introduced the

boys to each other, and Blister to Tyler Vance. Formalities
completed, Gibbs said, "What, Carl McDuffy run you out
of Greensboro?"

Tyler nodded. "On a rail."

"Can you dribble good?" Cullen Vance said to Blister.

"Well," corrected his father.

"Well," Cullen amended.

"Pretty good," said Blister.

"Will you help me with my crossover?"

"Whoa! I said pretty good. I can't crossover dribble."

Cullen smiled. "Then maybe I can help you. Daddy?"

"You know where the balls are, babe," Tyler said. "Be
sure to stay where we can make eye contact."

"Okey-dokey," agreed Cullen, and the boys were off.

Connor smiled at their backs. "That's the politest kid
I've ever seen."

"Ain't that the truth," said Glenn.

"Thanks," from Vance. "I hope you can still say that
when he hits his brain-dead years."

"When's that?" Glenn asked.

"Oh, thirteen. Maybe twelve since he's a mite precocious."

Glenn Barnes, not that long out of his teens, wasn't sure
he appreciated the sentiment, but he asked of Connor,
"What can I do for you today?"

"If you'll give me a second to talk to Ty, I'll let you
know."

"Sure." Glenn went to help another customer.

"I've got a little problem with matériel," Connor began.
Tyler gave rapt attention to the details, a personal trait; you
never had to tell him anything twice. In conclusion, Connor
asked, "So what're your thoughts?"

"You'll need two guns, at least."

"I don't have but one."

Tyler grinned. "How many would you like to borrow?"

"Heretofore, my GI .45 has handled whatever arose."

"It might yet, the way you shoot, but only if whatever
arises is within fifty yards or so. And that would depend
on your being able to see your sights. If Slade makes his

move at night, you might as well throw rocks. Your pistol sights will be worthless."

"How about tritium night sights?"

"You'd be able to see them, all right, but probably not what you're aiming at. Too risky, especially with a hostage involved."

"How about a shotgun?" said Gibbs.

"Still too range-limited. If you use buckshot, the spread past thirty yards will endanger everyone in the direction of fire. An errant pellet could drop someone two football fields away. If you choose slugs, you'll need a rifled barrel, and excessive penetration could rear its head. No, you need a rifle, preferably short, light, and scoped."

"I thought about using Holmes Crenshaw's AK."

"A conventional rifle round, even one a bit weak in the knees like the 7.62 × 39, would, again, be overpenetrative. You'd shoot through Slade, three yaks, and a fire hydrant. Still, I'd personally want a rifle, for the reach if not the power."

"I don't know why you'd want a gun at all. With only your hands, you're more lethal than a missile silo."

Vance smiled to acknowledge the compliment, but continued to focus on Gibbs's problem. "So unless you go with something like a 'spray and pray' Uzi, that appears to put you right back where you started, with a .45 in your fingers. But there are other options."

"And they are?" said Connor.

"You could go with a lever-action .357, like a Marlin or Rossi. But they work best with two hands in control, John Wayne to the contrary. If someone zaps you in an arm, you'll have problems. Besides, those cowboy levers are too slow to reload. Better," he said, pointing, "is one of those."

Connor looked where the finger indicated. There on a rifle rack, amongst a phalanx of disparate longarms, was an ugly, black, synthetic-stocked carbine with an extended magazine poking from its belly and a barrel not much longer than a gardener's trowel. "Ugh. Would I have to take it out in public?"

Vance chuckled. "Pretty is as pretty does. That's a Ruger PC9. It takes the 9mm pistol cartridge, but boosts velocity two or three hundred feet per second, depending on the load. If you choose your bullet carefully, excessive penetration is pretty much a nonfactor."

"Does it come with scope rings like the Ranch Rifle?"

"The receiver is machined for them, but they come separate. You could throw on a red-dot sight—if you buy 30mm rings—or a low-powered variable scope, and have your bases covered to at least a hundred yards. More if you take the trouble to test different brands of ammo for accuracy."

"Not enough time."

"You buy the gun, I'll provide the ammo."

"I can't let you do that."

"Connor, I'm a gun writer. Ammo companies send me stuff by the truckload."

And thus did Connor Gibbs part with more than six hundred dollars for a Ruger 9mm carbine, 30mm scope rings, and a Tasco Pro-Point optical sighting system, all of which went home with someone else.

"Cullen was really nice," Blister said, back in the van. "And so polite. Every time I showed him a new move, he always said thank you."

"Listens to his dad well, too, doesn't he?"

"Boy, howdy. I tried to get him to go look at baseball gloves with me, but he said no, he wouldn't be able to see his daddy."

Connor smiled. "Discipline. And Cullen dotes on his dad. Which is a good thing, because he's had some tough experiences since his mother died."

Blister glanced over. "Cullen's mother died?"

"Killed in a wreck. By a drunk. Just like yours."

Cody was quiet for a spell. "Did he ever get to know his mother?"

"Yes. He was four when she died."

"Has his daddy always . . . been there?"

"Tyler? You better believe it."

"But Mr. Vance seemed so . . . I dunno . . ."

"Aloof? Self-contained? Standoffish?"

"Not unfriendly, though. He shook my hand, and not many men offer to do that." He looked up. "I remember that you did."

Connor grinned. "Thanks for noticing."

Blister thought some more. "Is Mr. Vance . . . tough?"

"He's the most dangerous man I ever met, and I've met some deadly ones."

"Dangerous how?"

"In every way dangerous can be measured."

"Could you beat him up?"

"In a fistfight, possibly. Equally possibly not. And I'd sure hate to try. In any other kind of scrap, he'd leave me stone-cold dead. Knives, guns, hatchets . . . hell, *boladeros,* it wouldn't matter, the result would always be the same. Me bleeding a lot."

"But you're so much bigger."

"And that's my only advantage, except maybe a little extra strength because of my size. But Ty's quicker, more agile, more flexible, and more knowledgeable. Plus he has one major, major advantage."

Blister waited.

"I had to learn to fight," Connor finished. "Tyler Vance was *born* to fight."

They were still maybe ten miles from Wendover's city limit when Blister said, "Why'd you buy a gun today? Don't you have some?"

"Not some, one. I thought I might need something a bit more . . . versatile. When Jackson Slade makes his move, it probably won't be pleasant."

"You're a detective, I thought you'd have lots of guns."

"Why? I've got only two hands, and I need one of those to cover my eyes when the lead starts flying."

Broad grin from Cody, then: "But on TV—"

"My boy, one good gun is all a man needs in life. Except drink." Doing W. C. Fields.

An even broader grin. "Who's that?"

"Who's that? Who's that!" Gibbs shook his head sadly. "Is it that Fritos guy?"

"Just never mind. Back to guns, which I don't especially like and never will. But whether I like them is not the point. I don't like a dentist's drill, but life would be a pain in the tooth without a few around. I'm not deeply in love with stereo equipment, either, but I play a lot of CDs. My point is that a gun is a tool, for a specific purpose—like an iron, or a band saw—and until something better comes along for its purpose, I sometimes have to use one. But I never like it."

"Have you ever . . ."

Connor glanced sideways. "Ever what?"

"Killed anybody?"

"That's not a question one asks."

"Why not?"

"It's not appropriate. If someone volunteers that kind of information, then it's okay for you to listen, realizing of course that it may not be the truth. But asking, *broaching* the subject, is never acceptable."

"So you won't say?"

"I won't say."

The boy turned away, disappointed, and punched on the radio.

Connor let him listen to the end of "Big Yellow Taxi," then switched off the din. Blister, pouting, looked at him harshly, as in *What?*

"Guns generally don't solve problems. Nearly as often as not, they merely antagonize, can even initiate—and certainly escalate—hostilities. Then they become necessary of themselves, because they're there.

"On the other hand, a gun can be mighty comforting to a weaker party when a predator is trolling. And by weaker I don't just mean kids or women or old people, but men who aren't by nature fighters. There's no need for folks to have to yield life or property to aggressive people—or a group of aggressive people—when a gun could turn the tide. And remember, the police can't always be around. In fact, most of the time they aren't."

"Which is good for my dad, huh?"

"Right. One other thing," Connor continued. "Violence is seldom the best solution to a problem. Please note that I said 'seldom,' not 'never.' And even when violence is unavoidable, the results are almost always unsatisfactory, one way or another."

"Like how?"

Connor hestitated so long, Cody thought he wasn't going to answer. "Once I was heading home from Bennie's place and got stopped by a traffic signal. On the opposite side of the street, heading the other way, I saw my wife's car, stopped for the same light. My son—his name's Cameron and he was seven then—was in the front seat, between his mother and one of her men friends. She was driving. Cameron spotted me and hollered 'Hey, Daddy,' and waved, big smile on his face." Gibbs paused for a deep breath; this was obviously hard for him.

"The man saw him wave, and jerked his arm down. Cameron didn't like that, and tried to push the man away, which made the guy mad. He hit my boy right in the face, with his fist. I saw it, saw my little boy's head rock back from the blow."

More deep breathing now, several minutes' worth. Then: "I jumped out of my car, ran across the intersection, and jerked that worthless gob of spit out of the car."

Connor stared straight ahead, reliving, back at that intersection two years ago. "I beat the bastard so badly he lost twenty percent of the use of one arm, and the hearing in his right ear. I couldn't stop. I was in a rage. In my mind I kept seeing my son's head rocking backward from the man's fist, his little face contorted in pain and fear."

Cody never took his eyes from Connor's face.

"I probably would have killed the guy. I was told later that three men tried to stop me. I just batted them away. My wife clawed at me, and bit my shoulder trying to stop me, but I simply shoved her aside."

Deep breaths again.

"Know who stopped me?" Connor said.

"A cop?" guessed Blister.

Connor looked at him. "Cameron. He took my arm in both his little hands, tears streaming down his face, blood running from both nostrils, one eye nearly swollen shut, and said, 'Enough, Daddy. Please.' "

Connor rubbed his face. "Just that. 'Enough, Daddy. Please.' So I stopped, let the guy sag to the ground, scooped up my son, and took him to the emergency room. An hour later my wife had me arrested."

Nothing else seemed forthcoming. After three minutes Blister couldn't stand it. "So what happened?"

"We came to an agreement. Two joggers had seen my wife's friend hit Cameron, and agreed to testify. Plus, it was obvious that Cameron had been struck by something hard, and he certainly showed no qualms about telling everyone who'd done it. The guy was a state senator, so that was that, he dropped the charges, then dropped my wife. She'd always fancied herself moving in political circles, so she never forgave me."

"Well, that jerk got just what he deserved. And at least you didn't go to prison."

"No," Connor said. "But I lost my son."

THIRTY-NINE

One of Fangelli's imported thugs looked like Buddy Ebsen. The other didn't look like anyone Slade had ever seen, thank goodness; he was a most unsightly gentleman. His head was bald as an onion, his nose an open-pored clone of Cyrano de Bergerac's, his shoulders grotesquely wide, his hips incredibly narrow. He looked like a golf tee with a grape on it.

Slade said to Buddy Ebsen, "Bet you're a hell of a dancer."

Buddy grimaced. "Yeah, but I ain't rich. Don't even have a billy-yard room."

Slade liked him. Well, as much as he liked anybody. Onionhead said, "Got'ny joe?"

"Did you see the McDonald's when you drove into the parking lot?" Slade said.

"Yeah."

"Well then."

Onionhead went to get some joe. When he'd left the motel room, Slade said, "That's one ugly cocksucker."

"Looks don't count for much in this racket," Buddy countered. "You can rely on him. That does count."

"We need to come to an understanding right off the

bat," Slade said. "For starters, you take your orders from me."

Buddy said Fine.

"You guys will turn Sizemore over to the cops, but I'll deal with the insurance company, and get all the credit."

Buddy said Of course.

"We're doing this tonight at eleven. The longer we wait, the better the chance of some royal fuckup."

Buddy said Sooner the better.

Slade said, "You bring your own hardware?"

"Nah, but Fangelli's guy had some for us at the airport. We'll either give 'em back when we leave, or toss 'em in the drink where some kid won't find 'em."

"You're worried about kids?" Slade said skeptically.

"Shit yeah. I got three."

"Will wonders never cease. I'm going to take a shower, then get some eats. We have lots of planning to do."

Buddy said Have at it.

When Slade stepped from the bathroom fifteen minutes later, Onionhead was back with two large cups of scalding coffee. "Hey," Slade groused, "none for me?"

Onionhead said, "McDonald's is still right where it was." Asshole.

Connor Gibbs answered his door at 6:43 P.M. It was Odie Vance, Tyler's dad, holding an elaborate gun case: black, of some pliable synthetic material, with a long strap for carrying.

"Come in, Mr. Vance," Connor greeted.

"Hafta go," the elder Vance allowed. "Takin' Cullen to see *Hercules*. Here." He handed the gun case to Connor, then: "Ty said tell you the 115 Federal plus-P-plus holler points shot best, but the Cor-Bons were a close second. Box of each is in the bag. He said the scope is dead-on at ninety yards, so you won't be much above line of sight out to that far, even at mid-range, and holdover at a hundred is naught to fret over."

"Please tell him thanks."

"He don't need any," the old man said, and departed.

When Gibbs closed the door, Holmes Crenshaw was standing behind it with a 10mm Glock. He put it away. "What you got there, *sufi*?"

"This is the rig Tyler Vance was setting up for me," Connor answered, crossing the foyer into the library.

"Let's have a look."

"Oh no. You'd shoot off a metacarpus."

"One of yours."

"That's what I'm worried about."

Amid such banter, they checked out Connor's newest ordnance.

Connor's DCS phone rang at ten sharp. He answered it. Jackson Slade said, "Who's there?"

"Herman's Hermits."

Slade hung up.

"What the hell did 'Herman's Hermits' mean?" Noah asked worriedly.

"Connor's trying to establish some degree of control," Holmes said. "Otherwise you might get screwed."

"I'm screwed already. Don't get smart with him, Connor, please. I want Fatima back in one piece."

"We talked about that," Connor said. "And agreed there's a chance you won't see her again."

Noah laced his fingers behind his head, stared at Connor's ceiling, pacing nervously. "I know, I know, but—"

The phone interrupted.

"Yo," said Gibbs.

"You break wise with me again, I hang up for good."

"Okay."

"Now, who's there? Tell me everybody."

"Noah, his son, Vera McGraw, Holmes Crenshaw, me."

"Not Benella?"

"Oh, I forgot her."

"I figured the big bitch would be there. Okay, listen up. At 10:15, I want every single one of you to get in your van and start down the street. A car will flash its lights. When it does, stop. One of my men will check your vehicle. If all six of you aren't in it, the exchange is off and Fatima dies. How many DCS phones you got?''

"Mine and Noah's."

"Gimme his number."

Gibbs did.

Slade continued: "Drive around until I call. My guy'll give you a map. Follow it exactly. Drive the speed limit, no slower, no faster. My man will follow. If you lose him, Fatima dies. If anyone joins you, or interferes in any way, Fatima dies. If a cop stops you, or my man, she dies. If you deviate from my route, or go too fast or too slow, Fatima dies. If anything happens to my man, Fatima dies. I'll have three other cars in the hunt, off and on. One or more of them will be within sight of both you and my man. Between 10:40 and 10:50, I'll call you with further instructions. You don't follow them, guess what?''

"Fatima dies."

"Bingo. And Gibbs?"

"What?"

"Don't mess with me. We got a nice even swap going, here. You get tricky and it all goes to hell. You won't know who my people are, or where, or how many. Fatima's tied to a chair right now, sitting over a box of dynamite, you dig? I have the detonator taped to my wrist. Fuck with me and I'll turn her into a red mist. Understand?''

"Yes."

"Say it," Slade snarled.

"I understand. And the exchange will go as you say, under two conditions."

"You don't make conditions."

"Then keep Fatima, and I'll turn Noah in myself."

Silence for a count of ten. "What conditions?"

"First, I won't endanger anyone other than Noah, so don't try changing the rules at the last minute. Second, I want to talk to Fatima."

"Why?"

"You know why."

"She's okay, Gibbs. Why would I hurt her?"

"Because you're sick, cupcake."

Slade paused to regain control of his breathing, then said, "Don't make me angry."

"Why, what'll you do? Kidnap someone?"

More breath control. "I told you Fatima was all right, but she's not real talkative right now. I had to put her under so she wouldn't yell. I'm kind of exposed, now that you violated my home and all. Hiding in plain sight, so to speak. She couldn't talk right now if she wanted to. Show some faith. In an hour or two you can talk to her all you want."

Connor thought about it.

There was really nothing he could do.

So he agreed.

FORTY

Tate Sizemore seemed to be getting weaker every day, and spending more and more time in his wheelchair, but his mind still worked just fine. Not to mention his hand. In it now, as it rested in his lap, was his long black Taurus .357 Magnum revolver. Rex Jobie and Tank Top (pale lavender tonight, just the color for covert movement in the dark) were helping Tate into a Ford Bronco, the dying man intent on helping his youngest brother get his girl back. He had little idea how, but that didn't stop him, any more than it would stop most people from embarking on foolhardy missions.

Jobie climbed behind the wheel and the Bronco pulled out into sporadic night traffic, headed northwest, waiting for Noah to call.

Fat chance.

There was no way Estelle Lawson was going to allow Connor to handle the Jackson Slade situation without official help. *Her* official help. So at 9:41 P.M., she sneaked onto his property, stuck a magnetized tracking device onto the chassis of his van, and slunk away in the dark. Two blocks away she parked her unmarked in a driveway within sight

of Gibbs's house, opened a can of Sprite, and put the tracking monitor beside her on the seat. *Tonight you won't lose
me, jelly bean,* she thought, and took a swig.

Eleven minutes later a Buick LeSabre with a bad muffler
rumbled down the street from the opposite direction, did a
quick road turn, sided the curb, and shut off its lights. Local
resident? If so, why park on the street; no one else in this
neighborhood did. Visitor? Then why was he still sitting in
the car, smoking yet, a red pinpoint giving him away. Or
her. Nah. Felt like a him.

Estelle watched and sipped and listened to the Beatles'
White Album on cassette.

Manfred Hoolivich flipped on his Walkman; the radio in
this old Buick was broke. He took another drag on his
Winston with Carole King wailin' in his ear: ''Jazzman.''

Manfred loved ol' Carole. She'd been popular when he
was a jock at East Carolina. Football. Nose tackle. He was
big and he was good and he was slow. After two years of
beer and bread and cheerleaders, he was *real* slow. His
scholarship evaporated. Since then, the glory had been ab-
sent. The cheerleaders, too. Not to mention dough; hookers
cost money.

Tonight was gonna be an easy five hundred.

If he'd only known.

Connor was speaking to all those gathered in his home,
except Benella—currently upstairs slipping into a scarlet
bikini so brief as to be nominal. He said: ''We have no
way of knowing whether Slade will pick a secluded spot
or a public one. I lean toward secluded, since an abundance
of people could present him with more problems than it
would solve. If I were choosing, I'd go for out of the way
and dark. Holmie, your job will be taking out their vehicle,
assuming we can find it. If not, play it by ear.''

''Why did Benella go to get her bathing suit?'' questioned Cody McGraw, currently operating under the name
of Blister.

At that very moment the bathing suit in question sauntered into the room, containing (just barely) Ms. Sweet herself. Blister's eyes goggled and his throat tightened; Holmes, too. What male could help it? Connor simply averted his eyes; tumescence would serve no useful purpose. Not now, anyway. Bennie slipped into a royal-blue sweatsuit, to cover her distractions.

"Vera, you stay with Blister at the van, the whole time," Connor continued. "In fact, I'll probably send you and Blister off in it as soon as the show starts."

"Why can't I have a gun?" she said.

"You're too impetuous. Besides, it'll be dark. Target identification will be a problem."

Vera didn't like it, but she agreed.

"Bennie already knows her job, so I suppose that's all I have to say."

"Does *she* get a gun?" Vera said snidely.

"She never uses one," Holmes grunted. "A blade, now, might be another story."

Benella smiled sweetly. "Why Mr. Crenshaw, whatever do you mean?"

And then the phone rang. It was 10:15.

Estelle's monitor indicated that Connor was on the move. She took one last swallow of tepid Sprite, then crushed the can—tossing it onto the passenger-side floor mat—and switched off the CD, started her engine, waited to see which way Gibbs headed.

As soon as Connor's van hit the street, Manfred Hoolivich flashed his beams, one, twice, thrice. The van turned toward him, drew abreast, pulled in behind him at the curb. Manfred stepped out, swaggered to the van, and glanced inside, counting heads other than Connor's: two male, black and white; two female; one brat. Just like he'd been told. "You know the rules?" he asked the huge mo-fo behind the wheel.

"I wrote them on the back of my hand so I wouldn't forget. You know how to drive?"

"Whaddaya think?"

"I hope so, because if you lose me due to incompetence, and this thing blows up, you'll get ten demerits."

"The hell's a demerit?"

"A swat in the puss."

Manfred started to say "Yeah? You and who else?" but decided that this guy wouldn't *need* anyone else. So instead of exchanging lip, he threw Slade's hand-drawn map in the window and hoofed it back to his own car, with much less swagger on the return trip.

"Odd," Estelle said to herself, watching the driver of the Buick (big punk, nearly Connor's size) flash and halt and confer. Then Connor was on the move again, with the Buick in tow.

"Slade's eyes, I'll bet," she surmised aloud. So she decided to sit for two minutes, then trot along, see what developed.

Tate called Noah's DCS phone from the Bronco. "Hello?" said Noah.

"Where are you, boy?"

"Tate, I need to keep this line open."

"Got your cell phone with you?"

"Yeah."

"I'll call you right back," Tate promised, and closed out the call.

"What if he keeps calling, ties up the phone?" Noah groused.

"Tell him not to," said Crenshaw.

"That's like telling a possum not to shit," Noah declared. Then his cell phone chimed.

"Where are you?" Tate demanded.

"Stay out of this, brother. You'll only muck it up."

"You can't trust Slade, boy."

"I got no choice at his point."

"Sure you do. We can—"

"Tate, there's no time. You're out of this," Noah said, and rung off.

"Out of it, huh?" Tate said to his two cronies. "We'll

see." He paged Tab Sizemore, a nephew on the city force who happened to be patrolling tonight. Tab called back within five minutes.

"Uncle Tate," he said.

"Hi, boy. Listen up now, I need a fix on your uncle Noah."

"You know I can't—"

"Don't wanna hear 'can't.' This is blood kin we're talking about. You put the word out that I'm looking for Connor Gibbs. I just drove by his spread and his van's not there. You get his plate number off your DMT, and tell your buddies to call me at this number the moment he's spotted. Tell 'em don't do nothing else, just call me. It's important."

"Okay."

"And we need this in a big damned hurry."

"I'll get back to you."

Connor was just turning onto Market when Slade called. It was 10:49. "You at Market yet?"

Connor confirmed.

"Take Benning, then left on Siler. You know where the Coca-Cola property is, near I-40?"

"The hay field where the canning plant is due to go up?" Gibbs gave Crenshaw thumbs-up: secluded.

"Right. You're three minutes from there if you don't catch a light. I'll give you five. Turn left onto the dirt road just before you reach the I-40 entrance ramp. The guy behind you will follow you in, staying fifty yards back. Just keep driving very slowly along the tree line until you come to an orange garbage bag on the ground. Can't miss it."

"What if the bag's blown away?"

"I put a few rocks in it, Gibbs. I'm not an idiot. Now, as soon as you get there, I want all of you out of the car so I can look you over. I've got a night-vision scope on a .30-06 and I won't be far away. One of my men will flash a light. As soon as you see it, start Noah on his way toward the light. We're talking maybe fifteen seconds after you clear the car. No hesitation. As soon as you spot the light, start Noah walking.

"Fatima's tied to a chair. If anything goes wrong, I'll spread her over a half acre. Got it?"

"What does Noah do when he gets to your man?"

"He gets cuffed. First thing you know, Noah'll be gone and Fatima's all yours. By the way, leave this phone line open. That way I can hear if you call anyone."

Shit, thought Connor. He turned to Benella and whispered, "He didn't know exactly where we were, so chances are no one's monitoring us at the moment."

But she was way ahead of him.

She was already losing the sweatsuit.

The Gibbs party had stopped, so Estelle stopped. They were on Market now, only a half mile away from her. She could see them as she looked across a mammoth industrial parking lot.

Maybe I better get closer.

She did.

Maybe it's about to go down.

It was.

Maybe I better call for backup.

She decided against it.

Too bad.

"Mr. Tate Sizemore?"

"Yeah?"

"This is Officer Hollis Smythe, Wendover PD."

"What you got?"

"A blue Previa van, North Carolina license number JK1347-HG. I understand you wanted to know its twenty."

"Right."

"It's currently stopped for a light at the intersection of Market and Hedgecock. Would you like me to follow them, sir?"

"No! Stay clear, don't go anywhere near that van. It might be being watched. Thanks for your help, Hollis. If you ever want some good barbecue . . .''

The patrolman chuckled. "Not necessary, sir. I'm happy to do Tab's uncle a favor."

Some favor.

Manfred Hoolivich was stopped at a light, right behind the Gibbs van, with Kim Carnes's "Bette Davis Eyes" blasting away, and he simply was not prepared. Few heterosexual males would have been.

Someone had stepped from the van. Someone tall and golden and blond and regal, someone luscious as a tropical rain forest . . . wearing the teeniest, tiniest, reddest, *fullest* bikini Manfred had ever seen. His jaw dropped to about belt level, along with his libido.

"She'll let you take her home," the Walkman blared.

Manfred's eyes were twice the size of a giant squid's as she took one long-limbed, hip-swinging, stride . . .

"It whets her appetite."

. . . after another . . .

Until he couldn't breathe, didn't dare, as she came closer, closer . . . all visible fat centered high and out front, moving as if they had minds of their own . . .

. . . and suddenly she was there, smiling, radiant, tapping at his window . . .

. . . and he was opening it as if to some sumptuous, splendiferous, sensual vision . . . encircling his sweaty head with her long arms, pulling him to her bosom . . . and he, enraptured by the billowy sweetness, scarcely noticing being spun around, barely feeling the strong arms tighten constrictingly, was only peripherally aware of being . . .

    put . . .

       to . . .

          sleep. . . .

"Good grief," exclaimed Vera, her neck craned around, peering out the rear glass. "He didn't even struggle. Just opened the door like an idiot."

"Who wouldn't?" Crenshaw argued.

Vera gave him a look.

"Present company excepted, of course," he amended.

"I sure would," Blister offered, eyes popping as Bennie squatted down, draped Manfred across her back, stood easily, and carried him back to the van.

"God. That woman's an ox," Vera said.

"Doesn't look much like one, though," from Holmes.

"She's about to spill out of her top," Vera observed. "Cody, close your eyes."

"Aw, Aunt Veer—"

"You, too, Holmie," said Connor, stepping from the van to assist Bennie with her containment problem. A nip here, a tuck there . . . he had to give up; too much flesh, too little cloth. He took Manfred instead—still asleep—and heaved him in beside Noah. Holmes got out his side of the van, went to the dilapidated Buick, climbed in under the wheel.

"I got your back, *sufi*," he said loudly.

And away they went, with Benella in the back suiting up.

"Jeepers!" Officer Smythe, having viewed all this from a Bojangles lot, was agog. He decided to check this situation out further, maybe get another look at that goddess.

Maybe not.

It ought to be against the law to be that damned big, that damned gorgeous, and that damned strong, and still have only about ten percent body fat, Estelle thought to herself. *And look where that ten percent is. I'd shoot her if I had a gun big enough.*

But she needn't have worried.

Someone else was more than willing to do it for her.

FORTY-ONE

Connor spotted the dirt road—more a path, actually—and steered left onto it, with Holmes behind him in the ratty, radioless LeSabre. Manfred was coming around, slowly, Benella tending to him in the backseat, whispering into his groggy right ear that Vera—"seated on your left with your gun in her hand"—would shoot him in the knee if he said one, count 'em, *one* word. Further, that he was to do exactly as he was directed—"through sign language"—when the van stopped, or Vera'd shoot him in *both* knees. Meanwhile, by climbing back into her dark sweatsuit, Bennie was breaking the poor lad's heart. Blister's, too.

Vera simply sat silently, staring into Manfred's eyes, exuding an intense desire to shoot him somewhere, *anywhere*. Manfred, though dull and headachy, had not taken leave of his senses. He said not a word.

After Bennie had redressed, she smeared blackface all over Manfred's exposed parts, then leaned back to examine her handiwork. Whispering into his ear again: "You're not Holmes, but you'll have to do."

Holmes Crenshaw had his cell phone to his left ear, listening hard, the connection to Connor's van still open. After getting into the Buick, he'd removed the overhead bulb so he could open his door without benefit of light. He was now awaiting the opportunity.

Estelle Lawson watched as Connor pulled off the hardtop onto the Coca-Cola property, the Buick in tandem. She'd observed the exchange of drivers back on Market Street, though she wasn't certain what it represented.

She did feel certain of one thing: the trade was about to go down.

She scratched her armpit, where the Protech ballistic vest she was wearing chafed her, and drove past the turnoff Connor had just taken. Thirty yards on, the off-ramp from I-40 intersected. She turned down it—the wrong way—but kept to the shoulder to avoid causing a wreck. Not far from the bottom of the ramp, she spotted a parked car. It looked like a rental. She ran the plate on her DMT. Nope, not a rental; registered to Fangelli Enterprises.

Aha.

She U-turned and drove halfway back up the curving exit ramp until she lost visual contact with the car. There she stopped, parked, removed a twelve-gauge Remington pump from its bracket, jacked a shell up its chamber, got out, scratched her armpit again, then locked the car.

Four minutes later she was seated with her back to a small elm, across a ditch and barely twenty yards away from the Fangelli vehicle.

She folded a piece of Juicy Fruit into her mouth and waited, listening hard and watching westbound traffic.

Officer Hollis Smythe, Wendover PD, watched the Gibbs van leave the tarmac and disappear into a coppice. Then he watched the scruffy Buick LeSabre follow the van, it, too, vanishing into the umbra. A tryst in progress, little communing with Mother Nature? As he was pondering, a state-owned Dodge breezed by, slowed near the dirt road the previous vehicles had taken, then sped up, drove to the ramp from I-40, and went down the exit.

Hmm.

Officer Smythe did a three-point, zipped into the parking lot of an industrial building nearby, gathered up his gear—including the handset for his radio—and walked to the head of the dirt road/path.

He didn't wear his hat.

Or his vest.

But it really didn't matter in the long run.

Because neither would have helped.

"There's the bag," Connor Gibbs said, louder than was absolutely necessary. Holmes heard him just fine, and whispered from his end, "I'm going into the woods to my left as soon as I stop."

Gibbs pulled up to an orange garbage bag flapping in the breeze and cut his motor. The Buick stopped sixty yards back, with a wide, brushy hedgerow beginning fifteen yards on the right and running directly south for at least a hundred yards, and including a few sizable deciduous trees. As Connor shut off his lights, Crenshaw snuffed his, grabbed the AK-47 off the seat beside him, and eased out the door. As soon as he hit the ground, he low-crawled into the woods on his left. Once there, he knelt with the cell phone held tightly against his ear, breathing hard from both stress and exertion.

It had been a long time since he'd done this.

He was rusty.

A light flashed, briefly—on and off—at the far end of the field. Connor spoke loudly, not for the benefit of Noah on the seat beside him, but for Crenshaw, somewhere out in the night: "There's Fatima, at the opposite end." They were parked at the northern boundary of an open hay field roughly a hundred yards by one twenty. In the dim light, they could see at the southern edge of the field, hard against the tree line, a woman seated in a chair. Two men were standing at her shoulders, one on the left, one on the right, both slightly to her rear.

Connor trained binoculars on the scene, and said, "She's tied to a wooden straight chair, bound by her legs. Can't see her arms, so we'll assume those are tied to the chair as well. There's a small box under the chair, possibly explosives. She has what appears to be a large cloth bag over her head, but her head is up."

"I want all five of you out of the van, right now," Jackson Slade said over Connor's DCS phone.

Gibbs said, "I'm sending them out in pairs for you to look over."

"Bullshit! I said—"

"I'm not putting my entire group under your gun at one time, Slade. You think I'm nuts?"

"I have no intention of—"

"Sorry, can't trust you. Anyone who'd kidnap a child, slap a woman around—"

"Slap *her* around!"

"I meant Fatima, you never saw a time you could slap Benella around. But let's not argue, here come the boy and his aunt." Gibbs turned in his seat, placed the muzzle of his .45 against Manfred Hoolivich's upper lip, and one finger against his own. "Shhh," he sibilated. Hoolivich uttered not a peep.

Vera climbed out from her side of the backseat, Blister crawled over his dad and exited the passenger side, up front.

"You see them?" Gibbs said into the phone.

"Yeah," grunted Slade.

"Okay, boys and girls, back in the van. Noah, you and Holmes are next, but wait until they're completely inside before you get out," Connor instructed, then jerked Manfred close. "You make a wrong move out there, and one year from today, you'll have been dead one year."

Hoolivich believed him. He got out and stood beside Noah, the picture of docility and obedience. "All right, guys," said Gibbs, "hop back in."

"Hey," objected Slade over the phone. "I didn't get a good look."

"Me and Bennie next," answered Gibbs, and climbed out.

He had earlier instructed Benella to stay between him

and the van. "Why?" she'd asked. "Because the putz might shoot you," he'd answered. "But that would blow his swap," she'd argued. "You'd still be dead," he'd concluded.

So now she was doing as he'd suggested, keeping her chest against his back and her backside against the van as they stepped around it. Once abreast of the side door, she jerked it open and jumped back in, leaving Connor outside alone. He slammed shut the door behind her.

"Send Noah," Slade said.

"Daddy?" Blister said as Noah started to get out of the van.

"Yeah, son?"

Blister grabbed him, hugged him hard, kissed him on the shoulder, tears making a damp spot on Noah's shirt. Noah didn't care; he hugged back fiercely in return.

"I'm just getting to know you," Cody cried, voice muffled by his daddy's shirt.

"Vera'll bring you to visit. Besides, I won't be in jail forever."

That much was true.

Holmes Crenshaw had used his rifle's scope to check out Fatima as soon as Connor pinpointed her location for him. He was now moving northeast through the woods, swiftly but silently. If they heard him coming, this whole shebang could go south in a hurry.

No one heard him.

Noah was walking steadily. Cylindrical hay bales dotted the landscape; there must have been a dozen of them in the field, like giant fuzzy tin cans, erratically placed, all of them ten feet long and maybe five feet high. His eyes were adjusting to the darkness; he could see surprisingly well. Fatima sat very still, her hands obviously tied behind her. To her left rear was a short wide man with an onion-shaped head. He looked to Noah like a depiction of an oversized Rumpelstiltskin, or maybe Quasimodo.

On Fatima's right was a taller, thinner fellow. He resembled the guy on *The Beverly Hillbillies*. What was his name? Art Carney? No, that wasn't it. . . .

Noah was thinking thus to keep from having a heart attack from worrying about Fatima. Was she alive and well? Alive and not so well? Just alive? At twenty yards, he stopped and called, "You all right, baby?"

He couldn't see her face, of course, because of the bag, but she nodded once, in response. "She's got a gag on, stoopit," said the onion-headed guy.

That's okay, she can still nod, you ugly prick, Noah thought.

He started walking again.

Holmes Crenshaw had hit a snag. Fortunately it was just the right height, and not five feet into the extreme eastern edge of the woods, not far from the north end, where Connor's van was parked. Holmes was maybe seventy, seventy-five yards from Noah, with Fatima and her consorts a bit farther on.

He watched with mild alarm as Noah stopped and called out, but he couldn't hear what was said.

The thickset man said something in return, then his shoulder dipped slightly. Going for a gun?

Holmes rested his elbow on the snag, shouldered the rifle, quartered the guy's head *(Whew, that sucker's UGLY!)* with his scope's cross wires, and released the safety.

Ready.

Noah had stopped again. Something wasn't right. He was only ten yards away now, thirty short feet. He flashed a light, laid the beam on Fatima. She didn't appear to be breathing.

"Hey!" said Beverly Hillbilly. "Cut off the light!"

In lieu of that, Noah said, "Take off the bag. I want to see her."

"You're going to see bullets coming if you don't douse the light," the tall guy yelled, and whipped a gun out of his pants. His wide-body buddy did the same, only slower.

There was a hay bale not ten yards away, to Noah's right.

It looked inviting. He felt very exposed. Suddenly he intuited that Fatima was not okay, despite her nod.

He looked from the hay bale to Fatima. Back to the bale. Couldn't decide!

Others decided for him.

Crenshaw saw Noah's flashlight snap on. He also saw the taller of the two thugs pull a gun, then the squat one. He heard a verbal exchange, then saw the ugly guy point his gun (very small in his huge fist) at Noah.

Holmes shot the guy in the head.

Onionhead dug into his belt for the stoopit .380 automatic that Fangelli's mutt had given him, and dragged it out into the moonlight; the freakin' little thing made a hole like in the end of your pee-pee, but what the cannoli, it was better'n nothing.

"He said douse the freakin' light," Onionhead yelled, the beam bright in his eyes, his night vision shot now, the stoopit shit.

Hey, maybe *not* so stoopit . . .

He raised his gun.

Noah saw the guns come out, heard the shouted orders to douse the light, then saw the squat guy point his shiny little automatic at him. He doused his light exactly coincident with hearing a booming *crack!* from his left rear, a good distance away.

He didn't hear the flaccid *pop!* immediately afterward, directly from his front.

He did, however, feel its searing result, the punching impact, the spinning, rending sensation as a bullet tunneled between two ribs, through his right lung, and out his back. It didn't knock him down, and it didn't hurt for long, his upper body going suddenly numb in a low-voltage-shock kind of way.

He sought cover behind the hay bale.

•   •   •

Buddy Ebsen heard both shots. He also heard one of them strike home with a liquid *thwack* that he was quite familiar with. It always made him sick. And scared him shitless.

He fired the piece-of-shit Rossi that Fangelli's gofer had given him, then took to the woods, bound for his car and a quick getaway, partner be damned.

That was his plan, anyway.

Onionhead didn't hear either of the two shots, including the second one, the one from his own little gun. The reason he didn't hear the second one was that the bullet from the first one had impacted a corner of his mouth, blown a few teeth and a good deal of his left cheek all over this shirt, then gone on to remove his left earlobe. (His own gun had fired when his hammy fist convulsed from the hit.) He staggered, then looked for something to shoot. No dice; his .380 had jammed. He looked around for his partner, who had run for the hills—and with the car keys, too—leaving him here to die.

Not alone, he thought.

He was right.

Holmes watched the result of his shot. The squat guy jerked crazily, firing his gun, then spun half around and aimed his gun again, but didn't shoot. Jammed? Yes! The guy threw it into the woods in disgust, then dove into the woods himself.

The taller fellow had fired a shot of his own, then hot-footed it. Now there was nothing to shoot at.

Noah'd run over to a hay bale, was currently crouched behind it. He seemed to be okay. Fatima hadn't moved. Had the taller guy put a bullet into her?

Holmes had some decisions to make. He could sneak through the woods, get closer to Noah, but at various points he wouldn't be able to see him. Hard to cover him that way. If, in order to keep a watchful eye on Sizemore, he elected to creep along woods' edge, in the open, he'd be duck soup to anyone with a rifle, or even a slingshot. Ditto if he went straight across the field to Noah. Ditto in reverse if he called Noah to come to him.

Shit.

Probably best to sit it out, cover Noah from here. As long as Noah stayed by the hay bale, he might not get shot.

Holmes had no way of knowing that Noah had already been shot.

Jackson Slade was wedged into the fork of a tree, six feet off the ground, in the hedgerow that bordered the field's west side. From this elevated viewpoint, he watched Noah traverse the field, heard the heated oral exchange with the New Jerseyites, all the while keeping an eye on Gibbs's van. Over his left shoulder, he could see the Buick; if Manfred was still in it, he was lying down, the turd.

Now what's this?

A shadowy figure had emerged from the woods near the Buick. Slade put his nightscope on the figure. Cop!

Now where did—?

Crack! Pop! Pow! Three shots in rapid succession, behind him as he sat twisted. Someone had done something stupid. He hoped at least one of the three bullets had found Noah Sizemore, but he couldn't worry about that now. At the sound of the shots, the cop had squatted on his heels and pulled out a radio.

No, no, my friend, Slade thought.

And fired.

Officer Hollis Smythe heard three shots, including Buddy Ebsen's knee-jerk tribute. He never heard the fourth one. Hunkered down near the Buick, he was about to radio for backup when a bullet from a .30-06 rifle punched through him, making a mess of his thorax. He wasn't dead when he hit the ground, but he didn't last long.

His wife and two children were home asleep.

As soon as Crenshaw opened up, Connor Gibbs jumped out of the van, PC9 in hand. Bennie had already shifted Manfred to the back of the vehicle, securing his hands behind his back, his legs together, using duct tape. She'd also cuffed him to a seat support.

When Gibbs quit the van, she slid her long legs under the steering wheel. Connor put one hand on her arm, said, "Don't stop for anything," and stepped out of the way. She winked and took off, U-turning in the grassy field, the supercharger earning its keep, dew-saturated sod flying from the tires, rear end oscillating like a crazed marlin on the end of a saltwater line.

As she started to move, Connor heard the hollow *ba-room!* of a serious rifle.

A .30-06.

Slade.

Afraid that Jackson was firing at the van, Gibbs took a fix on the sound and opened up with his Ruger. *Bam! bam! bam! bam! bam! bam! bam! bam!* his bullets clipping branches and twigs and leaves as he charged, zig-zag, trying not only to distract but also not to get shot for his effort.

He made it to the trees unharmed, just as Slade fired again.

Noah watched Bennie digging up the field, watched Connor zigzagging across the turf, blasting holes into the night. *Now's the time,* he thought, and went to get Fatima.

Holmes Crenshaw also watched the excitement, and spotted the muzzle flash when Slade shot at Officer Smythe. He also saw Slade jump from his tree immediately after the shot and disappear into the undergrowth before he could bring his AK to bear.

"Missed my chance," said Crenshaw.

And he had.

Slade hit the ground running. The next thing Gibbs would try would be getting the noncombatants (including that big bitch) out of danger. Well, fuck that. There was a small open area between the hay field and the paved road. The van had to cross its upper end. . . .

And here it came, like a bat fleeing Satan.

Slade hit prone, dug in, swung the muzzle of his .30-06 onto the van, and fired.

The Previa was doing its best to remain upright as Benella Mae stood on its throttle and made for the paved road. Out of the corner of her left eye, she caught movement.

Slade!

She saw him hit the dirt belly-down, set himself—legs wide for stability, left elbow planted solidly under the rifle. *"On the floor!"* she yelled to her passengers. They were already there.

She saw the muzzle flash and knew Slade wouldn't miss, *couldn't* miss, not at this range and shooting prone, so she jerked the wheel clockwise, hard.

It was a mistake.

Noah skidded to a halt beside Fatima's chair, grabbed the cigar box from underneath, and threw it far into the woods behind them. Next he tried to jerk off the cloth bag, but something was binding it. Heavy twine ran out a hole at the rear of the bag, down the chair and around its lower rung, then trailed off . . . he was kneeling on one end of it! He jumped up, poked the string back through the hole, jerked off the hood.

Fatima's head was forward, the heavy twine wrapped tightly around her forehead like a sweatband. "Baby? You okay?"

No, she was cold . . .

Stiff . . .

Dead.

The thickset guy had used the string to make her nod her head.

Like a puppet.

Noah jumped to his feet and screamed into the night, *"Bastaaarrrddd!"*

Estelle heard Buddy Ebsen coming before she saw him, and released the shotgun's safety, but left the gun lying across her lap. When the guy popped out of the woods, he was within spitting distance.

Literally.

She said, "Evening," and he nearly shat his britches. He also flipped up the Rossi and pumped four .44 slugs at her at virtually point-blank range. She went over in a heap, shotgun clattering to the gravel. He was about to check her pulse when a Ford Bronco careened down the ramp, practically on two wheels. A guy was hanging out a back window aiming a rifle at him.

He took to the woods again.

Benella hadn't noticed the ditch. She did now, losing her steering as the right wheel dropped into it; her solidity as the van, going too fast, heaved precariously over; and her perch, since she'd not had time to buckle up. The van rolled heavily onto its right side. Bad break. But Bennie was very bright and very bold and not in the least indecisive.

"Out! Up here!" she ordered as soon as the van stopped moving. Blister and Vera scooted through the left front window, into the dangerous night air.

"You okay back there, mac?" Bennie said.

"Hell no, I ain't," assessed Manfred.

"Least you're not dead," she said. "Yet."

Drawing Manfred's gun from her pocket, she stuck her head through the window, saw Slade coming on the run, and unloaded the piece at him, the reports slamming her ears painfully.

"*Owww!*" screamed Hoolivich, since he had no protection for his ears.

Slade ducked for cover.

"Sorry 'bout that," Bennie told Manfred.

Then went out the window.

Connor was easing through the brush, intent on slinking up on Slade's backside. Going was slow; if not, given his size and this dense brush, he'd make more noise than a tap dancer in a submarine. Actually he was doing pretty good, considering that the moon had set and he couldn't see as far as his eyelids. Damn, it was dark. And Connor, despite all his strength and cunning and good intentions, couldn't see in the dark.

So he didn't see the lead-filled sap whip through the air, didn't feel it crash into his neck just below the point of his jaw, directly over the carotid artery, causing an instantaneous and precipitous drop in blood pressure. As Gibbs fell—dropping his rifle—Onionhead swung the sap again, striking a concussing blow to the back of Connor's head. When Connor landed on the ground, it drove the breath from his system.

But he didn't feel it. Nor did he feel the malevolent monster repeatedly kick, stomp, grind his ribs, nor yet feel them yield, crack—on both sides of his chest.

He didn't feel all this because he was out cold and helpless.

Vera had Connor's .45, and she had Cody to take care of, and that's *all* she had. She had no idea where she was, nor for certain just where to go. Nonetheless, she deduced that moving away from the shooting was probably wise.

They did. Heading north.

Holmes Crenshaw didn't know what to do either, but he did know where he was. And where Noah was, more or less, since he'd just heard him scream in primordial fashion. And he knew that Connor and Slade were west of him, somewhere in that forbidding, overgrown hedgerow. And he knew the van was out of commission, having heard both the crash and the shot that immediately preceded it. Was Benella dead? Vera? Blister? If not dead, hurt? Had Slade shot into the van's interior, or taken out its engine? Or had the shot been at Connor, and not the van at all? Had Bennie overcooked the van in her haste to get Vera and Blister out of danger, thus rolling it?

He needed answers.

He went to get some.

•   •   •

Noah stopped running through the woods when he heard shots. Four of them? Who was firing? His chest hurt and his breathing was irregular, so he leaned against a tree, tears streaming down his cheeks.

For Fatima.

He heard a crashing in the brush, coming toward him. A deer? No, two legs. He could tell the difference. He was in no shape to fight, not for long anyway, but he knelt on the ground, groping, searching for a weapon.

Any weapon.

Dead branch! Too small; not enough heft.

Another! Rotten; hit someone with that and it would come apart in his hands.

A rock! The size of a softball. Perfect.

But he'd have to do it with one swing.

Because that's all he had left.

Slade had dived into the brush when Benella (the bitch) opened up on him with a handgun. Now he sat, back to a tree, and waited.

Nothing. Five minutes later, more of the same. Ten minutes, nothing some more.

Then he heard a twig break. Behind him.

He lay the rifle across his lap and slipped a trench knife from a sheath at his belt. In addition to its six-inch blade— sharp on both edges, daggerlike—its grip was protected by brass knuckles, pointed ones—and it had a full-length shank, for rigidity and strength. All in all, a nasty weapon.

Another twig snapped, then a heavy *thwock* and a grunt of exhalation, then another blow and a louder grunt, then someone fell and there were repeated sounds of hitting or kicking.

Someone was getting the shit stomped out of them.

Slade didn't care who, just so long as it wasn't him.

He slipped away.

Benella also heard the ruckus in the brush. Connor and Slade? Maybe.

She went to find out.

• • •

"Oh God! It hurts so bad!"

"Take it easy, lady." Tate Sizemore was helping Estelle
off with her jacket, and her vest, and her blouse. Her ribs
were an angry red, from the impact of the bullets. One of
them had hit over a breast. That one was the most painful.

"It hurts!" she gritted through clenched teeth.

"You're alive. Rex just called 911. They'll have help
here in a jiffy. Try to relax."

"*You* relax! It *hurts*!"

Tank Top brought over a pill and a can of Pepsi. Tate
took them, offering the pill to Estelle. "What's is it?" she
asked.

"Morphine," Tate said.

"Where the hell would you get . . . ?" She looked at him
anew, at his thin pale visage, his 120-pound body.

"I'm sorry."

He shrugged it off. "Take the pill. It works."

She did.

Noah was flagging fast. Too much blood leaking out. He'd
better make this good. One blow, that's all he had the
strength for. He could hear the guy coming closer, not quietly, this jerk was no good in the woods. In too big a hurry.
Noah's eyes swam. He was nauseous. He was weak. He
leaned against a tree. He had to make . . . one blow . . .

   just . . .

      one. . . .

He slid down the tree and passed out.

As Noah slipped into oblivion, Buddy Ebsen (whose real
name was Carlton Seager) heard him fall. Off to the left.
Back toward the field. *Shit, probably the son on a bitch
that shot Goolah,* he thought. (Goolah was his partner.) He
was tempted to make a run for the car again, but he'd had
only five rounds for this piece-of-shit Rossi to begin with,
and he'd shot all those.

The empty gun was still in his pocket. He took it out,
dug a quick hole with his toe, and buried it. *Now's there's*

a gun that no kid'll find, he thought, and headed east, par-
alleling the interstate, which he could hear through the trees
to his right, not a hundred yards away.

Noah lay directly in his path.

When Bennie saw some guy stomping Connor, she took
three quick strides, jumped high in the air, twisted sideways, and with both feet kicked the man right in the spine,
catapulting the genetic mishap twenty feet, into a sizable
birch. The ghoul immediately climbed to his feet.

*Uh-uh. Adrenaline at work. Maybe a little blow. Good
grief! Look at that cheek, or what's left of it.* She could see
where a couple of teeth had been blown out through the
hole.

Hurting this guy won't work, she reasoned. *He's already
been hurt.* Out came the folding hawkbill; serrated four-
inch blade; sharp, sharp, sharp. The Neanderthal rushed her,
a bubble of blood ballooning from one nostril, but she sidestepped and grabbed an arm in a viselike grip, twisted the
wrist to expose tendons and vessels, then sliced them like
spaghetti with the blade. Onionhead didn't even grunt. He
simply reached over with his good paw, grabbed a handful
of hair and jerked. Benella, though not the least bit vain
about her tresses, went right along. If she hadn't, people
would be calling *her* Onionhead. While she was going,
however, she figured she might as well cut something, so
out flicked the knife as she passed, ripping her assailant's
abdomen from spleen to colon.

No stoicism this time. He roared in defiance and pain.

But he didn't let go of the hair.

So Benella did what she had to . . . she snipped off a
clump of her hair with the knife, then rolled upright to
block his menacing hand as it reached—still clutching her
amber locks—for her throat. She didn't grab the wrist this
time, just slashed it, which was almost as effective. He
missed her neck but got a shoulder and tried to dig in, but
his fingers weren't working properly. She flashed the knife
forward and down and deep, slashing across his massive
torso, upper right to lower left, unzipping him further. His

insides started to spill out as he staggered but didn't go down, lashed out with an oaken arm, used the last of his driving strength to smash her into a tree, robbing her not only of air . . .

. . . but of the knife.

As it spun away from her grasp, he charged, leading with his misshapen nose. She gave it her best shot, ridgehand to the heavy bridge, feeling it snap, *hearing* it snap, and then, as he closed the gap, she bent her legs to get low, then whipped foward a right hand, open palm, to that grotesque appendage, HARD, all of her strength and frustration behind it, driving bone splinters into his brain.

This time he did fall . . . like a stump, short and thick and malignant. . . .

And stayed fallen.

Buddy Ebsen passed within ten feet of Noah, where he lay on the forest floor, fluid oozing from his body, front and back.

Buddy never saw him.

Holmes Crenshaw found Benella bending over Connor. "How bad?" he said.

"I'm not sure," she answered, worried. "His breathing is raspy. There are broken ribs, maybe a punctured lung. But he's not bleeding from his mouth or nose, so then again maybe not. There's a hell of a mark on the left side of his neck, but the carotid pulse is strong. Good-sized bump on the back of his head, though. He could be out for hours. Guy didn't seem to kick him anywhere but the ribs. I looked for dirt on his pants, checked his scrotum, no swelling or contusions. I'm more worried about concussion and internal bleeding. We need to get him out of here."

"You bet. First, I'll speak with Jackson Slade about it." He moved over to Onionhead, or what was left. "Don't play, do you?" he observed.

"Neither did he."

Holmes looked at her hair, then down at the fistful beside the corpse, then back at her, arching his brows.

"I needed a trim," she said.

"Like the look. Here." He handed her his Glock. "I don't know where anybody is, so be careful who you shoot."

"Where's the fun in that?"

"Bye, Bennie."

And he went to look for Slade.

Slade was doing some looking on his own. Near the overturned van. He heard movement inside. Stuck his head in, pistol first. "Who's in here?" he said, low-voiced. "Tell me true or I'll be pissed."

"That you, Slade?"

"Manny? What the fuck—"

"They overpowered me, beat the crap outta me, dragged me into—"

"Shut up."

"Okay."

"You hurt?"

"Not bad. Wet myself, though, when this thing turned over."

"I'll be back for you," Slade promised, never intending to.

"Wait, I'm just—"

"Manny?"

"Yeah?"

"Shut the hell up, or I'll come back there and cut your fucking throat."

"You got it."

Manfred Hoolivich lay in his urine-stained trousers for another hour. He tried to sleep, but couldn't.

Life is tough.

Connor opened his eyes and looked up at Benella, his head cradled in her lap. "Call me sugar pie, will you?" She looked down; he hadn't moved, just spoken.

"Hey, sugar pie," she said. "How you feeling?"

"Like I mud-wrestled three rhinoceri."

She smiled. "That's not the plural of rhinoceros. Is it?"

"If it isn't, it ought to be."

"How's the head?"

"Still there. I can tell. It hurts."

"Big baby."

"If I take a deep breath, hell, *any* breath, my chest feels like its full of broken glass."

"Close. He got your ribs."

"Who?"

"This *reeeally* ugly guy with one cheek and a nose the size of a kumquat."

"You never saw a kumquat."

"As far as you know."

"That's a Chevy Chase line." He shifted his weight slightly, grimacing. "Bennie?

"Hmm?"

"I'm . . . sleepy."

She put the gun down, took his face in her hands, and kissed him gently.

Then, unlike Manny Hoolivich, he slept just fine.

For a while, anyway.

When Buddy Ebsen stepped from the woods onto Swaim Road, he saw an old pickup truck with an even older man standing on its bumper, peering into the engine compartment. A rusty metal rod propped up the hood. The old man had a wrench in one hand.

Buddy Ebsen walked over nonchalantly, debris clinging to his jacket, courtesy of his trek through the woodland. "Engine trouble?" he asked helpfully.

"No," said the geezer. "I just like to stand on my bumper with the bonnet up."

"Well, pardon the shit outta me," said Buddy. "I was just offering a hand."

"No you wasn't. You was lookin' to bum a ride. Been in them woods long, have you?"

"About an hour."

"What's all the shootin'?"

"Foxhunting."

"I reckon. Here, fetch me that screwdriver." The old

man pointed. When Buddy turned to "fetch" it, he averted
his eyes. When he averted his eyes, the old man applied
the wrench to Buddy's head, right behind his ear. Buddy
sagged against the truck, sighed, and collapsed.

"Foxhuntin', my raggedy ass," said Lawrence Sizemore,
and went to fetch his cell phone.

"Tell me what that feller looks like that shot the police
lady," said Lawrence. Then he listened a spell. "Uh-huh.
Uh-huh . . . That's him, all right. . . . Why, I got him right
here. . . . Uh-huh . . . You come get him whenever you're of
a mind to. No hurry. He ain't goin' nowhere."

Lawrence didn't say good-bye. He never said good-bye.
It wasn't his way.

Jackson Slade heard the sirens and knew his plan was bust.
He walked to the Honda—parked a half mile away behind
a cluster of industrial Dumpsters—and left the area before
it started crawling with cops.

Vera and Blister flagged down a squad car on Market
Street, nearly a mile from the Coca-Cola property. They
were taken to Estelle's location, where she was being
loaded into an ambulance. For the next forty minutes,
thirty-one people fanned out in search of Noah Sizemore.
When they found him, he was in very bad shape.

They lit up an ambulance roof and hustled him to a hospital.

Bennie kept the Glock in her hands until she could identify
the shadowy newcomers as police. Then she yielded not
only the pistol, but Connor Gibbs. A patrolman drove her
to the hospital, in a squad car right behind the ambulance.

She was debriefed in the waiting room. Soon Cody and
Vera joined her. An hour later, Holmes, too. Five minutes
later Tate walked in.

Around two A.M., a nurse asked Benella if Connor had
family. Bennie said yes. The nurse said Connor had requested they not be notified until it was certain he was

either completely out of danger, or about to die. Benella smiled; it was just like Connor not to want to worry anyone, which early-morning calls from hospitals tend to do.

"Should we call anyway?" the nurse wanted to know.

Benella's smile disappeared. "You mean ignore your patient's wishes?"

"I guess not," stammered the nurse, and went away. Benella just shook her head.

FORTY-TWO

"I don't care. If Zep can't come visit I'm not staying."

"He's just kidding," said Holmes Crenshaw.

"No he's not," Blister disagreed, winking across the room at Benella, sitting in a leatherette chair of indeterminate age and a color too horrible to describe. She winked back, causing his nine-and-a-half-year-old heart to go pitter-pat. Any minute he'd fall over from syncope.

"Who's Zep?" asked a nurse, tapping with a forefinger a syringe the size of a grain silo.

"His girlfriend," quipped Benella.

"Interesting name," the nurse said. "Is she foreign?"

Connor nodded. "South Carolina."

"That's not foreign," judged the nurse, obviously humor-impaired, and stepped toward the bed.

"You don't intend to stick me with that, do you?" from Connor.

"You guessed it."

He squinched shut his eyes.

"Big baby," Bennie gibed.

"Yeah," said Crenshaw.

"Yeah," said Blister, joining in.

"Any of you want a shot?" asked the nurse. She seemed serious. No one said anything else.

Twenty minutes later Vera came in. Unhappiness radiated.

Connor, floating on the ceiling, said, "Howsnoah?" His voice sounded very strange, to himself, anyway.

She shook her head. "Not good. He's lost a lot of blood. And a lung collapsed. They don't know."

She stood near the door, just the two of them in the room. He motioned her closer. "I can har'ly hear you," he said, drugged to the core. Well, at least nothing hurt at the moment.

"What if he dies?" Vera asked, eyes glistening.

"Dere's nuffin you can do aboudit," he slurred, eyes dull.

Crying openly now. "I threw his letters away, seven years of a man opening up his heart to his son. What kind of person would do such a thing?"

"One filled wif hate," his head nodding. "Hate's always bad. Always."

"If he dies, I'll . . ."

He raised his eyes to hers. "Wha'? Hate yourself? Wha' good'll 'at do anybody? Speshly Blis'er."

She ran from the room and Connor went away for a while.

FORTY-THREE

When Connor awoke, it was morning, and Bennie was in the room, beside his bed, face grave.

"Noah okay?"

She shook her head. She'd been crying; her eyes were puffy.

"Blister?"

"He's outside. Waiting to see you. He hasn't said a word, shed a tear, nothing. He just came right here after they . . . told him, and watched you sleep until the nurses finally ran him off. He hasn't slept a wink, just waiting for you to wake up. He seems to need you badly."

Connor nodded. "Okay."

Benella went to get the boy.

Cody was ashen, and seemed to have shrunk in on himself. He approached the bed as if it were used for immolation. No sign of tears, just dark circles under the eyes. This child was on the edge.

"Hi," Connor said.

Cody nodded.

"We found your daddy, you and I."

Cody nodded again.

"And he sure was glad we did."

Slight moistening of the eyes.

"Your daddy loved you, Blister. More than anyone alive."

"More than Fatima?"

Connor nodded. "I think so. But he loved her, too. And your momma, years ago. And Tate. Your daddy was filled with love."

Eyes distinctly damp. "You told me you'd find him."

Connor nodded.

"And you did. Everybody tried to stop you, and I was ashamed of you sometimes, but none of that bothered you. You just kept on, and on, until you found my daddy for me." Real tears now, rolling. Cathartic. "And now he's gone."

Connor was damp now.

"I just got him back and now he's gone."

Small hands reached out to grip Connor's big one. "I just got him back and now he's gone!"

Harder and harder the little hands squeezed, echoing the pain. *"I just got him back and now he's gone!"*

Connor grabbed the boy, hurt ribs be damned, and held him tightly, tightly, barely able to breathe from the pain . . .

. . . of the wailing. . . .

"I just got him back and now he's gone!"

"I just got him back and now he's gone!"

"I just got him back and now he's gone!"

Until Blister had cried himself to sleep.

FORTY-FOUR

Braxton Chiles called Connor his second day in the hospital, with news. After offering condolences, he said, "Slade was seen getting off a plane in Atlanta. Then getting on one bound for Dallas. He has family in Tupelo. We expect that's where he's headed."

"The cops are on it. Feds, too. Kidnapping."

"Yeah, well, I thought you might desire, ah . . ."

"Retribution?"

"Yes."

"I'm not in the retribution business. Unless of course it's a windfall. At this point I think it would stir things up that are better left as they are."

"I understand," Chiles said.

"I do appreciate your keeping me posted, though. Never know when I might be in Mississippi."

"If you need company . . ."

"Thanks for the offer. I might take you up on it someday."

"Oh, Mantra's giving up dealing. Noah was her source. No one else can work with her. She's a flake."

"What makes you say that? By the way, was Wacky a third partner?"

"Sure."

"Good grief. Can you imagine being in cahoots with those two," Connor said.

"I can, but I'd rather not. You being released soon?"

"Day or so. They tell me, anyway. But I have good insurance. They may keep me until it runs out."

"How's Noah's kid?"

"He'll be okay, I think."

"Tough. Finally finding a father that you can't even remember, and then . . ."

"I know."

"Take care, man," Chiles said, and hung up.

The phone again: Cameron, in California. "Daddy?"

"Yo, babe."

"Bennie called, said you were in the hospital, but not to worry."

"She was right on both counts."

"What happened?"

"A guy beat me up."

"Somebody beat *you* up?"

"Yeah, but he cheated."

"How?"

"He was meaner than me:"

"Did somebody have to pull him off you?"

"Yeah. Bennie."

"Did she hurt him?"

"Uh . . . you could say that. Where are you?"

"Danielle's."

"Danielle?"

Shy pause. "She lives next door, moved in last week."

"You like her?"

"She's great."

"Mm-hm. Pretty?"

Another pause. "Yes. You sure you're okay?"

"Tip-top."

"Wanna hear a joke I made up?"

"Love to."

"What do you call a female worm?"

Connor's first impulse was to say Felicia, but he denied himself. "I give up."

"A worman."

Connor laughed. "That's pretty good. Don't tell it to your mother."

"Already did. She didn't think it was funny at all."

Why am I not surprised?

"Daddy?"

"Hm?"

"I really miss you."

"Me, too, hon."

"Sometimes at night . . . I can't sleep . . . and . . ."

"I know. Just remember I love you, no matter where you are or what you do."

"What if you forget me?"

"Not a chance. And we'll see each other. I'll find a way," Connor promised.

"Did you find that boy's father?"

Connor's turn to pause. "Yes."

"Was he happy to see him?"

"They were both delighted."

"Good. Well, I better go. This is on Danielle's bill."

"Tell her thanks for me."

"Okay. Love you."

"Love you."

And he was gone.

"Guy's name is Seager, out of Jersey. Got a record of strong-arm stuff as long as my schlong," Holmes Crenshaw said.

"Never been arrested, huh?" from Gibbs.

"I got your 'never been arrested.' Anyway, the list of charges is, shall we say, extensive. Chances are he'll never see New Jersey again."

"Maybe that's why he did it."

"Hey, I got relatives in Jersey."

"I rest my case."

Holmes said, "Cracker. Oh, and speaking of which, Tate wants to see you. You want to see Tate?"

"Only if it has something to do with Blister. Trust fund for schooling, like that."

"Wouldn't be surprised. Old Tate doesn't have long, and the guilt is riding him. Maybe he'll offer Rex Jobie as a tutor."

Connor began to laugh, then stopped abruptly. "Please, no jokes. My ribs are killing me."

"Here's something that'll sober you up. The po-leece wish to speak with thee."

"Are they happy campers?"

"This is just a guess, you understand, but I'd say no."

"Well, send them in. We can all be unhappy together."

The next afternoon, Estelle Lawson was getting around pretty good, despite her bruises. Standing bedside, she gave Connor a peck on the cheek. "Slade's vanished," she said.

"Who's taking the fall for Smythe? And Fatima?" Connor queried. "Seager?"

"He's a nobody, a hireling. Slade's the *dybbuk*."

Gibbs chuckled. " '*Dybbuk*'? You're not Hebrew."

"So? I know a rabbi."

"How's your chest?"

"Watch it, jelly bean. I might just show you." She pumped her eyebrows rapidly, like Groucho.

"All bluff."

"Someday, galoot, I might surprise you."

"You already did. Showing up out at Coca-Cola to save my rump, then getting shot for your trouble."

"Kinda shot," she corrected. "But aren't you worth it?"

"Asolutely." Doing Rocky Balboa.

"Can you do Mickey?"

"I'm workin' on it." No Burgess Meredith, maybe, but he had Stallone down pat.

They spent ten minutes comparing body damage.

Connor won.

Benella came in after dark, to susurrate in an exposed ear. "I bribed the night nurse into letting me stay over."

"Vixen. You'll kill me," Connor said.

Lips touching a lobe, she whispered, "I shaved."
"Aw . . . Bennie. No fair, no fair. I'll die."
She found a way.
And he didn't die.
It may even have been therapeutic. . . .
Because he left the hospital the next day.

District Attorney Taryl Drexler was heading home from a meeting with the high sheriff, the chief of police, the county attorney, and his aunt Maud, the mayor. His mood was not insouciant. In fact, his spirits needed oiling. So he stopped at one of the hangouts from his youth to bend an elbow and growl at the barkeep, an old friend from his college days. He'd barely had time to dampen his tonsils when who should swaver in but his longtime nemesis, Able Johnson, already three sheets in the wind. Johnson took up residence at the far end of the bar and ordered: "Gimme a fucking Jack and Coke."

The barman looked over at Drexler, read his expression, and refused the order, whereupon Johnson grew surly. He was immediately shown the door by two brawny men. "Well fuckallaya," was Able's parting shot.

Drexler moved to a window to watch as Johnson reeled over to a Cadillac and urinated on its fender. The DA clenched and unclenched his fists, jaw muscles working, teeth grinding. The barman came over, put an arm around his pal's shoulders. "Let it go, Taryl. The dumb son of a bitch ain't worth it."

Drexler looked up. "I've been letting it go for seven

years, Luke. Letting it go and sucking it up and holding it in. I don't know if I can anymore.''

"Nothing else you can do."

"I'll see you," Drexler said, and stalked out to his car just as Johnson was peeling off, leaving a long black mark on the pavement to mark his passage. From the open bay of a defunct service station across the road bolted a big Chevy Suburban, hustling after Johnson's Ford. Taryl Drexler recognized the truck. He hopped into his own car and followed it.

Hanging well back from the primary players—running with his lights off and keeping his big German car between the verges by dint of bright moonlight and possibly divine assistance—Taryl watched the following events unfold: Noah Sizemore zoom up on Johnson's tail; blue smoke swallow Sizemore's Suburban; both vehicles enter Hawcourt's Curve going far too fast; two sets of brake lights flash on, the oscillations of one indicating near total instability; both vehicles slow almost to a halt, then the lights from the Suburban lurch as Sizemore rammed the Ford. Finally Drexler watched the Ford veer sideways, jerk from impacting the guardrail, then tilt . . . tilt . . . and disappear over the edge.

The Suburban hesitated briefly then sped away, nearly sideswiping an oncoming car, which in turn slowed, then accelerated. Going for help? If so, better hurry.

So he hurried.

Able Johnson had been in some doozies, but none like this. In the grips of tachypsychia, everything seemed to be happening in slow motion—his car rolling clockwise, over and over, seeming to take forever to get to the bottom of the fucking hill. Showered by shards of glass but secured by both his seat belt and his shoulder harness (not to mention being loosey-goosey and as drunk as two skunks), old Able rode it out, all the way to the bottom pretty much unscathed. Hell, it was kinda like being whipped around in one of them Tilt-O-Whirl things down at Myrtle Beach *when he was a kid. Except then he didn't end up with five pounds of glass in his hair!*

Nor upside down, either. Wasn't that just his fucking luck, to end up ass over nose hair with gasoline pouring all over, like monkey piss . . .

. . . Gasoline?

GASOLINE!

"Hello! Hello! Is anybody up there? I need help, there's fucking gasoline coming down!"

No one answered from above.

Able struggled with his harness, to no avail. Then the buckle of the seat belt, mostly obscured by his vast waist-line. No dice there, either.

He was beginning to worry. "Hello! Is any-fucking-body up there?"

Still no answer from above.

Beside him, though, a voice said, "Hi, Able."

"Oh God! Help me outta here! I can't get my seat belt undone and there's gas everywhere!"

"You're right. Just everywhere."

"So help me, asshole, don't just squat there on your fucking haunches!"

"Do you know who I am?" the man asked, knocking a cigarette into his palm from a nearly full pack. He offered the pack to Able Johnson.

"Hell no, I don't want . . . are you crazy? There's gaso—"

"You don't mind if I do? Wrecks make me nervous. Smoking helps me relax."

"I don't give a shit what helps you relax!"

"Able."

"What?"

"You didn't answer me."

"Answer you about what?" Able struggled against his bonds. No good. His bulbous belly hurt, and the stench of eighty-seven-octane was beginning to sicken him.

"I asked if you know me?"

Able looked at the man squatting there fifteen feet away,

calmly smoking a cigarette and making no move to help him.

"No, I don't know you. Am I supposed to?"

"Well, I was kind of hoping you'd remember me."

"Why should I?" Able was starting to sweat; something about this guy was making him very nervous.

Taking a long drag on the cigarette, then: "Because I have faced you in court, many times. Too many. Most recently you killed a pregnant woman. Her name was Christy Sizemore. That was her husband who just ran you off the road."

"Yeah? Well, when I get out of here, I'll find the bastard and—"

"Seven years ago you ran over a young girl. She was walking home from school. Three-thirty in the afternoon, you worthless bag of pus, and you were already shit-faced." The man took another slow drag and watched Able Johnson hanging there, reeking of broken glass and Exxon.

"But she didn't die!"

"No. She's just paralyzed from the waist down." Puff. "In a wheelchair. She can talk pretty well now, and the nightmares have stopped, but the colostomy bag still embarrasses her."

Able was really fighting the harness now, tears of frustration joining the gasoline streaming down. He ripped off a fingernail, but barely noticed.

"Listen, mister," he blubbered, "I promise I'll never drive again if you'll just—"

"And I promise you'll never drive again," Taryl Drexler said.

And flipped the butt. It bounced off the dashboard, sparks flying.

Able Johnson died screaming.